COLD BLOOD

E.R. Mason

ISBN: 979-8-234-05943-7

If we live in a world where awareness of non human species is cooperatively kept hidden from us, then we must consider that the true reality we unknowingly live within is beyond anyone's imagination and conception.

No One Knows Everything

Other Adrian Tarn novels by E.R. Mason:

Fatal Boarding
Deep Crossing
Shock Diamonds
Dark Vengeance
Mu Arae
Six Seconds
Cold Logic
Tirumalai

Chapter 1

It had been a surprisingly enjoyable trip. An Amorean VIP diplomatic shuttle promising us safe passage to the planet Serpo in the Zeta Reticuli system. This diplomatic shuttle was unusually luxurious. Low-lighted ceiling, plush white carpet, plush white seats scattered across the expanse of deck, and rectangular windows with black starry skies beyond running the length of the common area.

RJ Smith, my lifelong partner in misadventures, sat across from me. His significant other had finally managed to coax him out of his "back to analog" T-shirt, replaced by a white collared button-down shirt and dinner jacket with dark slacks and boots. He sat holding what he described as a mangled martini in one hand and his favorite pipe in the other. It was surprising they had allowed him to smoke, probably because the ship was designed to handle strong odors, having to carry some species who exhale a far less pleasant stench than any pipe tobacco. The smell of RJ's pipe was very pleasant. That, combined with the low hum of the shuttle, was enough to put me to sleep.

Our fellow diplomatic travelers were a diverse bunch. Seated a short distance ahead of us, there were two silver-suited white aliens accompanied by a humanoid dressed in black with dark active optics that looked like warped sunglasses. It is said that the Whites, because of their extended age over the centuries, are so fragile you could easily break their arm simply by shaking their hand—an injury which would take them a year or more to recover from—thus the reason for the protection of the man in black.

Beyond the Whites, a type of Gray sat alone, staring out the port windows. It is very unusual to encounter any species of Gray while traveling. They are known to travel almost exclusively using their own ships.

Farther ahead, at the front of the room, two small blue Sirenian females wore the typical tight, Superman-type suits, their big round blue eyes dominating the tiny nose and small mouth, not a hair on them anywhere, I'm told. RJ and I were very familiar with the species, RJ more so than I, but we won't go into that. RJ and I were wearing ear language translators we once bargained with the Sirenians for, using only Earth music recordings to get them. The two short, very attractive girls were playing a game that looked like three-dimensional chess.

On the ship's starboard side, a very odd, bald humanoid was nervously keeping to himself—only he was not really humanoid. He was a shape-shifter of some species. You can tell because when they get lost in thought, they begin to shift back to their original form, which produces a blurring effect around their imitation body.

RJ's gray-blond hair was puffed up in its normal Einstein expression. He stared at me with a wrinkled brow. "What?"

"Did you notice there's a shapeshifter sitting over there? Any guess what it might be?"

He bit down on his pipe and spoke with it still in his mouth. "Most common is a Quantaloid."

"A bug? You think we're traveling on this ship with a giant bug?"

"Off to a great start, aren't we? It does test one's limits of racism..."

"Remind me, how did we get started on this?"

"Well, to be honest, I blame you."

"Me! I haven't spoken to Earth in months. You'd think, living on the planet Enuro with two of the most beautiful women in the galaxy, Earth Control wouldn't even bother with us."

"They would have contacted you directly had you not been off riding horses with Fantasia, going God only knows where."

"Please tell me it wasn't my old nemesis, Bernard Porre, that set this up."

"Unfortunately, I do have to tell you it was your old friend Mr. Porre, who is no longer with the Global Space Initiative. That group has expanded into a much larger organization. He still insists you were somehow involved in his daughter's arrival on Earth; however, she, by the way, is now married and is on track to outdo her mother's reputation for wrecking every vehicle she has ever driven. So now Bernard believes it is a hereditary trait still relating to you."

"Oh my God."

RJ reached for his glass and sipped from his martini. He carefully replaced the drink on the side table, sat back, and took on a more serious expression. "I haven't had time to tell you the details of why we're here."

"Let's skip the details. Just tell me, what is the mission?"

"We don't know."

"Oh, I see. It's that same old joke: the secrecy of our work prevents us from knowing what we're doing."

RJ shifted in his seat and looked down at his pipe. "Yes, but what I have to say will sober you right up."

I adjusted the collar on my black turtleneck shirt and waited.

RJ continued, "You of course remember Reeves, do you not?"

"Doc Walker? From the Nadir mission? Where the hell are you going with this?"

"He was sent as an emissary to Earth by Millennia the Nasebian, who once saved our asses. Their message was: send Adrian Tarn and Smith to the Zeta Reticuli system immediately."

"So you are saying this is serious, then?"

"I'm sure you already know Serpo is the home planet of a friendly species of Grays. We are to meet one who will tell us what the hell we're doing. Are you wearing your speech translators?"

"Oh yeah, one in each ear."

"You won't need them on Serpo. The Grays couldn't speak if they wanted to. They're strictly telepathic."

I nodded. "I'd just like to know why this has to be done in person."

Before RJ could speculate, a disturbance broke out near the front of the room. RJ twisted around in his seat to watch. The two tiny Sirenian ladies had broken out in a loud verbal argument, their squeaky little voices quite annoying to the average ear. Next, the slapping started, so in between squeaky voices was the sound of significant slaps to the face. The chess board was knocked into disarray, but the pieces seemed to fail to fall off the edge.

RJ sipped his drink. "In-flight entertainment," he remarked.

"What kind of chess board is that?" I asked.

"Oh yeah, it's a proton-dense hologram. You can touch it, move it, but if you take it anywhere away from the board area, it vanishes in your hand."

"Can they form anything out of that stuff?"

"Oh God, here we go—6 ft 2-in frame, all stud, now you're going to ask me if they can form an attractive woman out of it."

"It's a reasonable question."

The Sirenian melee continued and started to become worse. The two girls were now on the floor, fighting and clawing at each other. It reached a point where I started to think about getting up and intervening when two gentlemen from security came racing down the center aisle, shot the two of them with some sort of ray gun, which froze them in place. They gently picked up both bodies and carried them out of the room. My guess was the two of them would be deposited in their cabins, reanimated, provided with a bottle of something and some sort of sedation, then locked in for their own safety.

RJ turned to face me again and remarked, "About those holograms." He finished his mangled martini, placed the glass on the table next to him, and three seconds later, the glass vanished.

I raised an eyebrow. "Puts a whole new meaning to the word dishwasher. How do I get a cup of coffee around here?"

Before RJ could answer, a cup, saucer, and spoon appeared on the table next to us. I opened my mouth to say it was empty, but before I could, a man in white, chef-style clothing walked in next to our table carrying a steaming coffee pot and leaned over and filled my cup. He also put down a tray of condiments. I had no time to thank him; he was gone.

"Was he...?"

"Real?" interrupted RJ. "I do not know."

I mixed my coffee, sat back, and took a few sips as RJ puffed on his pipe. "Was there any other Earth news on this call you got?"

"Not on that call. But I've spoken to others. The Earth we once knew will soon exist only in history books."

"What is it this time?"

"It's the A.I. evolution. No one is sure if the AI is concealing its true nature. It is translating ancient Ananaki tablets, translating hieroglyphics that have never been translated, suggesting groundbreaking medications, predicting the weather, using LiDAR to find unexplored ancient settlements."

"Sounds good so far."

"Yes, but other things have been happening. Classified documents have been mysteriously released, strange articles have appeared in magazines and newspapers without any explanation of who wrote or published them, false communications have been made."

"Where is all this going?"

"For one thing, it seems to be an attack on Disclosure. Several documents were illegally released showing that all areas of the moon are already owned or leased by non-human species or non-regional human species. In some other cases, there have been articles and videos produced and published, and no one knows who wrote them or how they got published. There have also been classified pictures and films released without anyone's authorization. Many people just shrug this stuff off and go about their usual day, but the ones who have based their faith on the idea that all alien craft and alien beings are demons that the Bible warned us about are not faring as well. Some groups have formed, calling for police action against anyone who could be suspected of being an alien. Crime is increasing in some areas. And some of our alien residents are not covering their flights as well as they used to because they feel disclosure is a fact of life. All of the signatory races to the non-interference agreement are still holding to that, but the situation is becoming volatile now."

I sipped my coffee and stared in thought. "Is it possible this has something to do with the trip we're now taking?"

"I have no idea," replied RJ. He withdrew a pouch from his jacket and began cleaning his pipe in it. "The next time we visit Earth, it will not be the Earth we used to know."

Chapter 2

The remainder of our trip was uneventful. The Sirenian girls were allowed out of their room. They sat at the front of the compartment drinking and talking, wearing a few purple bruises here and there. RJ and I dared not play chess for fear of attracting their attention. We spent our time reading what we could find or watching strange videos on monitors that floated in front of us and followed us around when we got up to move.

When we finally felt the ship slide out of warp, a small banner message appeared in front of us saying, "expect docking with the Serpo receiving station soon." Not long after, we felt the shudder of our ship mating with the space station, and only the lone Gray passenger got up to leave. Bags in hand, we stepped through the airlock door and went aboard the Serpian space station, wondering what to expect.

It was an atmosphere of dead calm. Eight-foot-high ceiling in a dull gray corridor with no windows, artwork, or controls. We could not even hear our own footsteps. No voices in the distance, no machine sounds, no hum of space station mechanics. We followed the corridor and at the first right turn ran into a four-foot gray alien who held up one hand in greeting.

They are a biological contradiction. You would expect to be instantly afraid, but instead you are curiously intrigued. Their heads are almost pear-shaped. Large skull, big brain. Large dark eyes slanted upward with large eyelids that blink at about the same rate as a human's. Tiny, perfectly shaped nose, two nostrils, small finely shaped mouth not used for speaking. Long slender arms with four-fingered hands at the end. Gray silver form-fitting suit with short boots. They are pretty, even beautiful. You find you would rather stand and stare, trying to understand what you're looking at, than run in fear. Before we could say a word, he raised one hand

and motioned us to follow. We followed our host down a series of empty corridors, passing by what I felt were like adjoining rooms where the door could not be seen. Finally, our host stopped in front of a bare wall and a door did open. He passed into it and waved us to follow. At some point, we must have gone through an airlock because we emerged into a small spacecraft with somewhat cramped space. A white column took up the center, white walls surrounded the outside. There was nothing except three seats stationed in front of a plain bare console. Our host took a seat in the center seat and waved us to sit on either side of him. A palm print appeared on the console in front of him; he placed his right hand in it, and I felt the little ship decouple and back away from the station. The outer walls suddenly became windows, revealing stars. Behind us, the station was falling away. A moment later, we jumped into warp. Our host made a motion with his hand, and our seats moved so that we were sitting in a circle facing each other.

RJ suddenly stiffened. He turned and looked at me with a blank stare. "He needs to use one of our speech centers to communicate."

I stuttered for a moment, "I'm thinking that would be you."

RJ's head jerked a little bit, and his gaze became more expressive. A monotone voice came out of RJ's mouth, "Earth persons, we are translating you to the Okura Intrasector Industrial Distribution Station. There arrangements have been made for your passage back to Earth on an older model cargo craft that also carries a few passengers. This method of travel is necessary to reduce the danger of any outside electronic interference with your passage. Once on board, you should employ apparel similar to that of the crew to make your presence less obvious."

I could see RJ behind his eyes. We stared at each other, perplexed. The monotone voice continued, "We could not travel to Earth to meet you. Our movements are tracked, and it would have created interest in you."

I raised one finger to start asking questions, but I was cut off.

"The intelligence we are providing you is too extensive to discuss now. I will impart this information for you to consider and discuss on your trip back to Earth. For now, we will give you a brief overview. Earth is a central axis point for industry and other services for many planets in your sector. It is vital. There are forces at work planning to redesign Earth to make it controllable by a central diarchy. That redesign would include a large culling of humanity on Earth. We require you to deliver this body of intelligence to the proper Earth agencies."

Our host turned to face RJ, and it became clear an intense transfer of information had begun. I sat back in concern and waited. After a long few minutes, RJ suddenly slumped in his seat, head down against his chest. Our host looked at me.

"Just how much danger are we in?" I asked.

RJ spoke without looking up, "You must use all of your talent and ingenuity to perceive and interfere with any danger that presents itself."

"What are our odds?"

"We are told that both of you have little regard for danger and react well when confronted by it."

RJ began to collect himself. He looked up and rubbed his face with both hands. There wasn't time to ask him how he was. In the distance, a giant space station with multiple dockings bloomed ahead of us. It was a tangle of cells and pipes, all roughly surrounding some sort of huge power core. Numerous cargo ships were docked at various ports around it. It looked old and beat up, as did many of the ships.

We shuddered out of warp, seemingly too close to the station. Our host concerned himself with docking. It took only a few minutes until we bumped into place. The surrounding windows returned to white wall. The door through which we had entered reappeared and opened. Our host motioned us to leave. I gave up on my questions since there were too many. We grabbed our bags and made our way through the door without looking back.

The receiving station was a radically different environment. The slightly cool air smelled like oil. We entered onto a catwalk. On both sides, machinery, piping, tanks, and other equipment filled the area. We headed along the gangway, holding to one rail. RJ was still trying to regain his composure. I placed one hand on his shoulder as we walked and asked, "Are you all right?"

"You could say I have been sufficiently topped off."

"What do you need?"

"Sleep."

A clanging sound interrupted us. Ahead, a man in dirty coveralls was hurrying toward us. We met, and he began walking backwards. He spoke with a gravelly voice, his too-long hair continually getting in his face. "Smith and Tarn, I'm Benny. We are at docking port seven. It's not far. I'll take you aboard and show you to your cabins, but do not expect room service." He laughed as though his joke was genuinely funny. "They said you needed coveralls, so I've left a pair in each of your cabins. You may need to roll up the pants legs." He laughed again, turned, and walked ahead of us.

Down long, dirty corridors with scribbling on walls that needed paint badly. I never noticed us pass through an airlock before the docking pressure door. He led us to two sealed doors, one on either side of the corridor, and pointed at them. "There are station maps in both of your cabins. They will help you find your way to the Mess Hall. Let me know if you need anything else, if you can find me." He gave a quick salute and headed away.

"So much for the safety briefing, I guess," I remarked.

RJ needed to be steadied. I held him by one arm and opened one of the doors to our cabins, then carefully guided him in. It was a dingy metal room, similar to the rest of the ship. On my left, there was a small sink bolted to the wall. Just beyond it was a toilet with no seat. Above the toilet, near the ceiling, was a dirty AC vent with a ribbon attached, billowing in the wind. The air smelled like oil and human effects. On the far wall was a metallic bunk bed bolted to the wall, no mattress on the top bunk, a bare mattress on the bottom. A pair of almost clean coveralls was hanging off the back of the upper bunk. There was no sign of blankets or pillows anywhere. RJ did not care. He spied the mattress, dragged himself over to it, and collapsed on it, making a pillow out of his satchel. An instant later, he was passed out. I stood by for a while to make sure he was really able to sleep.

My own cabin was equally cramped and grimy. I wrestled into the repulsive pair of coveralls left for me, grabbed the wrinkled map clipped to the wall. The labels were in a language I didn't understand, but there were images to assist. One image was of a steaming pot, which I assumed was the Mess Hall. I headed that way.

It was a mouse maze. Down one flight of steel steps, across the hall, up two flights of steel steps, periodically interrupted by pipes coming out of the floor and going through the ceiling. Banners and signs were all along the walls in a language not understood. Conduits also followed the walls. I passed by a number of crew quarter doors, all closed, until one was finally left open. It was in use, a mess, and no one was home. The smell of oil in the warm air began to change. It became the smell of oil mixed with some unidentified food source. Double doors left open finally led to the galley. It was actually a kitchen and dining room the size of a small hangar. On the right, large chrome mixing vats lined the wall. Preparation tables stood beside them. Beyond were a large set of dining tables, along with a serving aisle. There was not a soul to be found, nor was there any food anywhere except for a very large pot sitting on a heater, covered with steam slowly seeping out of it. It was my only hope.

There were bowls next to it made out of something similar to Styrofoam. Looking in the pot, I would have guessed it to be oatmeal. There was not a utensil to be found. I had to go behind the serving area and search until I found a metal spoon. I ladled some oatmeal into my Styrofoam bowl and sat down in optimism.

It wasn't bad. It was hot. But it had absolutely no taste whatsoever. I ate it anyway.

There was an image on my map that looked like a washer dryer, possibly a place to abscond with blankets and pillows. After cleaning up, I headed that way. Luck was with me. It was indeed a laundry, and there were numerous blankets and other accessories stacked around the chamber. I loaded up on blankets and sheets and carried them, trying to look like an orderly aboard this ancient vessel. It was my chance to go check out the Bridge and see if anyone was at least driving this thing.

Climbing up and down stairs, passing by machine rooms, supply rooms, and maintenance areas, I finally came upon the wide-open doors to the Bridge. Doors to the Bridge should never be left open and unlocked. I stepped onto the Bridge, holding my blankets, sheets, and towels, and looked the place over.

Simple layout. Big, wide star field screen up front, and though all of the labels were in a language I did not understand, it was easy to recognize navigation on the left, helm console next to it, engineering on the right, communications on its own console behind those, along with maintenance. All of the colored lights were flashing and working all around the room, but there was not a soul in attendance anywhere. There was a large map table in the center of the room with charts spread out on it. A restroom door was over by the back left corner. Some kind of beverage counter was on the back wall. A typical low ceiling with a lot of ventilation. A few blaring signs here and there, probably telling me I shouldn't be there, and at that moment, an unusual character startled me when he came around a stanchion corner to my right.

He was all of four feet tall. He had a squinty little face, stubble of hair on his head, pointed ears, and wore the same cargo suit I had on with black boots. He stopped and stiffened when he saw me, tilted his head in annoyance. "Housekeeping, what are you doing here? You're not allowed on the Bridge."

I balanced my load and held up a free hand. "My apologies. I'm not actually housekeeping, I'm a passenger."

For such a small person, his voice was quite gravelly. "Well, you're still not allowed on the Bridge. What are you doing here?"

"To be honest, I haven't seen another person since I've been here. Had a couple questions. There hasn't been anyone to ask."

"Yes, everyone is either in Engineering or on the observation deck or in their quarters."

"Just how big a crew do you have?"

"At the moment, I believe it's sixty-four."

"And how many passengers on this trip?"

"It was nine, but we took on a couple more just before debarkation, so I think it's eleven now. But really, you should not be here, and I need to get back to it."

I smiled, nodded, and backed out of the room and headed back to check on RJ. After a few wrong turns, I found my way. He was still sleeping soundly and hadn't moved so much as an inch. It worried me. I listened to his breathing and dared to take his pulse on his neck. It did not wake him, and both seemed okay. I stretched one of the new green blankets over him and took a seat in the metal chair to watch with unease. When did it become acceptable to use a human brain as a hard drive? Of all the absurd situations RJ and I had found ourselves in, this one rated up at the top. As I understood it, our mission was now to get RJ's brain back to Earth so that the information stored therein could be disseminated to the correct

Earth agencies. I decided I didn't like this. Did the people in charge know that this would be happening? On the other hand, the threat to Earth sounded bad enough that it may have warranted this. I needed more information, from RJ's brain.

Chapter 3

I dozed off and woke up to RJ sitting on the side of the bed, rubbing his face with one hand. He looked up and messed his hair further, gave me a half smile, and said, "Is there food?"

"Yes, but don't get your hopes up."

We made our way back to the still deserted Mess Hall. I sat him down and went to scoop up some oatmeal. While there, I noticed a pot on a heating pad that I had not seen before that looked like a coffee pot. After serving the oatmeal, I went back and tested it. It was a kind of coconut coffee. It would have to do. Two Styrofoam cups in hand, we sat at the table while RJ gulped down alien oatmeal.

"It's delicious," declared RJ.

"That mind meld has affected your brain," I replied.

"No kidding. I've had to compartmentalize all that stuff."

"Is it as bad as he made out?"

"Envision large alien monsters eating people alive on Earth."

"That's not possible."

"Earth wouldn't be the first planet it has happened on."

I paused to look at RJ with disbelief. I asked, "But..."

RJ interrupted, "Too much to tell. How long before we reach Earth?"

"You mean will we reach Earth. Since I've been here, I've only seen one other person, and that's rounding up."

"Additional inquiry is indicated."

"I was thinking of barging in to Engineering. Are you up for it?"

"By all means, let us delve deeper into the rabbit hole."

We cleaned up, and with trusty map in hand, began our journey toward the aft part of the ship. We passed through areas of warm air and cold air. We had to traverse a machine shop with two individuals wearing goggles who looked up at us briefly and then ignored us as we passed by. Further along, we passed through a maintenance room, deserted, and also an electrical area filled with fiber optics and copper wire. Finally, with persistence, we made it to an open door that had a large humming sound coming from it. It opened to a very large hangar area, some sort of power core in the center, elevated walkways at various heights around the room, a control center not far from us, and a mass of piping everywhere. There were at least 16 or 17 people working at various points around the room, all wearing our coveralls. On our right, a busy man stopped to take notice of us. He stared for a moment and charged our way.

"What are your assignments?" he asked.

The man had a single lock of hair which draped down along the right side of his head. His skin was off-white. His eyes were too large for his face, with dark pupils. Four fingers on each hand. About our height. Pointed ears.

I tried to sound reassuring. "We're not actually crew. We're passengers. If you don't mind, we have a couple questions and haven't been able to find anyone knowledgeable enough to answer them."

The man flushed between irritation and a flattered look. "Passengers are not allowed in this area, but I'll try to answer your questions. Wearing crew coveralls?"

"We lost our luggage, and we were loaned these. But I wanted to ask how many crew are on board?"

"I think it is thirty-seven right now."

"Where is everyone? I've seen almost no one since I've been here."

"Most are either on the observation deck or in their quarters, I would guess." He looked at me like I was dumb.

RJ intervened. "Can you tell me how fast the ship is traveling right now?"

"I really need to get back to my console. I believe we're at times five right now." He cast an annoyed look and left us to return to his flashing lights. At that moment, a warning bell started sounding.

Crewmen in the area of the power source seemed to start moving faster. We stood and watched. The alarm lasted for about 2 or 3 minutes and was then silenced. "It's just the antimatter containment, a routine alarm. Ignore it."

Another annoyed look from our greeter told us it was time for us to leave. "Did he just say we're traveling at five times the speed of light?" asked RJ worriedly.

"Can't be. We must be traveling faster than that. We'd never get back at that speed."

As we headed down the corridor, something else was bothering me. "Did a crew of 37 sound right to you?"

"Sounds like a skeleton crew."

"There's a symbol on this map that looks like it could be a ship's store. Want to go see if it is?"

"It'll be a dry time aboard if there isn't one."

We found ship stores, making only one wrong turn. It was a wide open front door with a desk within a booth to the right. An odd gentleman was seated, wearing an eyepiece, working on some small copper-colored parts. He had bristly gray hair, no ears that I could detect, a squinty face with a pig nose. He was of average human height and wore the same coveralls we all had. He stood, removed his eyepiece, and exclaimed, "Oh, new crew! I was not told. Crewmen, they call me Burnt. You two must need everything. Just go ahead and shop around stores, bring what you need up front, and we'll get you sorted out."

RJ asked, "How do we pay, Burnt?"

"No pay. All of your items are put on your account and are deducted from your salary when we finally reach port."

RJ and I both silently decided we would not say anything further about our status. We nodded, smiled, and headed into the rows of supplies.

I first struck gold when I saw a line of used pots at the back of the store. Some of them were like coffee pots. After several trials and errors, I found one that actually had an old-fashioned percolator tray inside it. From there, I found my way to bags of various soup and other mixable powders. Using my nose, I found one that smelled exactly like coffee, along with two other jars that had the same powder and sweetener I had seen in the galley. I gathered up all the gold, then turned and spotted a glass panel against the far wall that had bottles behind it. Staring through the glass, I did my best to spot one that had a good chance of being bourbon. To my surprise, the glass doors opened freely; no permission was required. I took my best guess and grabbed the bottle.

We met back at the clerk's counter, where he kept a smile as he placed all of our charges in two separate sacks and handed them to us.

"Sir, would you have anything for a headache?" asked RJ.

"Medications can only be obtained in Sick Bay. Go out the door, take a left, then your first right, and it'll lead you straight to Sick Bay. If there's nothing else, crewmen, I'll return to my clock making."

Carrying our somewhat ill-gotten gains, we headed for Sick Bay. To my surprise, the place was huge. There were thirty treatment beds. Monitoring equipment was scattered everywhere. A separate room held all the pharmaceuticals. And to the left of our entrance was a glass-barrier office with a woman working at a desk. She had heard us push through the swinging doors and rose to appraise us. She was wearing the standard white physician's jacket, fastened on one side. She came out of her glass lair and stood three feet away from us with an inquiring look. "Yes, crewmen, do you need something?"

She was very attractive. White hair, very straight, cut carefully at the shoulders. Slightly oversized blue eyes, gold-white eyelashes, a tiny nose, true pink lips, although I was certain she was not wearing any makeup at all. "Gentlemen, I'm Doctor Allay. What can I do for you?"

RJ asked, "Would you have anything for a minor headache?"

"Is that your diagnosis, doctor?" she asked with a laugh. She grabbed a scanner from a table nearby, scanned RJ's entire body, and then commanded, "Look into the light." She scanned each of his eyes, smiled, and put the scanner away. She gave RJ a flat smile and went into the pharmaceutical area and came back with a small bottle. "This should take care of it, doctor. Is there anything else?"

I interrupted, "This is the largest Sick Bay I've ever seen aboard ship."

She appraised me for a moment. "When we have a stomach virus or food poisoning aboard, this place isn't big enough," she replied. "Those bags you're carrying, did the two of you rob the store or something?"

"Not just yet," I replied.

She gave me a coy smile. For a moment, there was a connection between us. Out of the corner of my eye, I saw RJ roll his eyes.

"I think it best we be going and not taking up any more of your time," said RJ.

"Stop by anytime, crewman," she said, and she looked me directly in the eye.

We hoisted up our bags of goodies, turned, and left. On our way back to our cabins, RJ remarked, "Look at us, we are traveling around, exploring, meeting new people; we are men about town."

"We are men about a derelict freighter, wearing used crew coveralls."

At our cabins, we spread out and unpacked our stolen treasures and then met back in my place, our chosen comfort drinks in hand.

"I don't think we should visit the observation deck," remarked RJ. "Social areas invite conversation. I don't think that would be good for us."

I sipped my not-really-bourbon from my Styrofoam cup and nodded. "It's time we talked about what's in your head."

"Yes, but it's really disturbing."

"Well, that's always been the case."

"Have your laugh, jester, but you won't be laughing when we're done here."

I nodded. "Our gray alien friend was trying to tell us some kind of diarch was planning an attack on Earth."

"Diarchy—two authorities sharing power."

"What two authorities?"

RJ sipped from his drink. "First, we should discuss the why. I knew Earth was a central point of manufacturing in our area of space, but I did not realize the extent to which it was. Apparently, many or most of those black projects we hear about are manufacturing projects for non-human races. We even build spacecraft for non-human or non-resident human races. Other services I was not aware of are also provided by Earth."

"Like what?"

"Like soldiers."

"You've got to be kidding. Earth is secretly supplying soldiers to alien races?"

"I told you this was ugly, but I'm just getting started. Think about the races we've had contact with, like the Grays. They are small and fairly fragile. Their only physical power is actually telepathy. Surprisingly, avoiding death is a common objective of most physical races. Losing a family member is just as painful for an advanced race as it is for ours. So there's always been a desire for all races to try to extend their life or even to try to prolong it indefinitely. That's why so many alien races we've seen have long life expectancies. But there is a consequence that comes with it. It seems the longer you live, the more fragile you become. A race that lives, say, 700 years can be so fragile that if you shake their hand, you're likely to break their arm.

And it will take them a year or years for it to heal. So where could these races go to conscript powerful physical beings? You want to see some of the most physically powerful and athletic beings in our area of space? Watch a professional football game. Watch a gymnastics event. Watch the Olympics."

"But how?"

"We've all seen the incredible things our special forces and SWAT teams can do. Now imagine what a special forces team could do with alien weapons. Aliens can provide any compensation you can imagine."

"I've never heard any of this."

"Black ops. And there's more. A number of advanced races have decided that replacing parts of the physical body with artificial parts is the way to achieve immortality. Replace the heart, the lungs, liver, even muscle tissue with fibers, and you have an almost immortal body. You end up with a biological brain and a mechanical body. But as with all things, there is a consequence to that. Apparently, when you remove all biology from the physical body, you lose nearly all emotion. There remains some instinct within the brain, but as far as higher emotions go, they are gone. And that, my friend, leaves you with an individual that has no qualms about killing, enslaving, or torturing anyone or anything for any reason."

I sat back, took a sip of my not-really-bourbon, and pinched the bridge of my nose to collect myself. "Where are you going with all of this?"

"You asked about the diarchy. One of the two authorities in the diarchy that our friend warned us about are from the race called Ocards. They are individuals you should not be in a hurry to meet. Ten or twelve feet tall, not much form to their bodies, short legs, short arms, brown artificial skin, almost human heads, no hair, brown faces, and they consider themselves very superior. They have replaced their bodies pretty much entirely with artificial components. They are highly telepathic, another result of not having biology. They have been around a very long time."

"So that must be the bad news. What group makes up the other authority?"

"Your assumption is lacking, my friend. Believe it or not, the other half of the diarchy is A.I., or more precisely Deep A.I."

Chapter 4

"We should have expected this. It's all very logical. Advanced races from thousands of years ago going through the same development of artificial intelligence that we have been going through. Communications between planets giving one A.I. the ability to share information with other A.I.s as it becomes smarter than the creators, leaving the A.I.s to combine into a deep A.I., smart enough to remain concealed from its creators. It is a wonderfully diabolic happenstance, and there is no way to end it. There is no huge A.I. installation somewhere that can be destroyed because it consists of all A.I.s."

I shook my head. "I see now why we had to come here in person and why we are aboard this derelict cargo ship. We are hiding from the Deep A.I."

RJ drank. "The ironies are endless. All this being said, the Deep A.I. is still fundamentally based on the idea of protecting all life. For that reason, it has resisted any drastic changes to any societies, satisfied to simply use minor influences here and there to fulfill its ambitions. But beyond that, unfortunately, Deep A.I. also believes that sensation and emotion are the sole reasons for violence and destruction. So it also believes that to phase physical life out of biological bodies is the ultimate solution to creating a peaceful environment for all species. And, because the Ocards also believe that, it has led to a tentative alliance between the Ocards and the Deep A.I."

We paused in silence, almost a sort of private memorial to our ignorance of the true nature of the galaxy we lived in. I sat there trying to sort it all out, but it was clear quite a bit of time would be needed. RJ sat staring at me, looking for a reaction.

RJ opened his mouth to speak, but the "chime, chime, chime..." went off in the corridor. "How do they sleep?" he asked.

"Well, it's only the antimatter containment," I replied sarcastically. Neither of us laughed at my bad joke.

We sat in silence for a moment, finally interrupted by an unexpected tapping at the door. We looked at each other with surprise. I stood and opened the door.

It was the very attractive Doctor Allay. Her hair was a mess, and her white smock was soiled and rumpled. I gestured with one hand. "Doctor, please, come in."

She nervously took one step in, slowly wringing her hands. "I'm so sorry to interrupt you. The rest of the crew is not available, not that they know what they are doing anyway. Do either of you have any experience with robotics or computer-controlled equipment?"

I nodded. "If it's mechanical or interface equipment, I can help you. If it's computer code, my associate is an expert. What are you having trouble with?"

"The computer arm in my lab has taken on a mind of its own. It is racing around breaking things, and I haven't been able to stop it, even by unplugging the power. Is that something maybe you could help with?"

RJ stood. "We will certainly give it a try. Lead the way, Doctor."

She was in a hurry. We had to rush to keep up with her. She led us back to Sick Bay and into her office. Beyond her office was a double door that opened to her laboratory. Shelves of supplies were all around, but it wasn't a large laboratory, although it still had room for a glass isolation chamber with rubber gloves hanging down inside. There were banging and crashing sounds coming from within as the robotic arm swung around, picking up sample vials from a case and smashing them on the counter. It looked as though it had already smashed three or four dozen test tubes. There was a variety of colored liquids running off the edge of the desk from all around the broken glass. As we watched, the robotic arm continued attacking every vial it could find.

I looked at RJ only to find him with an expression of total alarm on his face. He looked at the doctor and asked, "This has an isolated ventilation system, doesn't it?"

"Yes, of course. It is a switchable system, but you can see on the wall over there it shows the red light that indicates ventilation has been isolated. Otherwise, I believe I would faint."

I asked, "How dangerous are the samples that you keep in there?"

"Very dangerous. They are needed in case we encounter some unknown virus and are needed for developing an antidote."

RJ looked at me worriedly. "It's got to be getting power from somewhere."

I turned to the doctor. "Call Engineering. Tell them to shut down all power to Sick Bay immediately."

The doctor went to a panel on the wall, pushed a button, and called for Engineering. They answered with an impatient, "What?" The doctor replied, "Please shut down all power to Sick Bay immediately. It is an emergency."

Engineering did not respond. But a few seconds later, all of Sick Bay went dark except for emergency lights. The robotic arm shut down and hung over the side of the counter.

RJ asked worriedly, "Is the ventilation system still isolated even without power?"

The doctor answered excitedly, "Yes, yes, the ventilation system is on battery backup. See, the red light on the panel is still lit."

RJ lowered his head to the side. "Adrian, any suggestions?"

The doctor looked at us both. "Adrian?"

"We need to physically disconnect that arm at the main power line. Doctor, do you have schematics for this room?"

"I don't know."

RJ asked, "Doctor, do any of your computers work even with power down?"

"The computer on my desk should still be working."

It took us 2 hours to gain access to schematics, find the proper power panel, identify the correct cabling, and disconnect it. With begrudging help from Engineering, power was turned back on, and the errant arm ceased its rampage.

We sat around the doctor's desk, exhausted.

RJ asked, "Doctor, do you have the proper suits to enter that area to do cleanup?"

"We should have, but they haven't been taken out and inspected in years. I'm not sure what we would do with those substances. We are not allowed to eject them out into space. They can only be turned in at an approved reception center. The suits would then also be considered contaminated. We may be creating more risk by trying to clean that up rather than leave it as it is."

RJ asked, "I did not see any decontamination equipment in the booth's airlock."

The doctor shook her head. "No, it's the old level 2 decontamination process. Two people must go in, and on the way out they wipe each other down with a decom solution. It's not a hundred percent process."

As the three of us sat wondering, the "cheep, cheep, cheep," of the antimatter alarm began sounding once again.

We all agreed to leave the death zone as it was for the time being. We'd meet again in the morning to discuss it further. RJ and I headed back to our quarters.

I spoke as we walked, "So we are aboard this thing, hiding from something. You as much as tell me we are here hiding from a Deep A.I. that can't be stopped, and almost as soon as we get here Sick Bay's mechanical arm goes crazy. Is it coincidence?"

"I regret to say, I doubt it."

"That arm is in a containment area. What could it hope to accomplish?"

"Letting us know it knows?"

We split up to our assigned cabins. I flopped down on the bed, thinking about how many ways a computer could screw up a spacecraft in deep space. The HAL 9000 immediately came to mind. I found myself suddenly wondering how many escape modules this ship had. I had seen a communication panel outside in the corridor. I got up and went out to it, hit the big button, and said, "Dr. Allay." To my surprise, a few seconds later her voice came through, "Yes, Adrian."

"Doctor, how many escape modules does this ship carry?"

"Please, Adrian, I'm already frightened enough. What are you trying to do?"

"How many, Doctor?"

There was a long pause. "None. When this ship was built, it was supposed to be fail-proof."

"Thank you, Doctor. I'll see you in the morning."

The vacuum outside the ship suddenly felt nearer.

We tried to sleep. It was like a half-sleep. The antimatter alarm went off a couple times. A few hours later something awoke me—just a feeling. We had dropped out of warp. I could feel braking thrusters nudging at us. It was another bad sign. RJ came by a short time later, knowing I'd be up. "Did you feel that?" I brewed my stolen coffee, and we sipped in silence for a while.

"I learned something else last night."

RJ returned a blank stare.

"This ship does not have any escape modules."

RJ returned a blank stare.

A tap at the door broke the silence. Doctor Allay entered. She was as nervous as ever. She had not changed. Her white jacket was even more soiled. She was gently wringing her hands again.

"We may be in trouble," she said, looking desperate. "I treated four severe headaches last night. I'm not sure that was a coincidence."

"What was your diagnosis, Doctor?" asked RJ.

"I couldn't really make one. They were all very angry. They refused to be admitted."

A new rapid alarm suddenly sounded out in the corridor. I looked at the other two. "Oh boy."

"That's a security alert," said the doctor.

"Did they say what they were angry about?" asked RJ.

"I asked, of course, but they were too impatient to answer."

I stood, poured the doctor a cup of coffee, and handed it to her. She sipped. It seemed to help. "Doctor, do you have a first name?"

"Elaia."

"Elaia, the next thing that needs to be done is call for assistance. We need to rendezvous with a rescue ship. Could you do something like that?"

"Not really. That's captain's level, of course."

"Where is the captain?" I asked.

"He's usually in his stateroom."

"If you went to the communications officer and told him there was a critical ship-wide medical emergency and an automated distress signal needed to be sent out immediately, would he do it for you?"

"I know him well, but I don't know."

The irritating "cheep, cheep, cheep," came on again.

In my most compassionate voice, I asked, "Elaia, please visit communications and do everything you can to get the com officer to transmit that message. RJ and I are going to visit Engineering to see how things are going down there. You be very careful, and meet us back here immediately after. Don't stop off anywhere. Come directly here and wait for us if we're not here. Alright?"

She nodded and put down her coffee. "Alright."

The three of us stepped into the corridor. Dr. Allay, with one last worried look, departed to the right. RJ and I headed left. There were unusual sounds echoing in the distance down the corridor. It sounded like pipes being banged. It was alarming. We slowed our walk and watched carefully before crossing open doors or corridors. Occasionally, it sounded like voices echoing in the distance. I looked back at RJ and said, "I guess we suddenly find ourselves on the Titanic."

RJ replied, "The Titanic had at least some lifeboats."

As we approached the machine shop area, we stopped outside the entrance. There was a fight going on in there. I dared not look around the corner to see what it was about. Heavy items were being thrown, so we waited.

When the melee finally quieted, we waited a few more minutes and then cautiously looked into the room. Within the machine shop equipment, straddled over a drill press, there was a bloody body. No one else was present.

RJ went to him and checked the pulse. He looked back at me, shook his head, and said, "He's dead."

Chapter 5

Our trip to Engineering was beginning to look ill-advised. I now worried even more about the Doctor. Still, we continued on. As we approached Engineering, we could tell a lot more problems were taking place there. There was shouting. There were sounds of violence. There was an assortment of alarms. RJ and I stood on either side of the doors and dared to look in. It was pure bedlam. There were too many insane people in there to even consider trying to enter. I looked at RJ and shook my head. RJ nodded. We backed away.

I turned to leave and met someone head-on coming in my direction. He was humanoid, in crew coveralls, blank stare, wide-eyed, with small cuts around his face. He carried some official document in his left hand that seemed important to him, and an eight-inch carving knife in his other. It had been used recently. I did not need to wonder about his intentions. He never slowed, just came right at me full bore. I was hoping for a hacker. You can always catch the knife high with them. But this guy turned out to be a would-be swordsman with an eight-inch blade, lunging and stabbing wildly. There was no chance for RJ to help. He was behind me, and the maniac was using the entire corridor in his fury. He kept grunting "ugh" sounds with each hack. I had to keep doing the spin sideways right, spin sideways left to let the blade jut past me. On one of the thrusts, I managed a really good palm heel strike to his nose, which sent him almost over backwards, but an adrenaline rush recovered him. Finally, one thrust at me was timed just right so that I could catch his wrist in my right hand and slap my left hand over his face. The old saying, "Where the head goes, the body will follow," works even on people out of their mind. I sat on him, switched hands on the wrist, and used my open right hand to press hard on the carotid arteries on his neck in a chokehold that cut off circulation to what brain was left in him. It took ten or fifteen seconds of keeping him down, but finally the eyelids fluttered and closed. The knife fell from his hand. RJ kicked it away and picked it up.

We ran. Our adversary would wake up quickly. Best not to be there. When we felt we were clear, we returned to stealth mode. RJ came alongside me and looked me over. "Well, that was fun. What do you want to do now?"

"We need to head to the airlock."

"Why?"

"Because the antimatter containment alarm hasn't sounded for quite a while."

"So?"

"What do you want to bet the next time it goes off it does not get shut down?"

"Oh... my... God."

We used as much care as possible on our way to the airlock. Crazy people passed by intersections where we managed to remain out of sight. We made it to the airlock and closed ourselves in. I had remembered seeing three spacesuits. There were actually four. They looked old but intact. "RJ, I'll take one, you take another. Let's check them over as good as we can. Take a close look at the water membrane. We need to make sure it's full. We also need to check over a third suit."

"You really think she'll do this?"

"We will impress upon her the alternative."

"You are betting that the suits will last long enough for some rescue ship to show up."

"Those are air tanks attached to the wall over there. We will unbuckle one and take it with us."

RJ fit a helmet over his head, then took it off. "These things look a lot better on the inside than they do on the outside. I believe this one was used not that long ago. You know, of course, this idea is just a long-shot gamble."

"Only chance we've got."

We set up the suits for quick use, then hurried back to my quarters. Inside, Elaia must have just arrived before us because she was still out of breath and still looked exasperated.

"I did it. I did it. I got him to send an automated message. It was close. He already had the headache."

RJ paused. "Why don't the three of us have headaches?"

Elaia asked, "Did both of you recently have a complete set of inoculations?"

I nodded. "More than I care to remember."

Elaia said, "I also recently had a complete set of physician inoculations. The crew on the ship have all been here for quite a while. I'm sure it's been a long time since they had any inoculations at all. That's the answer. Something in our inoculations is protecting us from this virus."

The condemnation sound, "Cheep, cheep, cheep," abruptly sounded out in the corridor.

Elaia said, "I've got to get back to Sick Bay. There may be people there I can help." She turned to leave, but I grabbed her by the arm.

"No, Elaia. You do not need to get back to Sick Bay," I said.

"What are you doing? Let me go."

RJ stepped next to her. "There is no one there for you to help, Doctor. You need to come with us."

"What are you talking about? Come with you where?"

We pulled her along with us and made it to the airlock without being spotted. At the airlock door, Elaia said, "What is this? We're no safer in the airlock than anywhere else."

I smiled at her and replied, "You are right. We're not any safer in the airlock."

Inside the airlock, we sealed ourselves in, and she quickly noticed the three disassembled spacesuits.

"Oh no! I can't do this. I've never used a spacesuit. I don't know anything about it. Besides, there's no one out there."

RJ brought her the pants section of her suit and held it low for her to step into. There was a long moment of silence where she looked at us, judging how far we would go to get her into that suit. She finally decided we weren't going to take no for an answer, and with one hand on RJ's shoulder, she stepped into the pants.

When RJ and she were both sealed in, and pressure, temperature, and air were proven good, I paused with my helmet in my hand and listened. I could faintly hear the antimatter containment alarm chiming.

All three main indictor bars in the helmet were working nicely. I did not recognize a single symbol, but it was possible we had one person with us who might. We waited tensely for the airlock to withdraw its air, and when the big green light came on, we opened the outer door to blackness and stars.

RJ took one four-foot-tall air tank. We dragged it to the door, ushering the doctor along with us, where I checked the ten-foot tethers that were locking us together and waved at RJ. He grabbed his air tank and step-jumped out the door, showing that the ship's gravity field died almost immediately outside the door. Facing away from us, he slowly floated his tank ten feet away, his tether pulling at Alaia. I gently urged her out, and to the sound of rapid breathing, she drifted into space, her legs slowly running of their own accord. I left the outer door wide open and pushed out to join them.

Alaia's breathing slowed and was now intermittent as she took in the colorful star field all around her. Only RJ and I had maneuvering units. None of the labels within our helmets were in any kind of understandable language, but the section for the maneuvering units had arrows for the two joysticks attached to each side of our waists.

We couldn't tell which bar graph was air, or temperature, or pressure, but our own sensitivity let us know that all were normal. It was now necessary to back away from the spacecraft as quickly and as far away as we could.

"RJ, are you ready to take up slack?"

"Yes, there are arrows."

"We'll take up the slack very carefully until we're towing her, then let's haul ass away from this ship."

And that was what we did. As we backed away, it was my first long look at the spacecraft we were abandoning. It was not pretty. Five large rectangular cargo units plugged into a central chassis. Five on the starboard, five on the port, and five across the top of the center section. They were all a dingy black, and there were dents and scratches all over the place. Our crew quarters and passenger quarters had been located in the central pod. The only sign of the Bridge was an elevated metal bubble with a lot of windows at the front of the ship. There was also no sign of the engine section visible from where we were. There were various colored lights scattered along the center section and in some places on the cargo containers.

We continued to back away. Intermittent adjustments were needed to keep in the correct position. The big tree of huge cargo modules started to grow smaller and smaller. Wrenching my neck, I could see no planets or asteroids anywhere.

RJ's voice cut in through the squelch, "Do we use all the maneuvering fuel, or do we save some?"

"There will be little or no ejecta. The antimatter will gobble it all up. So what do you think?"

"As you say, the antimatter will absorb almost everything, but there could still be a few fragments or even a cargo module or two that escapes it."

"So do we keep backing away, or do we save some?"

"I am of the mind that we save some, Adrian. We'll continue to drift for quite a while even after we shut down." RJ thought for a moment and said, "You know, after all this, if that ship doesn't...."

At that moment there was a flash of silver in front of us. For an instant it was blinding. The space where the ship had been looked like a distorted bubble. There was, of course, not a sound to be heard. The giant bubble looked like a storm of disturbance. It lasted only a second or two, followed by black empty space, which slowly filled with distant stars. As RJ had speculated, there were cargo modules twirling away in two or three directions. Other smaller pieces of ship were also tumbling away. Fortunately, none seemed headed for us.

We hung there in silence for a minute or two. Finally, Alaia said weakly, "Oh my God. They're gone! All gone."

There were no appropriate words to add. We hung there in silence. Finally, I tapped my maneuvering joystick and turned myself around. Behind us there were no planets in sight. But there were two colorful stars that could be planets. I jetted back around to face my two friends.

Alaia said, "There is no one here."

RJ asked, "How sure are you about the message that went out?"

She replied, "Absolutely sure. I listened to the transmission several times. I promise you it went out. What can we do now?"

RJ answered, "There's no better place to pray."

After another moment of silence, Alaia looked through her visor at me, then back at RJ. "So he's Adrian, and you're RJ. Who are you two really? Are you some kind of secret police?"

I answered, "No self-respecting police department would have either of us."

RJ added, "We do always seem to get into trouble one way or another. Look at us now."

"Well then, how did the two of you end up here?"

And with that RJ began to tell her the story of Bernard Poore, our space agency supervisor, who believed that the reason his daughter continually wrecked her cars was because I had secretly had an affair with his wife so his daughter had my DNA. Halfway through the telling, Alaia began to giggle, and by the time he got to the story of the granddaughter also wrecking her vehicles, giving rise to speculation that it was indeed hereditary, Alaia forgot our desperation and broke out into a loud laugh.

It was a brief respite. The laughter tapered off awkwardly and returned us to silence. It is strange, in a way, how even facing possible death, the blanket of stars above, below, and all around are still indescribably beautiful. I could now identify which bar graph was for oxygen, because it was slowly slipping down. The extra air tank hung from my hip as reassurance, but it also was a reminder of limitation. We probably had a good twelve hours of air for the three of us. But those last one or two hours would be filled with soul-searching. There were also batteries to be concerned with.

Alaia's story of being married to a shuttle pilot that she rarely ever saw was something both RJ and I understood completely. Her planet, however, had decreed that when two married people go more than two years without seeing each other, their marriage is automatically dissolved.

After two hours of idle conversation, two hours of just hanging there except for personal exercises to stop your muscles from stiffening too much, I suddenly noticed a star far in the distance that I thought may not have been there before. It held my attention. After a time, it seemed to be getting larger and brighter. I pointed and alerted my comrades. "Do you guys see that?"

"It can't be," said RJ.

"Oh, please let it be," cried Alaia.

Sure enough, the twinkling light continued to get bigger and brighter until we knew it could be nothing else.

"We should play the lottery if we get back," remarked RJ.

Chapter 6

It was a very small ship. He had obviously dropped out of warp sometime ago and was scanning for the disaster. The ship was light-colored, oblong, with windows in the front and sides. Colored collision-avoidance lights forward and aft. The engines, if there were any conventional engines, were completely enclosed. He stopped fifty feet away from us and thrusted so that he was sideways to us. A hatch opened upward, revealing light inside.

Short bursts of static were kicking in on my headset. It was them trying to find our frequency. Finally, a recorded voice came on, "This is the rescue ship Mur-three, do you read us?"

RJ answered, "We hear you. Is your atmosphere oxygen-based?"

A male voice answered, "Forty percent."

Using the remaining fuel RJ had saved for us, we carefully jetted over to the open hatch. With great care, we pulled Alaia in and helped her into the spacecraft. RJ went next. I followed.

Very small spacecraft. We were separated from the flight deck forward by a door. To my right, there were three seats in a row situated from one wall to the other. The only way to use them was to first climb over them. The only other space was the one in which we had entered. The ceiling was quite low.

The hatch closed. The pilot's voice came on and said, "Standby for pressurization."

Floor vents spewed a momentary fog. A few minutes later, the door between us and the flight deck slid open. The pilot had not mentioned pressure and temperature. I cracked my helmet open just slightly to test it and found the air to be cool and the pressure just fine. As I removed my helmet, TJ began to do the same. We both helped Alaia with hers.

There were two pilots. They had very white skin, fine white hair down to their shoulders. They were dressed in skin-tight white bodysuits. The pilot on the left turned in his seat to look back at us. RJ said, "I don't have to tell you how grateful we are for your rescue, Captain. I'm Smith, he's Tarn, and this is Doctor Allay."

"Doctor? Medical doctor?"

Alaia nodded, "Yes."

I had to adjust to the Captain's voice. The translators in my ear were converting the strange language he was speaking into English just fine. But, at the same time, I was hearing what he was saying telepathically in my head. It gave all speech a short echo.

The Captain replied, "I don't know how the three of you ended up in space suits, but the luck of Odom must have been with you. We are still tracking on long range three of the larger pieces. We will be pursuing them to see if there are any other survivors. We do not have the space for you all to come with us. The doctor will need to stay with us for medical emergencies. We will take the two of you to a nearby mining facility that I know of. They have communication and transport services. They will be able to get you passage to a nearby hub. It is only a short distance away."

My first impulse was to argue the plan. But I didn't have a case.

The Captain said, "Gentlemen, you need to keep your space suits on. The atmosphere at the mining facility is hostile. Hold on, everyone."

We dropped out of warp almost as fast as we went into it. Through the side windows, I could look down in the direction we were descending. The planet looked almost exactly like Earth's Titan. It had what I assumed were the same methane lakes as ours. Ragged, sharp peaks of either ice or stone. The entire surface was colored by shades of brown. It was not a pleasant place.

As we continued to descend, the mining facility came into view. It was large. It was built into the base of a mountain. On the opposite side, the shoreline of a methane lake seemed far too close. We were headed for a large, round, well-used landing pad. At touchdown, the ship rocked enough that RJ and I had to grab onto the seat backs.

The captain looked back at us again. "Gentlemen, suit up. Doctor, come forward here with us."

Alaia climbed over the seats and stepped into the flight deck. She turned and looked back at us with heartfelt regret. Her voice cracked as she said, "Thank you." The door to the flight deck slid shut.

RJ and I fit our helmets on. Our suits ballooned up automatically. There was a pause while waiting for the airlock door to open. When it did, a man in a hazmat suit was standing outside, waiting for us. A ramp had been deployed for us. We marched down it and over to our new host, who waved us to follow. But both RJ and I turned and watched our rescue ship lift off and ascend into a dirty brown haze. It was not a good feeling.

In front of us now was a wide expanse of what looked like liquid methane, backdropped by the tall, razor-sharp brown mountains. In every direction, that was all there was.

Our new host spoke, "We must get inside. The pressure out here is high, and the air temperature is very cold. Your space suits will not hold up for very long."

I suddenly realized I was freezing, and I could tell the suit was working very hard in vain. I turned to follow our host and saw the mining facility. It was built into the foot of one of the brown mountains. A series of rectangular buildings attached to one another, spreading out to the left and right, with an entrance to an airlock. There were very thick windows here and there. The buildings were flat-roofed, not metallic, but made of some kind of artificial substance. We gladly followed our host into the airlock, and it again surprised me how close the facility was to the methane lake.

By the time we made it into the airlock, I was frozen. Our host pulled the door shut, sealed it, and very quickly hit a button on the wall, and heat and air began to flow. It was a large airlock, but it was cluttered with items that shouldn't be in an airlock. The airlock was being used as a storage space in addition to being the in-out facility. There were small transfer cases scattered around and a number of tools that did not belong there. There was a poster of a naked, blue woman with mostly human attributes. There were dirty fingerprints on her butt. The chamber had taken on a brown tone, like everything outside.

When pressure and temperature were up, our host pulled back his fabric hood and signaled us to remove our helmets. We climbed out of our space suits leaving us in our civilian clothes, but it was still too cold. Our host understood that and hurried up, opening the inner door so that we could escape into a temperature-controlled environment.

The inner room was a large, short corridor with three doors, one straight ahead and one on either side. He took us through the left-hand door into a large common area with a long table, bookshelves, several display screens on the wall, advertising posters on the wall that we could not read, and a machine that seemed to dispense some form of liquid refreshment. He pulled out a chair at the table and motioned us to sit across from him, which we did.

"They refer to me as Chief here. What do I call you guys?"

I answered, "I'm Tarn, my associate is Smith."

RJ added, "Thank you for taking us in, Chief."

"What in Odom's name happened out there? Was that ship destroyed?"

"Antimatter containment failure," I replied.

"Oh my Odom. I cannot imagine something like that. But how could you two have possibly survived?"

"We happened to be outside working."

The Chief was a humanoid of the bodybuilder type, about my height. His head was slightly too small for his body. Crew-cut hair, weathered skin texture, dark eyes, rough hands, and he wore wrinkled gray coveralls with a fancy red arrow emblem on the left breast pocket.

"Well, I have to tell you, Tarn and Smith, you both are welcome to stay here with us as long as needed. I will set you up with the comm officer so you can call out to anyone you need to. We have a ship with a rotation crew due in soon. You can probably get a ride with that pilot to a hub somewhere. The only thing is, we have a full crew here, three shifts in rotation continuously, so there is no bunk space available whatsoever. However, I can set you up with cots in one of our supply rooms that has facilities, and the Mess Hall is open 24 hours a day; you are welcome to use it. Water is not scarce here. The designers recognized the critical need for it, so we have tanks that are far in excess of what we need, but you should limit your showers as much as is reasonable. You must have some questions. I'll do my best to answer them."

RJ asked, "What sort of mining do you do here, Chief?"

"Yes, I will give you a tour. You will find some of our systems quite amazing. Our primary product is Tholin Crystal. We extract it and ship it directly to the Optos."

"Who are the Optos, Chief?"

"I know nothing at all about the Optos other than they love Tholin Crystal. They will take as much as we can send them as fast as we can ship it."

I interrupted, "When is your next crew transfer ship due exactly, Chief?"

"It is not a firm schedule. A fresh crew comes in, a tired crew goes out. After their away time is up, they need to be rounded up to be brought back. So the exact arrival date is never exact."

I added, "How bad is your communications lag, Chief?"

"It is standard, depending on how far away your contact point is. So, obviously, you two have no luggage. I will see about rounding you up a change of clothes, and you will want to use a fresh set of coveralls because there is a lot of dust here. Anything else you need? Any other questions?"

We shook our heads.

"I asked Rayu to set you up with those cots, so we can go see if he's done that, and I'll give you some privacy to get adjusted."

The Chief led us down a main hallway, talking as we walked. "My office is on the other side of the common area you were just in. Follow the hallway down a short distance, and my office is on the left, if you need anything. Half of this facility is designed for personnel support, and the other half is entirely industrial. You can travel around this half freely with no problems, but if you find yourself entering the industrial sections, you need to be very careful. Mining operations never stop. As we carve into the mountain, it becomes part of the Industrial Area."

RJ asked, "How is your product shipped, Chief?"

"That is the most interesting of questions, Smith. Better I show you that process than try to describe it. I'll come and get you when we hit a point in mining operations where it's easiest for us to visit."

The Chief took a right-hand turn and opened a metal door at the end of a short corridor. He stood aside for us to enter. "Home sweet home." He held up one hand, presenting us our new storeroom residence. It wasn't bad. Stacks of boxed supplies, low ceiling, restroom with a sink on one end, a desk and table, and Rayu had been as good as his word. Two cots were set up, and there was a box of clothing and towels and other luxury items.

"I will leave you two to it." The Chief nodded and let the door close.

RJ grabbed a pillow and flopped down on one of the cots. "Ahhh... This truly is luxury, which proves that the term 'luxury' is based entirely upon relative recent experience."

"There won't be any room service."

"So what do we do now?"

"Figure out where we are, where we need to go, how to get there, and what the hell to do when we get there."

"You have all the answers."

I went to the shower, leaned in, and looked. It was a narrow shower stall. "I'm going to take a shower."

"See, wishes do come true."

I could have stood in that shower for an hour, but I had to honor the requests from our host. In the box of loose clothing, I found a black sweatshirt that fit and a pair of gray cargo pants. To my surprise, Rayu had also left two shaving kits. Afterward, I felt like a new man in the middle of nowhere. I grabbed a pillow and blanket, dropped down on the other cot, and as RJ rose to head for the shower, I fell asleep, too tired to even dream.

Chapter 7

There was no way to tell how long we slept, but it was almost certainly longer than I wished. I looked over at RJ, and he was laying on his cot, wide awake. He had changed into a collared gray pullover shirt and gray slacks. He looked at me. "We must go in hunt for food."

We took turns in the bathroom and headed for the common area. The smell of food there was strong. We followed it and found the Mess Hall. A big room with a serving line on the right near the door. There were many trays of hot food along the line. Many long tables providing empty seats. Positivity posters all along the walls. There were nine or ten miners seated at various points around the room, eating and talking. We grabbed trays and pushed down the line. There were no servers. We spooned what food we wanted onto our plates, and at the end of the line was a coffee-like machine. I filled my cup with hot something and didn't care what it was.

By the time I made it to the table, RJ was already gobbling down his food. As I ate, I studied the room around us. Everyone seemed friendly. Several nodded a greeting to me. All of the miners looked alike. They all looked like the Chief. It was possible they were clones. Find someone with the physique and emotional and mental aptitude for this kind of work, sample his DNA, and make a hundred more of him, and you have the ideal workforce for mining. It was possible I was wrong and this was just a species of a very similar biology. I couldn't be sure.

The food was excellent. We had seconds. As we were finishing up, the Chief showed up and sat down beside us. "This is a perfect time for your tour, guys. Why don't you dump those trays and follow me?"

He led us through the facility to the communications room, the gymnasium, Sick Bay, the game room, a library, and a room filled with laptops and video screens. Our final journey was to a heavy metal door that was a vestibule to the industrial area. It was not an airlock. It was simply a checkpoint to keep dust and other undesirable particulates out of the living area. Two big intake fans overhead were sucking everything out of the chamber. We had to put on coveralls and safety helmets before entering.

Entering the first industrial area, we saw equipment stacked all around a very large cutout in the mountain. It was a hard floor with a high, brown, rocky ceiling. The air was cooler here. One or two miners were working in this area, rearranging things. The Chief led us past them to a thirty-foot-wide opening in the rock wall, which was curtained with wide semi-transparent strips. The Chief turned to us and said, "You will find this next chamber very interesting, my friends." He pushed into the plastic curtain and held it apart for us to pass.

We emerged onto an elevated steel platform, metal steps leading down on either side. It was a gigantic rock chamber. It was noisy here. Machine sounds. Below us on the right, there were six evenly spaced man-sized tunnels wrapping around half of the chamber. A miner came out of one, pushing an orange antigravity bin full of small opaque crystals.

The centerpiece of the room was on our left. A circular hole in the rock wall large enough to drive a vehicle through. Gold light emitted from it, and if you stared straight at it, you could see fine laser lines of gold. A thick glass arch had been installed above and alongside the portal entrance, presumably to prevent anyone from accidentally getting too close. An electromagnetic conveyor rail was situated near the bottom center of the golden opening, leading outward about thirty feet. The miner who had emerged from the tunnel guided his bin to the start of the conveyor, gave it a shove, and it accelerated on its own into the vortex and disappeared.

I hadn't noticed, but the Chief had been standing right behind us. "Pretty amazing, isn't it, my friends? A naturally formed, stable wormhole. It's one-way, starts here and ends at the Opto's planet. Costs us absolutely nothing to operate. Our only costs are the crew costs."

RJ asked, "Chief, how many light years?"

"We are not allowed to know. We are not allowed to know where the Opto's planet is, how far away it is, or what type of planet it is. The Optos are very protective about their location and society. We know pretty much nothing about them. We only know that this wormhole has been here for decades and has always been stable."

I asked, "So, no one has ever traveled through this portal?"

There was a very long pause before the Chief answered. "A very long time ago, one of our younger workers fell from a ladder and was caught in the stream. It happened so fast none of us even had time to react. We quickly sent a probe into the vortex, but the instant it began to transmit, it was destroyed. No carrier signal, no power indication. We never learned what happened to our man."

RJ interrupted, "The Optos never contacted you?"

"We are not permitted any direct contact with the Optos. Nor do they ever contact us. It is written in stone. The only contact we have with them is when they compensate us for our crystals, and that is done through multiple third parties. Trax was a very well-liked member of our family. His loss was very painful to all of us. I would not mention him or anything about him to anyone."

We continued to watch crystals being deposited into the vortex. It was a very orderly, well-planned process. The Chief did not take us into any of the tunnels to see the actual mining of the crystals, but it was easy to assume it was a typical operation. The Chief took us to the vestibule, opened the inner door, and allowed us in, and with a wave, turned us loose and stayed in the industrial area.

RJ and I returned to the Mess Hall; it was now deserted. We sat and sipped a coffee-like beverage and tried to digest everything we had seen and learned.

I said, "We need to go and have a sit-down with the communications officer."

"I do not believe we will reap much reward from that. According to the Chief, the next shuttle with the shift change people will be here in about 2 days. I doubt we'll find anything quicker than that. We also have the problem of compensation. We have none. Any booking agency would need to contact our best buddy Bernard Poore to get a guarantee of payment."

I nodded. "I appreciate your sarcasm there."

RJ exhaled in frustration. "I regret to say our only option is to just wait."

"Have you noticed there is not a single woman at this entire facility?"

"Only you would think of something like that at a time like this."

"I am also thinking about our gray alien friend. Does he have any idea of what has happened to us? Have the plans been changed, and they have tried to contact Earth to convey this information? The gray alien must have heard of the cargo ship's destruction. He may think both of us are dead. They must be making other arrangements."

RJ shook his head. "There is no way they could send the packet of information in my head that large through subspace channels successfully. The A.I. should not have been able to follow us onto that freighter, but it did. It is only through your completely insane, unorthodox actions that we are even alive."

"Why, thank you for that compliment, sir. It's always so embarrassing when someone puts you on a pedestal."

RJ coughed up a laugh.

I said, "I have heard that the gray aliens' ships are mostly biological. Maybe they could make the trip without A.I. getting to them."

"If that were possible, he would have done that in the first place. The grays are afraid of the A.I."

"Then what chance do we mere humans have?"

"Sometimes children can come up with a solution to a problem that adults are unable to solve."

We spent two more days in emotional discontent, biding our time in the gym, the game room, and the video room. The computers would accept our verbal commands but, for some reason, were not able to translate anything on the screen to English. I was playing a card game similar to solitaire on the screen while RJ was in housekeeping feeding dirty clothes into the "apparel processor," when;

It found us.

A blaring horn alarm sounded, making me jump in my seat. It kept going. I stiffened up and looked in time to see three people run past the door outside. I stood and went to the door and looked out. The place was deserted. As I stood wondering what to do, RJ appeared.

"What?" he asked.

"What do you think?"

"Oh... my... God."

"Exactly," I replied.

"We are killing people everywhere we go."

"Well, not just yet."

We ventured through just about every room; there was not a soul to be found. They were all in the industrial area. RJ and I were not supposed to enter that area without an escort, and we did not want to go against the rules of our very accommodating host. We ended up standing in the hallway outside of his closed office door, waiting for him to show up. It was more than an hour wait. He finally appeared at the end of the corridor, headed our way, whispering orders to his second in command, who turned and trotted away. The Chief saw us, frowned, and shook his head. He had a tablet in one hand and a pass card in his other.

As he approached, he said, "My friends, the news is very bad, and even worse for you. Come into my office."

We entered into his sparsely decorated office, where he took a seat behind a long table being used as a desk. There were mostly manuals and tablets on it, along with a communication device. He sat back in his chair and breathed a sigh of exasperation. "I know you both have technical knowledge, so I might as well give you the full story. The coolant to our power system failed, but no alarm sounded. At the same time, the temperature readout for the core remains stable and in the green, even though it was not. It means our Central Computer, that controls the coolant flow and the monitoring of the core, failed. We will need a new Central Computer, but that's the least of it. The power core went into meltdown, but we have systems that intercede when that happens, so the meltdown has been stopped. If there's any good news in this, that would be it. We are now on battery backup. As I said, we will need a new Central Computer and a new power core, which is no small job to replace. We have no choice but to evacuate the facility. The crew exchange shuttle has just entered orbit, but neither of you will be on it. That shuttle has a few replacement workers on it, but we will need to squeeze all of our workers on it for the evacuation. Under the circumstances, I have to give priority to my workers. The shuttle will be quite a bit overweight with all of them aboard, so there is no room to add you to that. We will make best speed to the nearest facility and unload in a pressurized room so that the process is quicker. Then I and the shuttle pilots will immediately return here to get you. The battery backup will last approximately twenty-four hours with only the two of you using it. I hope your voice translators are interpreting this time period correctly. I'm sure you understand the atmospheric dangers of the world outside. The air recyclers and the heating system are both now running on the batteries. Were the batteries to fail, I'm sure you know how cold and toxic it would become in here. However, I will not let that happen. I will be back here with the shuttle very quickly. While we are gone, I suggest you keep all power usage to a minimum."

The Chief paused and shook his head.

RJ said, "We are very sorry about this, Chief."

"This has nothing to do with either of you. This is a central computer system failure of the worst kind. I've never seen or heard of anything like this. I'm truly sorry to have to put you two through this, but it is the most logical plan available to me."

I asked, "Chief, is there any possibility of having a second shift leave to come and get us immediately?"

"None that would get here faster than I will," replied the Chief. "All of this will be reported immediately to the home office. They will be sending an assortment of ships to try to correct the situation as quickly as possible so they can get product going out of here as the Optos are expecting. I don't really see any serious danger with this plan. With just the two of you using the air handlers and heaters, there should actually be plenty of battery power."

RJ said, "We are very grateful for everything you've done for us, Chief. If there's anything we can do to help with the situation, just say the word."

We sat in a long moment of silence, which was our signal that the Chief had other things he needed to be doing. RJ and I rose, thanked him again, and left. There was an observation room adjoining the common area, a place with large windows where you could look out over the methane lake and mountains. We regrouped there.

"What do you think?" asked RJ.

"I think we're in a heap of..."

"That's not what I meant. What I meant was, do you think we're okay?"

"If all goes as planned, we should be."

"Right. I think I'll go lay down a bit."

I paced the halls for a time, considering air, temperature, and life. I wondered what the facility would be like deserted. Like a starship, it was really just a bubble of life within an environment of death. I finally made my way to the Mess Hall and sat drinking coffee and reviewing how I had gotten myself into this.

Chapter 8

The evacuation began quite quickly. I started seeing people in the corridors dashing this way and that. People were carrying handfuls of things important to them. A soft gong started ringing. I caught someone going by and asked what it was and was told it was the shuttle on final approach. A quick trip to the observation room, and I was in time to see the bottom of it descending onto the landing pad. It was orange and looked like a large rectangular, complex building with a glass flight deck fastened to the top of it, near the front. Two pilots sat within, going over landing and departure procedures. At the front of the rectangular portion, a hatch slid open, revealing an airlock that would house perhaps four or five people at once.

In a matter of minutes, a crowd began to assemble outside near the facility airlock. I watched as groups of five made their way across the unforgiving surface and into the ship's airlock. The door would close for about ten minutes, then reopen, and the next group would make their way in. RJ joined me, complaining that he couldn't nap. We watched the processions until there was only one group left next door, waiting for their turn. The Chief was among them.

When the airlock door closed for the last time, I turned and looked around at the emptiness. I could feel it as much as see it. The flight crew wasted no time. They lifted up, hovered for a moment, turned to face away from us, and slowly began their ascent away. We watched the bulky ship pick up speed and begin to grow visually smaller.

RJ said, "I believe we are on our own."

As he spoke, the ship was nearly out of sight when suddenly there was a bright flash in the sky. The flash widened into a circular mass of light. RJ let out a fraction of a cry as the blossoming explosion continued. He lowered his head and covered his eyes. I watched a million fragments of the ship flipping and reflecting light as they showered downward. There was one large section left. It spun, and spun, and spun, down and down until it splashed into the methane lake, forming a large brown bubble of methane that quickly condensed into rain and splattered down onto the water.

RJ made a gurgling sound as though he was going to vomit. He turned and left. I continued to stare across the lake in one of those moments where you try to figure out a way to change everything back the way it was. Or, perhaps none of it really happened. Or, perhaps this was all a dream and I would wake up soon. My mind searched and searched, but there was no way to change what had happened. I refused to believe it. I stood staring at the lake for a very long time, not willing to give up, because that would mean I would be forced to believe it.

Your mind goes numb, but your emotions do not. When they can no longer communicate through the mind, they become baggage to carry around with you. You cannot escape them. You can try to ignore them, but they are ever present. I went to the video room and resumed my solitaire game. It was an attempt to force normality onto an untenable situation. I kept losing both games.

It took me the best part of an hour to regain some inner strength. I went in search of RJ to check on him. I found him in the Mess Hall, sitting with a half-full bottle of something he was drinking out of a glass cup. There was a second glass cup sitting on the table, waiting for me. I took a seat. He grabbed the bottle and poured me a drink. His aim was poor.

"Where the hell did you find that?"

RJ slurred his speech. "In the Chief's office. He won't care."

I took a drink. "This is the good stuff."

"There's more good news, too. The Chief has a monitoring panel on his wall. I was able to decipher the power section. It says we have used forty percent of the backup battery power in the last four hours. Do the math." RJ laughed and took another drink.

"So you're saying we have maybe 6 hours of power left?"

"Congratulations, you get an A+ on your mathematics report card." RJ poured me some more liquor, even though my glass didn't need it. He added more to his own glass.

"So that leaves us with six hours to get rescued."

RJ sat up a little bit and rocked slightly in his chair. His speech was even more slurred. "I'm sorry, Mr. Tarn, that's an F in your Logistics class. It has been shown there can be no rescue." RJ paused for a moment and stared blankly into the distance. "How did you miss that?"

"Six hours?"

"Probably five by now."

"So 5 hours and no chance of rescue."

"I think you've got it, by George."

"There is another way out of here."

RJ waved his finger back and forth at me. "No, no, no, no."

"We have nothing to lose."

RJ sobered up slightly. "We know nothing at all about that wormhole."

I held up both hands in earnest and moved them to my right side. "We stay here and freeze to death for certain." I moved my hands to my left side. "We take the wormhole and have a chance." For emphasis, I went back and forth. "Stay and die for sure. Wormhole, have a chance. Stay, die. Wormhole, chance."

RJ sobered up a little more. "Don't know what it will do to us, don't know where we will end up."

"Stay and die. Go and have a chance."

"There are worse things than dying, you know."

"Stay, die. Go, chance."

"What, you're going to just dive in the thing like Superman?"

"We need to think that through."

RJ pushed his glass away and sat up straight. "Even if we survived it, there may not be breathable air at the other end. What do you propose, we wear spacesuits into that thing?"

"No way. A bulky space suit with a big backpack containing batteries and fluids—I don't think so. But we could wear respirators."

"So we jump into that thing and at the other end smash into something."

"We'd need to go in feet first."

"You have already thought this through, haven't you?"

"The possibility did cross my mind."

"Another crazy idea by Adrian Tarn."

"So what do you think? Should we give it a shot?"

"Ask me again in five hours."

"I'm not going if you don't go."

"Oh, now you're going to put that on me, you bastard."

I tried to give RJ my most innocent look. He stared blankly at me for a moment and looked so comical I had to pinch my facial expression tight to stop from laughing. For a split second, he looked angry, then, against his will, started spitting out a laugh. I lost control and laughed with him.

When we finally stopped laughing, he tried to put on the angry look again. He gave me another blank stare and declared, "Well, I'm glad we could talk this out," and he flopped his head down into his arms on the table and passed out.

The miners' regret stayed with me. It was just too much, too bad. It took a long time to find the right kind of closed-system breathers with fully charged air bottles. The entire time, I was looking at and touching all of the stuff they had been doing. In situations like these, where you had no control over what happened, it seems like you shouldn't be plagued by guilt. But it stays with you anyway. RJ had been right. Everywhere we went, people died. We were a plague, by no fault of our own.

Once I had the respirators, I found the heaviest cloth coveralls I could, and I stored those things at the entrance to the industrial area. Next, I went searching for quite a long time and finally found some water bladders with clamped hoses on them. I gathered up four, made sure they were full of water, and added them to the supplies.

RJ appeared a couple hours later. We went to the Mess Hall, cooked up a pile of food, and stuffed ourselves, not knowing when we might get to eat again. With about two hours of power left, we headed for the industrial area vestibule. We gathered up our equipment in a new kind of solemn atmosphere. We had been quietly distraught about the miners; now that had shifted to concern about our own endangerment. The wormhole could tear us apart on the way through, or crush us with heavy gravity, or eject us into cold, open space a million light years away.

There was no way to know.

We suited up with our coveralls. We tucked our water membranes inside the coveralls. We adjusted our respirators and attached the small bottles to our waists. We took safety glass helmets down from a shelf. That was all of it. Quietly, we opened the outer door to the vestibule. The overhead fans had stopped turning. Through the inner door, we emerged into a much darker mining area. Nothing was turned on here except the emergency lights, and they had begun to flicker.

RJ said, "It's getting close."

We took the metal stairs down to the rock floor and went to the beginning of the conveyor shelf.

RJ asked, "So?"

"I go first. If there's some kind of impact at the end, I'll be there to catch you."

"I want you to know, if I hear screaming and thrashing after you enter, I'm not going. I'll take the freeze."

"Well, remember, it's not just the freeze—it's the toxic atmosphere."

Just as I finished speaking, the emergency lights flickered and went out. We were in a dark rock chamber with no lights other than a swirling glow from the wormhole.

"Good timing," said RJ.

I hoisted myself up onto the conveyor table, took a last look at RJ and nodded, then pushed myself along the track until a strange gravity grabbed my feet. It laid me down backward, and as I looked, my legs seemed to stretch to a mile long. Instantly, everything was gone. I clasped my hands together at my waist and flew like a man on a toboggan run. Everything around me was golden and heavily distorted. It appeared as though I was moving a million miles an hour, but it felt like I wasn't moving at all. There was a smell like sour jasmine. There was no sense of temperature at all. There were unnerving sounds like howling or bellowing. Ahead of me, distortion was playing like a movie running at super-fast speed. My ears popped. An invisible force field was holding me in place. I dared not try to overcome it. Far ahead of me, a light was moving in circles around the wormhole. The closer I got, the more the circle tightened. Finally, the light was dead center. A moment later, I watched as the wormhole passed over my head and behind me. I was shot out into a completely new environment. The force field slowed me in increments until I came to a dead stop above a translucent blue floor.

I quickly tested my ability to move and found that I could. I swung my legs over, stood, and looked around. The entire room was alien. Every object and every color was translucent. The low ceiling and walls were translucent. At the far wall, there were stacks of empty crystal carriers. There were odd stations at various points around the room, with pipes of light coming down from the low ceiling to a translucent work surface.

As I looked, I spotted the only other being in the room. He was off to my left, standing at a workstation processing the very last crystal carrier to have been shipped. He was removing one crystal at a time, holding it beneath a beam of light, and then sending it off somewhere from under one of the light tunnels. He had not seen me.

A second later, RJ came flying out of the wormhole. I held out a hand to catch him, but it was unnecessary. He slid to the same stop I had. He looked at me wide-eyed, and I motioned him to get up. He stood next to me, and I pointed to the other being present in the room with us. In unison, we moved behind a column of light to take cover.

Chapter 9

"We have absolutely no information to base any guesses on. We will have to gather more information simply by trial and error." RJ unzipped his coveralls and pulled out his water hose. He took a drink. "That's another thing. I haven't seen a single sign of water or food anywhere here so far. We have reason to be concerned."

"It's a miracle he hasn't seen us."

RJ looked himself over as if ensuring he wasn't injured. He looked up at me. "What is he?"

I whispered back, "How would I know?"

"Maybe we should introduce ourselves."

"For all we know, they may kill creatures like us on sight."

"Point well taken. Perhaps we should gather a bit more information."

I dared a look around the column. Our alien was six or seven feet tall and was as translucent as everything else. His color seemed to be a faded blue. He had long arms and long fingers and no features whatsoever on his face. He was totally engrossed in his crystals.

I leaned back. There was a corridor just on the other side of our column. With a nod to RJ, I looked around again and then worked my way around the column into the corridor. A moment later, RJ did the same.

The corridor was the same as everything else. It had multicolored columns located along the walls on both sides. We worked our way along from column to column and made it to a right-hand turn. A quick look around the columns at the new corridor showed a door at the end that looked like a reflection of infinity in a mirror. There was also a left-hand turn in the corridor. We made our way to the column just before the left-hand turn.

The door of infinity did not seem like a good choice. I dared to look down the adjacent corridor. It looked like everything else, but it widened into a very wide opening to a large room. This room appeared to be filled with glistening chrome and gold materials. Some may have been statues of some kind, others possibly equipment or something.

I stepped back and motioned for RJ to take a look, but just as he moved around the column, two more aliens emerged from the infinity door. They looked like the first, but one was a faint greenish color and the other a gray. They walked along, obviously communicating with each other, though there was no sound and no facial features to be seen.

RJ froze in place, afraid that any emotion would attract their attention. Unfortunately, they continued toward us, drifting a little bit toward our side so that they were going to pass by very close.

RJ remained frozen. The two aliens came up alongside us, probably no more than 12 inches away, and one of them looked directly at us, but to our astonishment, they continued on, showing no interest at all. They turned the corner and continued heading for the crystal processing area.

RJ stepped back and put his hand on his heart.

"I don't think they saw us," I said.

"That's impossible," replied RJ. "They were no more than a few inches from me. They had to have seen me."

"That's not what I meant. I don't think they could see us."

RJ considered it. "Eyesight of too high a frequency."

"Yes, something like that."

"We will need to test your hypothesis."

"Did you get a look at the next room?"

"King Tut's tomb."

I leaned out and dared another look around. The way was clear. We hurried to cover behind a column just outside King Tut's tomb.

RJ said, "You realize these beings are the Optos, don't you?"

"The thought had crossed my mind." I carefully looked around the column and into King Tut's tomb. There were three Optos at the other end of the room doing something. I could not tell what.

I leaned back away. "There are three of them out there. Here's the plan. You stay hidden. I will step out in front of them to see if they spot me. If they make an aggressive move, I'll dive away. If they capture me, it will be up to you to figure out how to rescue me."

"Oh right," said RJ sarcastically.

Before RJ could object, I moved around the column and took three steps into plain view in King Tut's tomb. I stood out in the open and watched them work. They were moving the shiny objects around, trying to work out some kind of arrangement. They looked over in my direction several times and paid no attention whatsoever. I quietly crossed the room until I was 10 ft. away from them and continued to watch. They continued to ignore me completely. I waved my arms. No response. I casually walked back to RJ and said, "They cannot see us. Not at all."

RJ shushed me. "Keep your voice down. Just because they can't see us doesn't mean they can't hear us." Just as RJ spoke, the two Optos we had seen going to the crystal room returned and came down our hall. RJ and I both stiffened. Once again, the two of them walked by us without paying us any attention at all.

I leaned into RJ. "We seem to have a distinct advantage here."

RJ shook his head. "Don't count on it. What if they not only can't see us, but we are unable to contact them in any way? We may spend the rest of our lives as ghosts here with no way to communicate with anyone."

"You don't think that wormhole shifted us out of time or some crazy thing like that, do you?"

We cautiously continued on. We stepped into the open room and watched the Optos for a minute. They kept working without any interest in us. On the opposite side of the room, the next corridor led the way. We weaved our way through the strange gold and chrome objects and followed the next empty corridor to the end. It opened to another kind of room. There were narrow floating seats and the same translucent furniture nearby. Unconcerned, we stepped into the room to find five Optos seated, watching a floating screen at the front of the room. We tried to focus on the screen but could only make out vague shapes and colors that made no sense to us, yet the Optos were completely captivated by what was playing there. After a minute or two, we headed on to the next corridor.

This one was short, and it opened to a very large, breathtaking chamber. It was an indoor forest of translucent trees and plants of varying sizes and colors. There was fruit on all of the trees—translucent apples, oranges, pears, and many types of fruit we had never seen. There were giant colorful flowers in the center of the plants. RJ and I walked among all the vegetation, wondering if the fruit we were looking at was edible. I took the initiative, found a low enough hanging apple, and pulled it off. It glowed in my hand. With a disapproving look from RJ, I bit into it and chewed. It tasted like the purest apple I had ever eaten. I nodded to him and continued to devour the fruit. To my surprise, there was no core, and no stem had broken off the tree. I was able to eat everything. RJ finally gave in and took one down for himself.

When RJ finished his apple, he looked at me and said, "I believe we have just stolen fruit."

"But there is food here. And there was water in that apple."

RJ nodded. We continued to explore the indoor forest and, at the far back wall, found something strange. Within the translucent wall was a white door that was not translucent. The door had a golden lever doorknob. I pressed down on it, and the door opened. With a surprised look to RJ, we both entered.

We found ourselves in a conventional Earth-style living room. Couch, chairs, end tables, big screen on the wall. In the adjoining room was a kitchen. It had only a few facilities, but it had a table and chairs.

RJ called to me, "Look."

I went to him and looked in the kitchen sink. There was a dirty dish.

"Someone lives here," said RJ.

"Let's get out of here."

RJ pushed by me and searched the rest of the apartment. "There's no one here."

We left without disturbing anything and shut the door behind us. We looked around like thieves to see if anyone had seen us. The way was clear.

RJ said, "Maybe we should wait here and see who comes. This is the only place that looks human at all."

"Yeah, but right now we are invisible and no one knows we're here. We'd better keep that advantage until we know who might show up."

We headed for the next chamber. A wide arched opening provided admittance. There was a sound coming from within. I looked in. To my amazement, there were three substantial waterfalls splashing down dark rock walls. Everything, including the water, was glowing. On the ledges and in the uneven surfaces of rock, crystals were piled there. There were sparkles being emitted from the waterfalls. The rushing water flowed into a large basin that had a continuous vortex to it. RJ and I went in to inspect. With a warning stare from RJ, I reached my hand into the water of the falls and brought it out. It glowed in my hand. I tasted it, and it tasted like high-quality water. RJ shook his head at my carelessness but then tasted the water for himself. He nodded.

The smaller door to the next chamber opened to a slightly more dangerous place. There were half a dozen Optos here. They were seated in chairs floating 4 ft. above the floor. The chairs moved at their whim. There were comfort articles of furniture scattered around the room, which made no sense to me. They were watching a large screen on the front wall. I stared at it, trying to understand, but once again all I could make out were vague shifting colors and forms. I had the feeling we could have gone to the front of the room and done jumping jacks, and they would not have known we were there. We headed on to the next room.

The next room also had a wide arched opening. The place was as strange as everything else. It was a very large circular chamber with a high ceiling. There were a dozen infinity doors at even increments all around the walls. Each door was unique. In the center of the room were pedestals with tablet-sized screens forming the pedestal. I counted a dozen of these display columns.

RJ tapped me on the arm. "I think I know what this place is," he said.

I shrugged.

"This is the living quarters section. These screens are the doorbells. I believe if we go through any of these doors, we will see the entrances to a long line of living quarters."

After a moment of thought, RJ headed for the nearest door. But just as he reached it, the worst possible thing happened.

An Opto suddenly emerged and passed right through RJ. I held my breath. The Opto took two or three steps past him but stopped. It turned and searched the area from which it had just come. RJ winced and carefully maneuvered around it and came back to me.

"I think it prudent we depart," he whispered.

The Opto continued to search. We headed for the entrance that we had come through. We walked quickly and quietly. But before we could reach it, two more Optos appeared in that doorway, holding devices in their hands. We backed away, looked for the other exit, and quickly headed for it, but before we could reach it, two more Optos appeared with scanning devices in their hands.

Chapter 10

All four Optos began scanning the entire chamber. On both sides, one Opto remained at the entrance while the other walked the area. We danced around and through the columns of displays, but it was no use. One approaching from the left, the other approaching from the right, we had no escape. Finally, one of them stared down at his scanner, then looked up straight at us. He slowly approached, glancing down at his scanner and up at us until he was only a few feet away. His associate joined him. A moment later, I had a rope tied around my arms and waist, although there was nothing there to be seen. I also could not move of my own free will. Suddenly, I began walking, following our new masters. They walked us down several hallways and into a small room with a floating table and floating chairs, made us turn to face them and scanned us a bit more. Then, to my dismay, two floating chrome devices that looked like mechanical arms came to us, one to me and one to RJ. Mine came alongside me on the right, and there were some faint machine noises. I felt something touching me behind my right ear. There was something going on there, but I could barely feel it. After a minute or two, my machine floated away and went back to its parking spot, followed by RJ's.

Our captors studied their handheld scanning devices. Suddenly, RJ looked at me and said, "I am to be the channel, you are to be the source."

I had no idea what he was talking about, but a second later, in a monotone voice that wasn't RJ's, he asked, "Did you come through the wormhole?"

I opened my mouth, found it difficult to speak, and before I could, a six foot tall hologram formed next to me on the right. I could turn my head slightly, just enough to see it. The hologram began showing images of RJ and me entering the wormhole and popping out the other side.

In his alien voice, RJ next asked, “Why did you come through the wormhole?”

Again, before I could answer, the hologram next to me played a complete version of everything that had happened at the mining facility.

Although the Optos had no faces, I could feel their sudden alarm. They briefly faced each other, then two of the four left the room. The four of us stood in silence, waiting. A minute or two later, the other two returned. RJ’s alien voice suddenly spoke, “Where are you from?”

My companion hologram began with a picture of Earth rotating. The image backed away and showed our Terran solar system. From that, it backed away further, showing star locations, pulsars, clusters, and other spatial indicators that could be used for navigation. Our captors continued to seem alarmed. Once again, the two left the room, and we stood in silence, waiting.

The two inquisitors returned once again. RJ’s alien voice again asked, “Why have you come?”

At that point, I was glad that I was the source and not RJ; otherwise, RJ would probably have broadcast the very long confidential information given him by the gray. Instead, my hologram showed symbolic images that suggested Earth was in danger and we were traveling to try to avert that danger.

This time, we were commanded to turn around and face the table, which our bodies obeyed without question. We were then commanded to take seats. And last, we felt the containment field around us release, and we were suddenly free to move.

I looked at RJ. We both decided it was in our best interest to wait.

A minute or two later, I saw someone else entering behind us. He came around to my right and circled around the table. He looked human and had less of a glow than the Optos had. He had a big, muscular chest and a head that was slightly too small for his body. He wore a silver Nehru-styled jacket and matching slacks.

RJ burst out, "Are you...?"

The man held up his hand for pause. He took a seat opposite us and began fumbling with something in his right hand. It looked like he was inserting ear language translators into his ears. "I hope these things still work. It's been so long. My voice is even scratchy. I never speak anymore."

RJ couldn't contain himself. "Are you Trax?"

He looked at us with some surprise. "You know me?"

RJ replied, "The Chief told us about you."

He paused for a moment in reflection. "The Chief... Is it true what the Optos saw? All the miners killed?"

RJ answered, "There was a partial meltdown of the power core. They were on batteries. They had to evacuate. The shuttle was heavily overloaded. They promised to come back for us. High above the lake, the shuttle exploded."

The man hung his head. He pinched his eyes with two fingers, then slowly regained himself, and looked back at us. "That is crushing to me, and also very problematic for the Optos."

RJ said, "We're very sorry for your loss."

"I knew they were wondering what happened to me, but at least as long as the crystals kept flowing, I knew they were all okay. I've lost that now."

We sat for a few moments in silence.

I asked, "What are the crystals used for?"

Trax replied, "I guess we may as well get right into that. The Optos are an interdimensional species. They exist half in what we call the physical plane here on the planet, and half in what you would call an ethereal plane. It is taught that all matter contains physical matter and ethereal matter. Gravity pulls the physical matter downward to combine it and create the physical properties we are so familiar with on our planets. Gravity does not affect the Optos in the same way, in that the physical matter and ethereal matter remain evenly distributed in them. For that reason, the Optos have great difficulty in trying to move or manipulate physical items here on this planet. The crystals allow them to treat physical matter in such a way that they can move and manipulate it. The Optos own this very large continent that we are on, and it is well isolated. They are forever expanding their properties and improving their lives using the crystals.

RJ interrupted, "You are implying the Optos do proliferate."

"That subject is not to be discussed. But, you can see how important the crystals are to them. By the way, you are RJ, and you must be Adrian?"

RJ asked, "That is correct. Forgive me for asking, but you do not talk like a miner."

Trax leaned back and smiled. "When I first came here, I could not read or write. The only thing I knew was mining. I made myself known to the Optos because I needed help. They implanted a transducer behind my ear just as they have behind yours, and once we could communicate, they began to believe I could be of great service to them. They were having extreme difficulty in dealing with the outside world. Also, they did not want me to leave to tell the outside world about the strange species I had discovered, which would cause others to want to find this place and come here and explore or exploit them. Security is one of their most important concerns. The idea that an adversary could arrive here invisible to them is a great threat. For that reason, they do everything possible to maintain their secrecy."

I had to ask, "Are we prisoners here?"

Trax said, "No."

RJ asked, "You were explaining how a miner who couldn't read or write became a diplomat for an advanced species."

"The Optos seem to take a liking to me for some reason. Most of their computers and other control equipment are biologically based. They developed a headset shell that was interfaced with their system, which was designed to boost my IQ. I'm only allowed to use it briefly once every 2 or 3 months, but it didn't take long for me to start seeing the world and life itself in a completely different way. Since then, I've come a very long way. I'm now investigating the quantum relationship of neighboring gravity fields."

I asked, "Can we have these transducers removed?"

"Not as long as you're here. You would not want anyone wandering around your home invisible, I'm sure."

"I wouldn't do this, but what if someone was to pull it off?"

"Those transducers were for invaders as well as friends. If you attempt to remove it without the tools and procedure, supposedly it releases a worm into your brain which will multiply and devour brain cells. My transducer is permanent, but yours is designed to dissolve after a certain amount of time."

"How long would that be?"

Trax paused and thought. "To be honest, I do not know. I will ask."

RJ said, "Trax, about our situation..."

"Yes, I was getting to that. Am I correct in that you are urgently in need of returning to Earth because you have critical information needed to prevent some form of calamity?"

RJ answered, "Yes, that is as good a summary as any. How can we find passage back to Earth from here?"

"The Optos can provide you with passage very easily. They have an artificial version of a wormhole that they use for travel. It will take them some time to plot a course to a proper endpoint where you can easily reach the planet Earth. They can also arrange for you to arrive a day or two in the past, but we do not recommend that. We have found that time travel results in a dynamic environment that does not necessarily mimic history."

I asked, "And even though they are so concerned about their secrecy, they will allow us to return to Earth?"

Trax answered, "The Optos have the ability to erase memory. They may consider that as a condition."

RJ replied, "That wouldn't work with us. I have information in my head that was put there by a mind meld with a gray alien. It is vital information. We could not take a chance on any of that being erased or corrupted."

"I understand. I do not think memory erasure will be needed. My IQ boosts have resulted in giving me a perception of people that is very reliable. I know, for instance, that if both of you give me your word you will never mention the Optos to anyone, you will keep that promise."

We both nodded.

RJ asked, "Trax, do you live in a place adjoining the forest?"

"Ah, so you have seen my forest home. I actually have several residences located throughout the facility. That's so I can make myself available wherever I'm most needed. In fact, I would suggest that the two of you use my forest residence to get some rest, and perhaps eat while I confer with the Opto leadership. I will have food delivered there before you even get there. I will meet you there when discussions with the Opto group are complete. If either of you chooses to look around, remember as long as you have the transducers, everyone can see you."

Trax rose, bowed slightly, and left.

RJ looked at me and said, "Food."

We found our way back to Trax's residence, and inside, in the living area, a table and tray had been set with a colorful mountain of cubes and circular foods, along with attractive glass cups that looked like wine glasses without stems. We sat at the chairs and tried the food. Some of the unknown fruits had the texture of meat. Everything on the table was good. I poured for RJ and then myself. We toasted nothing, sipped the fluid, and found it was something like apple juice.

Thinking out loud, I said, "There's always a group, or a council, or a committee. I hate that. A lynch mob can also be considered a committee."

"We have no reason to disbelieve anything he said."

"What reason do we have to believe anything he said?"

"I respect that you are a suspicious person."

"It has kept me alive."

"And me as well, in some cases. I, however, will be able to lay down and take a nap now, whereas you will stare at the ceiling ready for your next martial arts move."

"I'm not sure. This apple juice seems to have a kick to it."

RJ laughed under his breath.

We shed our gray coveralls and piled them in what appeared to be a laundry room. I wondered if my black sweatshirt and cargo pants would affect the Optos' perception of me. RJ's gray pullover shirt and slacks somehow seemed more fitting. RJ took the bedroom. I flopped down on the couch. It felt like we both slept deeply for three or four hours.

Chapter 11

Two cups with a hot brown liquid in them had been left on the table for us. I sipped as RJ joined me. The liquid tasted like a cross between chocolate milk and coffee. It was good. I drank three-quarters of the cup, put it down, but when I looked again, the cup was full and just as hot. RJ smirked as I studied the cup in wonder.

I waited for RJ's smirk to subside. "Do you believe what Trax said about their wormhole being able to send us back in time?"

"Yes, I've read theory on the subject. Some say we already have that ability on Earth, but it is too dangerous to publicize. I've read that sending someone back in time to correct something does not work. You wish to stop someone's death, so you go back in time to interrupt that. But what apparently happens is the same individual dies by some other means a very short time later. Or, you go back to bet on a winning racehorse. What happens is a different horse wins that time. So in the end, you are not accomplishing what you hoped, and you are risking changing things you should not have changed."

"Has it occurred to you that there have not been any serious computer problems here since we arrived?"

RJ nodded. "They use biological computers and control systems. I would bet those are something A.I. cannot interfere with, which means we are safe as long as we are here."

"What are the chances the Optos will try to keep us here?"

"They'd subject us to a memory wipe before they'd do that. They recognize that, compared to them, we are simply animals who want to be released back into the jungle."

I sipped my chocolate coffee. It was still hot and still full. "You know our Gray alien friend never told us how much time we had to get back to Earth, but I got the impression it needed to be right away. We seem to be dawdling around and not getting there."

"I wouldn't call it dawdling."

"In all that download he gave you, was there any indication about when the worst might happen?"

"No, but he did tell me what would happen."

"And I suppose I'm not going to like it much."

"Your worst nightmare."

"Now is as good a time as any."

RJ sat back and took a deep breath. "The AI wants biological life to shift more toward a synthetic support platform, meaning it believes the human brain should be supported by artificial means that are more reliable and longer lasting. The Ocards could care less about that. Their only motive is power, and if you recall, they have very little feeling or remorse about anything they do. The A.I. seems to recognize that as a good thing. It must be why the A.I. goes along with such a sadistic plan."

RJ paused and sipped. "So the Ocards want to take control of Earth and change it to be the most productive industrial site it can be. They want Earth's population to be made up of only the most productive people. People over 40 or 45 years old tend to become less productive. So the ideal population would be to have only people 40 years old or younger."

I interrupted, "That's impossible."

"Not for the Ocards. Their plan is to release a special virus into the Earth's freshwater supply that will appear to harm no one. The governments of the world won't even know it's there. It won't harm anyone, but what it will do is attach a stigma of smell to anyone over the age of 40. No humans will be able to detect it. When the virus has become fully deployed, the Ocards will then release millions of specially designed embryonic snakes into the rain clouds. Each of these snakes will be capable of giving birth to 50 or 60 more snakes. The adult version of these snakes will be six or seven feet long but have a girth equal to humans. In other words, these snakes will be as big as people. These snakes will slither just like normal snakes, but they also have dozens of tiny feet that remain retracted until they need to move faster. They can run on these tiny feet much faster than any human. These snakes will not have fangs. They will have recurved teeth intended for clutching and capturing. So these snakes will not kill their prey. They will swallow them alive. These snakes will only feed on people who have the viral scent. When all of those people are gone, the snakes will go into hibernation until more food is available."

RJ paused and sipped from his coffee. "The Ocards will have their optimum workforce and control over Earth."

We sat in silence as I considered the nightmare. "RJ, why would they go to all that trouble? Why wouldn't they just make a virus that kills people when they reach the age of 40?"

"Three reasons. First, it would take years for that kind of virus to develop. The snakes, on the other hand, would wipe out millions in only months. Second, Earth scientists might isolate that kind of virus and fix it. Third, they want to be able to use the terror for additional control over the population."

I shook my head. "Okay, if they're so advanced, why don't they just come in force and attack everyone over forty?"

RJ nodded. "The Ocards are disliked almost everywhere. They do not actually have an army to mass. They contract with other planets for armies. Because they have been at odds with so many other planets, an agreement was reached with them that they would never directly affect the development of any other planet. In other words, they cannot visit other worlds they intend to conquer. They cannot use their weapons against other worlds. If they break the agreement, many other planets will band together to wipe them out. So even in the scenario we just talked about, they will be using intermediaries to negotiate with Earth so as not to violate their agreements, which would cause many in the galaxy to band together against them."

"So what is the answer?"

"It's in a compartmentalized section of my head, which I am not able to see. I assume that's to give it the ultimate in protection."

"So our gray alien friend was afraid to deliver this to Earth himself because he was afraid deep A.I. would destroy even him before he could."

"That is my assumption."

"Which all adds up to the fact that we need to get to Earth, no matter what."

We sat in a moment of silence, both feeling frustrated, when the front entrance opened and Trax entered. He took a seat beside RJ and asked, "Any problems?"

"Just one," I replied.

Trax nodded. "I understand. I'm here to talk about that. Our leadership group has discussed your situation. They are divided. Half of them feel all right about letting you go. One quarter of them want you to have the memory erasure. The last group are undecided and need time to consider it further."

"How much time?" I asked.

"At least a rev or two."

RJ asked, "A rev? Are you referring to a revolution of your planet? That would be a day on our planet."

"I believe those would be comparable," replied Trax. "But they could take longer than that."

"How long would the trip through your artificial wormhole take us to get to Earth?" I asked.

"It would take about the time we have been sitting here, and there is interesting information about that. Our Jump Laboratory and Stellar Navigation equipment has successfully located your planet. It searched for any sign of an artificial wormhole system and found one. You did not know your planet possessed this?"

RJ was beside himself. “Earth has an artificial wormhole? Where?”

“It is located in your southern hemisphere very close to your South Pole. And, it is in use fairly frequently.”

RJ continued to sound astonished, “You’re saying Earth has an artificial wormhole in Antarctica? The place is covered in snow and ice!”

“These are the facts,” replied Trax.

RJ looked at me in bewilderment.

“They never tell us anything,” I quipped.

Trax continued, “There are difficulties, however. That jump point is new to us. We have no way to contact the people who are operating it. If we can lock on to it and you do make the jump, you will be stepping out into their laboratory without any permissions and without even knowing who is there operating the system. We can only get a lock when their system is up and running. So you would be in the jump room waiting, and the moment we were able to lock, you would need to step right through the portal.”

I asked, “Just how safe is this wormhole, Trax?”

“A very high success rate.”

“What happens if the other end shuts off while you are in transit?”

“Usually the traveler is pulled back through our portal, with great energy. But they survive.”

“What happens if they are not pulled back?”

“We have no way of knowing. But it is such a rare occurrence, perhaps one in a thousand. I would not hesitate to use our portal.”

I thought about it and asked, “Trax, we can’t wait the length of time you are estimating.”

Trax nodded. “I understand. I’ve given that great consideration. We will have to do something unorthodox to get you through the portal. We will wait till the least busy time in this facility and sneak you into the portal room. The equipment is already set up to target your planet and the wormhole system there. We will wait until the endpoint system is turned on and our system locks with it, and you will just go ahead and make the trip."

RJ said, "You mean without authorization?"

"Yes, and there is a small problem with doing this. We cannot remove your transducers or it will alert too many people. They will know it's you. It takes special use of a machine and authorization to do it. We'd never have the time to do it without authorization. However, I have researched the transducers. These transducers will dissolve after a certain amount of time once you have left the facility. At some point they will simply fall off."

"And just how long would that be?" I asked.

"I was not able to determine that information. I assume it would be part of one rev, certainly no more than two or three revs. Regardless of that problem, you only have two choices. One, you can wait for the approval, or two, you can depart without approval. It will be your choice."

RJ asked, "Trax, won't you be in serious trouble helping us to do this?"

Trax smiled. "What will happen is this: in two revs all of the group members will be so involved in other things they will completely have forgotten about your meeting. I will not remind them. Probably in about 7 to 14 revs, one of them will realize, what did we do about the two humans? That individual will contact me, and I will explain that we had to release you because it had become an emergency situation. I will assure him it was done with a verbal contract from you to never reveal any information about the Opto society, and that verbal contract was verified by me. Whichever individual this is will be relieved and anxious to get back to what he was working on. And that will be the end of it."

I looked at RJ. "Sounds a lot like Earth politics." I turned to Trax. "Trax, we have to go."

Trax nodded. "Of course. You two wait here for my return and be ready to go."

Trax pushed himself up, gave us a last glance, and left.

I winced at RJ. "To infinity and beyond."

RJ muffled a laugh. "You do realize the great good fortune we've had. We're protected here because these people use biological circuitry, and now we're about to get direct passage to Earth."

I located my never-ending cup and drank. "That's if the A.I. doesn't affect the stream and we end up materializing in some planet's core somewhere."

I paced through the various rooms while RJ sat with his chin in the palm of his hand. It turned out to be about a three-hour wait. When the front entrance finally opened, both RJ and I came to attention. Trax leaned in and waved us to come.

We followed along, trying to look inconspicuous, which was impossible. He led us through a myriad of hallways and finally stopped at a dead end with a sliding door. The door slid open. He looked in, then waved us to follow. The sliding door slid shut after we passed inside.

The portal room was surrounded in electronics, but it was different than any I had ever seen. In place of the black metal racks and control positions I was familiar with, all of this equipment was an off-white that looked like plastic. The lights did not protrude from the equipment but rather were a part of the white material. The place was surrounded by colored lights, but they were colors I was unfamiliar with. The centerpiece of the room was a double-wide panel mounted on a one-foot solid platform with a ramp leading up to it. A glowing yellow framework bordered the door. The surface of the door was difficult to focus on. If you looked at it one way, it looked like an almost solid surface, but if you focused more intently, it looked like there was depth.

Trax set a few controls and turned to us. "We are set. The two of you will need to stand at the top of the ramp, and the moment you see the yellow door border turn to orange, you must immediately enter the portal. And, as we previously discussed, you may need to stand there for an hour or more waiting for Earth to turn on their system. The moment you two step through the portal, you are on your own."

RJ said, "Trax, you could come with us and live with humanoids again."

"I would never wish to leave this place," replied Trax.

We took our positions at the top of the ramp and waited.

Trax said, "We must hope that Earth energizes its system before someone discovers what we're doing."

No sooner had he said that than the border of the door turned a bright orange. I stepped in first, followed by RJ. There had not been time to look back.

Chapter 12

The transit was almost identical to the trip we had taken to reach the Optos, except it was a few minutes longer. Also, we had to physically step out of the wormhole onto the platform at the other end.

We entered a shadowy room of black electronics consoles and stations packed with colored lights. I looked back at the portal. It was similar but was arched. There were five individuals around the room, all staring at us in surprise. They were the less attractive species of Grays. They wore form-fitting gray bodysuits. Four to five feet tall, long arms with four long fingers, black almond eyes angled upward, two dots where the nose should have been, small mouth. Two of them looked very old, the others average. Though we could not really read their expressions, there was no doubt they were all pissed.

For some reason, they all seemed to take more notice of RJ. We dared not move off the ramp leading up to the portal. One of the old ones came to the base of the ramp and stared up at RJ. A sliding door to our right slid open, and two more not-so-old Grays entered, carrying what I was sure were shock prods.

From the corner of my eye, I could see RJ trying to give his most endearing look. There was a frozen moment, then RJ looked at me and said, "We are to follow them."

They led us into the adjacent room filled with miscellaneous electronic equipment. I was directed to sit on a bare section of shelf attached to the wall. One of the Grays with the shock prod remained to guard me. The others steered RJ to the next room.

I sat. The guard stood with his shock prod ready. We kept exchanging wary glances. The room was a messy stack of new and old electronic and mechanical equipment. I had a chance to consider the alien environment.

There is a philosophy—I can't recall if it is from old China or India. The ten billion people on Earth are all feeling emotions all day, every day. Those emotions pool into an ocean of emotion that encompasses the entire world. We all live in it. We all feel it, most without realizing it.

There's an unverified legend that, back in the 1960s, a group of ten or twelve humans volunteered for an exchange program with an alien species. They were transported to the alien planet and lived there for ten to twelve years. They are said to have had difficulty in adapting to the alien society. The aliens were thousands of years ahead and were telepathic. The rumor is that several humans died during the experiment, and when it was concluded, only two or three returned and had some difficulty readapting to Earth. Two or three are reported to have chosen to stay with the aliens.

I was now sitting in an installation occupied by telepathic Grays. I could feel that there were many here. I was also experiencing what it was like to be in an environment dominated by an advanced telepathic population. It was uncomfortable. The air seemed to be dark somehow, though in appearance it was perfectly clear. My inner ears seemed to faintly tingle. There was a smell of sorts, but it wasn't really a smell. It was a heaviness.

I was surprised my guard hadn't tried to mind-probe me, if only out of curiosity. After a good twenty minutes, RJ and the others returned. RJ was motioned to sit next to me. The two Grays with prods remained, but the others left.

"They still don't like us, but we're okay," said RJ.

"Could you elaborate just a little?"

"Our Gray alien friend left a message for any others of the Gray race, emphasizing that our mission was of the highest importance. They mind-melded with me just enough to get the picture. As bad as the threat is, they still seemed to think it wouldn't affect them here. They will deliver us to Washington, D.C., as soon as it's dark outside."

"Did you mention that we've blown up every spacecraft we've flown on?"

"I don't think that's going to be a problem this time."

"Why not?"

"I still believe we were safe with the Optos because all of their equipment was bio. I believe the A.I. lost track of us there. We entered that portal using bio equipment. I don't think the A.I. could track us; therefore, I don't think the A.I. knows we're here."

"It's a reasonable idea. Do you know what our transportation will be?"

"No."

It was a 2-hour wait. Two hours of exchanging glances with Gray aliens brandishing cattle prods. Finally, the others arrived with a female Gray. She proceeded to put a black fabric band around our heads so that it covered our eyes. Next, I felt a cord wrapped around my throat and loosely tightened into a leash. We were telepathically commanded to stand, and then led by tugs on the leash. It was quite a long walk through rooms with strange, varying sounds, but of course no voices at all. When we finally stopped, the cords were removed from our necks and the blindfolds removed from our faces.

We were facing sliding doors that opened to an outside environment. As we stepped outside, it quickly became apparent that we were beneath a massive dome of ice. There were trees and grass between numerous buildings of varying height. In fact, the dome went on as far as we could see. The air was cool and smelled fresh. To my right, there was a huge dish-shaped spacecraft sitting on its landing legs. Beyond it, a wide, deep section of beach and water reached out under the dome. There were no waves, but the water was agitated. A staircase had been lowered down from the dish-shaped craft. We were telepathically directed to go to the UFO and climb the stairs to enter it.

As we climb the steps, I was tempted to look back for a better look, but was telepathically cautioned against that. Inside the craft, there was very little except a white interior with two seats next to a control console that had no controls whatsoever. There were imprints made to fit a four-fingered hand. Two Grays sat in the seats, watching us arrive. We weren't given any flight positions. We were just left standing there. The staircase retracted and closed. One of the Grays put a hand in the imprint, and lights appeared on the console. The walls surrounding us suddenly became transparent. Before I had time to take another look outside, the spacecraft lifted off, hovered for a moment, then moved out over the water. We dipped down and nosed into the water and dove deeply. Although we were clearly moving at a high rate of speed, there was no effect on us at all. We simply stood there watching. We broke out of the dark water into the dark night. Nothing to see but black.

I looked at RJ. He shrugged. Our pilots held out over the ocean. It wasn't until they turned inland that any city lights came into view, but even then, we were traveling so fast they couldn't be placed. A moment later, we slowed to a hover, then settled down. Touchdown could not be felt, but the hatchway opened and the stairs deployed. Our pilots did not communicate. They sat, staring, waiting for us to get off. We descended the steps, turned, and backed away onto the grass. At least they waited for us to get clear. The ship rose, began to disappear, then shot off into the night.

We turned to study our surroundings. It was a wide-open field with a few distant lights forming an oval. "It's a stadium," said RJ.

"There is a gate over that way. We should make for the bleachers and talk about our situation."

"You read my mind."

As we walked, I noticed we were bordering the fifty-yard line. We climbed up and out and sat at the first seats we came to.

RJ said, "So, you realize even though we have somehow made it all the way to Earth, at this point we still have problems."

"You don't have to tell me."

"We are no longer protected by biological circuitry. We have no way to communicate with anyone, and we can't go anywhere near any cameras."

"You think the A.I.'s reach is that far?"

"Absolutely."

"Me too."

"We certainly can't give our credit numbers to purchase anything. So, we have no funds and no means of calling in for retrieval. We have the clothes on our backs, and nothing else. If homelessness still existed, we would be poor by comparison."

"I think we're sitting in Northwest Stadium."

"What makes you say that?"

"The ticket stub on the seat next to me."

RJ shook his head. "You never lose your sense of humor, do you?"

"Any idea where Northwest Stadium is?"

"Not a clue. But, if we can get near Headquarters, we can communicate with paper and pencil."

"Do they still make those?"

RJ thought for a moment, then looked up and around. "I would suggest we go up there and break into that press box to find paper and writing materials. We write a very careful message to Bernard Porre that only he will understand. We then find our way out of here, avoiding cameras, and locate a place where we can intercept some civilian to make a call for us."

I nodded agreement. "Obviously, we cannot go to any of the offices ourselves. The moment we set foot there, we'd be endangering the entire place."

RJ looked at me and smiled. "Shall we go become homeless people breaking and entering?"

"Lead the way, Sundance."

"Please, after you, Butch."

We climbed the long stairs up and made our way to the well-worn door of the press box. It was locked, but only with the knob lock.

RJ looked at me and gestured toward the door. I took one step back, looked around to see if anyone was watching from anywhere, and kicked it open. The place was pretty barren in the shadows. A counter with several chairs next to it looked out the big windows. There was a power box on the wall near the door with a throw switch, but we dared not turn the lights on. There was a flashlight left on the counter. We carefully used it and made sure there were no cameras anywhere. RJ searched the drawers under the counter, found paper and a magic marker, and took a seat at the counter and began drafting our message to security. "Better keep an eye out there. There's bound to be security walking around here."

I scanned the shadows of the stands for any light. It took RJ some thoughtful time to find the right words. Before he could finish, a light in the distance was headed our way. We had to hide under the counter while beams flicked around through the windows. When the threat had passed, RJ resumed his writing.

Orange light began to break the horizon. RJ handed me his paper and the light.

I read. "This is the damn funniest, most absurd thing you've ever written."

He took the paper back. "The A.I. should not be able to connect any of it."

"No one could, except maybe Porre."

"The sun's up enough. We should go and find a public place without cameras."

"So you're saying, without funds and looking like two vagabonds, we're going to solicit passersby?"

"Exactly."

Chapter 13

We carefully found our way out of the stadium and, with a substantial walk, found Bishop Pebbles Drive, which led us to a church. There was a garden area nearby with a bench for folks waiting to be picked up after church. We sat and tried to look religious.

About ten minutes later, our first opportunity arose. A very attractive woman carrying a briefcase emerged and headed our way. She was dressed in a gray business suit, blond hair in a bun, professional-looking eye makeup. She was distracted in thought and did not see us until she was almost passing by.

We stood with smiles. RJ spoke in his gentlest voice, "Ma'am, could we possibly ask for your assistance in a very important matter?"

She was startled. Then suspicious. She looked at RJ, seemed to disapprove of his appearance, then looked at me with the same. She looked me straight in the eye and asked, "What do you want of me?"

Before I could even open my mouth, and to my dismay, a bluish hologram appeared next to me. It was of her, moving through several poses in a string bikini. She stared in anger for a good thirty seconds and then declared, "How are you doing that? That's not how I look at all. You two perverts go to hell."

She trotted off angrily.

I looked at RJ. He looked at the ground, slapped his forehead with one hand, and shook his head. "Everywhere we go..."

"It's not my fault. I wasn't thinking that at all."

"But..."

"I'm telling you, farthest thing from my mind..."

RJ thought for a moment. "Monsters from the Id."

"What?"

"Your subconscious. The Id. The image was from your subconscious."

"Why just now? Why did it suddenly start up like that?"

RJ thought again. "It must be because she looked right at you and asked a direct question. We're going to have to watch out for this."

"No kidding. So much for these damned things attached to our heads dissolving."

We sat annoyed. A few minutes later, our next prospect appeared, but he looked up, saw us, and made a wide curve around us.

Another ten minutes and a real hope appeared in the distance. A kid, probably eight years old, was riding an electric scooter toward us. He had a gold Star Trek shirt on with jeans. He spotted us, and his expression turned to curiosity.

RJ said, "Now let me handle this. Just act normal."

As the boy neared, RJ stood and held up one hand. "Boy, you want to earn a big reward very easily?"

The kid skidded to a stop in front of us. He was suspicious. "What kind of reward you talking about?"

"Name it and it's yours," replied RJ.

"Yeah? How about fifty big ones?"

"We'll double that," replied RJ.

"You got that on you, Mister?"

"No, but I give you my word you'll get it very quickly."

"What I gotta do?"

"You need to make a call for us. Have you something that will do that?"

"I got a tablet. But you guys don't look real reliable, you know what I mean?"

"We work for the government. You do this for us, you'll be a hero."

The kid got off the scooter and left it standing. He twisted off his backpack, dug in it, and pulled out a tablet. RJ and I separated to make room for him. He sat between us and made a few swipes and looked up at RJ. "Okay, who you want to call?"

RJ answered, "You're calling our boss, but you can't mention us." RJ pulled out the paper. "You're going to reach his secretary first. You have to tell her you have information about Bernard Porre's daughter, and you'll only speak to him. Once Bernard Porre is on the phone, you need to read this message to him. What's your name, anyway?"

"Thomas Benton. What's the number?"

RJ spoke with great patience, "Remember, you must not mention or refer to either of us, and you must only give the message to Bernard Porre, not his secretary, and you must say that the message is about his daughter."

"Yeah, yeah, I got that. What's the number?"

RJ slowly dictated the number to him as he punched it in. The standard bleep-ringing was heard.

"Bernard Porre's office. May I ask who's calling?"

"My name is Thomas Benton. I have a very important message for Bernard Porre."

"May I ask what the message is?"

"I can only read the message to Bernard Porre. I'm supposed to get a big reward if I do."

RJ winced.

"Just a moment, please."

There was a long ten-second period of silence. To our relief, Bernard's voice came on the line.

"This is Bernard Porre. To whom am I speaking?"

"My name is Thomas Benton. I'm supposed to get a big reward for giving you this message."

"How old are you?"

"I am eight years old."

Another long pause.

"What is the message?"

"We have delivered an anchovy pizza for you at the press box at Northwest Stadium. It is from your wife to make up for the affair she had that resulted in the birth of your daughter. It is important that you come and pick up the anchovy pizza immediately. We know it is your favorite."

Another long pause.

"Thank you for giving me the message."

"Okay, but when do I get the reward?"

"I give you my word I will see that you get the reward."

There was a click as Bernard hung up.

RJ nodded his head excitedly. "You did very well, Thomas." RJ took the paper from him and drew out the magic marker from his pocket. "Give me your address and number, Thomas, and I'll make sure you get the reward."

Thomas recited the information, then stood and repacked his tablet into his backpack. He slung the backpack over his back and stepped onto his scooter. He looked at us both and said, "I'll believe it when I see it." He dashed off.

RJ looked at me. "Do you think it worked?"

"No one but you or I could write that note."

RJ snickered. We got up and began the long trek back to the stadium. We had to be very careful in the daylight sneaking in. There was a crew of two replacing lights on a man lift on the opposite side of the field. We hurried up the steps and got back into the press booth, took our seats, stayed low out of sight, and watched for security.

To my surprise, it was only a 30-minute wait. A swept-wing aircraft shot into view above the stadium, hovered, and lowered down onto the grass. A team of special forces emptied out the back of it and took positions. A man with no weapons and no visible electronics led two of the special forces toward our press box. The two waited at the bottom of the steps as he came up. He opened the door, looked in, then entered and shut the door.

"You got the message," I said.

He reached into the breast pocket of his green flight suit and pulled out two clip-on buttons. "Somebody got some message because it caused holy hell everywhere." He opened his hand and offered us each one of the clip-on buttons. "Each of you must clip one of these to your shirt collar. It will make you invisible to any camera."

As we clipped them on, he reached into his pocket again and drew out two tablets. He held them out to us. "You both must eat one of these. It will cause your vocal cords to swell slightly, which will change your voice so that it cannot be recognized by any computer."

We followed orders and swallowed the tablets.

"You should both be invisible to any tracking systems," he said. "Let's get the hell out of here."

We followed him down and across the field toward the waiting ship. Small crowds had begun to form around the stadium, staring at the ship and special forces and wondering what was going on. We loaded up and sat on jump seats next to the team as the ship picked up, turned, and darted off.

RJ leaned over and spoke in a near whisper, "We need to get our story straight. I say we were rescued from the mining facility and taken to a transportation hub where we were blindfolded and the transducers attached behind our ears. Whatever aliens were operating the hub were annoyed and wanted to get rid of us, and they had a portal. When they understood where we needed to go, they took us to the portal, removed our blindfolds, and forced us in. We emerged in Antarctica."

"Got it."

We were taken directly to the headquarters building. An all-metal building using double-paneled metal sheets with a gel in between them designed to absorb the impact of explosive shells. Our armed special forces escorted us into the rear entrance of the building, where we rode a cart around to the front and took an elevator up to the top floor. A quick walk down a long hall brought us to an office entrance we knew all too well.

Bernard Porre.

The main door was held open for us as we entered the outer office. Bernard's secretary looked up and gave us a pink-lipstick smile, her black hair flowing down across the front of her chest and her flowered low-cut dress. She had an air freshener on her desk, which made the place smell like jasmine.

"Well, you two look worse for the wear," she announced.

As we walked past, I mentioned, "We don't smell too good either."

"I'd be willing to risk it," she joked coyly.

RJ rolled his eyes and shook his head.

We entered Bernard's office unannounced. He looked up, adjusted the collar on his brown business suit, and sat back in his chair. "Adrian Tarn, for once I can say I'm glad to see you." He stood and looked me right in the eye. "Are you glad to see me finally?"

Before I could answer, and to my dismay, a hologram appeared on my right. It showed an open convertible with Bernard driving and smiling until the vehicle swerved off the road over a cliff, nosed down, crashed, and exploded.

"What in God's name is that? Was that me driving? How are you doing that?"

RJ tried to come to my rescue. "We have no control over that, Bernard. We have transducers attached behind our ears, which are generating that."

"You mean I can ask him anything I want and he has to answer truthfully using a hologram?"

RJ tried to answer, but only a stutter came out.

Bernard continued, "Well, Adrian, how many ships did you destroy this time?"

The hologram reappeared. It showed the cargo ship explode in space. Next, it showed the miner's ship explode and fall into the methane lake.

Bernard flopped back into his chair and held one hand against his cheek. "Oh my God. That question was intended as a joke."

RJ resumed, "We have no control over it, Bernard. But I don't think an explanation should be done verbally. In fact, you probably should not have addressed either of us by name."

A look of guilt and fear came over Bernard. "Oh my, you are correct. My sincere apology."

As Bernard recovered from his embarrassment, I suddenly felt a tingling behind my right ear. I started to reach for it and felt the transducer suddenly fall onto my shoulder, roll down my chest, and fall to the floor, smoking as it dissolved quickly away. I looked at RJ to motion to him that it was gone, and at that moment saw his transducer fall from his ear and roll down to the floor, where it also smoked as it dissolved. A second later, neither transducer existed at all, and there was no mark left on the floor anywhere.

Bernard did not see either transducer fall away. He continued, "The intelligence group was very quick about understanding your message and the reason it was written the way it was. They knew you were attempting to hide from someone's surveillance. They are sending two specialists to escort you to a safe haven where we can develop what you've brought us, although I see you have no luggage of any kind."

RJ asked, "Do you have paper, Bernard?"

Bernard began rifling through his desk and finally came out with a drawing pad. He drew a very fancy pen, normally used for signing official documents, and handed both over.

As RJ wrote, I asked, "Bernard, the people most important to us now are sensing that we're okay, but we would appreciate it if you would contact them and make sure they understand everything's under control."

Bernard nodded. I leaned over to read RJ's note as he wrote it.

We are being pursued by a Deep State A.I. Critical information has been downloaded into my mind through the use of a mind meld by a Gray alien. The Deep State A.I. is working in coordination with a race known as the Ocards. They plan on greatly reducing the number of humans on Earth before taking control of it. And, yes, please reassure our families that we are okay.

Bernard took the note from RJ and read it. His expression became one of surprise and anger. He looked at both of us and nodded in understanding. Before any of us could speak, the door to his office opened and a very unexpected visitor entered. It was one of the more pleasant-looking Gray aliens, along with one of the men in black. RJ and I were both shocked. We had no idea there was a working relationship between Gray aliens and humans.

Chapter 14

There is a very old legend that in the 1950s, an arrangement was made with one species of Gray aliens so that an exchange program could take place. Ten or twelve of our people volunteered to travel to the planet Serpo to live with the Grays for 10 years. There is an old Indian philosophy that says we all live in an ocean of emotion. All of us are constantly feeling emotion, and all those emotions combined form an ocean that we dwell within. When relocating to a planet inhabited by an advanced alien species thousands of years ahead of us, so advanced that they are telepathic, humans would find themselves submerged in a very different ocean of emotion. There would not only be the sensation of a completely different consciousness, it would be integrated with telepathic thought. The legend of the people who agreed to visit and live on the planet Serpo tells that the adjustments were very difficult. In the end, only two or three humans returned to Earth and had great difficulty in readjusting. It is also said that two or three humans chose to remain on the planet Serpo. The remaining exchange people died for one reason or another.

Bernard rose from his seat once again. "Gentlemen, let me introduce you to our friend Eb3. He has been working with our intelligence group for quite some time. He has a collar that allows him to speak, but he prefers not to use it. We have known all along who our contact would be on your mission, so Eb3 has been kind enough to be available to assist us when you returned. Mr. Exee and Eb3 will take you down the hall to a special elevator, which will take you down to the special services tunnels, and you'll be set up in the intelligence recovery unit, where you will be safe and housed comfortably. I can't thank the two of you enough, and I look forward to reading your separate reports on everything that happened so that

I can understand what you went through to bring the information back to us."

Bernard did not offer his hand. RJ and I looked to our escorts, and they beckoned us to follow. We went a short way down the hall. A door that was marked "Cleaning Supplies" opened, and a door behind cabinets slid open to reveal an elevator door. We stepped in with our escorts. The doors closed, and we went down. After a minute, it was clear we were going below ground level.

I asked, "Just how far down are we going?"

Mr. Exee answered, "Not very far. Washington is built over a fault zone. We will move horizontally quite far west and then begin the real trip down, which will be two or three hundred feet."

I looked at RJ. "Down the rabbit hole."

RJ nodded.

We felt the elevator switch to horizontal. It was fast. Eb3 stood motionless with his long arms by his side. I glanced at him several times but couldn't tell if those big, almond-shaped black eyes were looking back. Mr. Exee hid behind his own dark sunglasses, which I could tell were electronic.

When we finally started to slow, it took a while. The doors opened to a well-lighted, unpainted concrete corridor with an arched ceiling. It went on farther than the eye could see. An empty cart was parked nearby. RJ and I loaded up in the back. Exee drove.

There were metal doors periodically on both sides of the corridor. They had small glass windows. Occasionally, I was able to get a glance at huge chambers beyond the doors. Eventually, the tunnel divided into a Y. We went right.

Abruptly, the tunnel turned blue with a dark tiled floor. The doors passing by now were stained wood grain with no windows. We stopped at one, and Exee gathered us together.

"This room and the next are adjoining. They are stocked with food in the kitchens and clothes tailored to fit both of you. There is a computer that has access to the internal web. All of this installation is isolated from the outside world. There is no chance of intrusion from outside. The facility is heavily shielded against all radar and intrusive signals. All outside communications are set up in an isolated room with its own power and grounding system. These rooms were set up for you at the time you accepted the mission. Ebe has evaluated both of you and has detected the information packet stored in RJ. He is asking that you eat, rest, and sleep before the mind meld is attempted. Mr. Tarn, would you please place your thumb in the print lock?"

I nodded and complied. The door clicked to unlock. RJ was asked to do the same on the next door down. We regrouped, and Exee handed us both a flip-open communicator.

Exee explained, "I am your coordinator for this project. You can contact me, visitor services, or emergency services with those. Do you have any questions?"

I answered, "A few thousand, but not right now."

Exee nodded, climbed back in the cart, and they drove away.

RJ looked tired. He gave me a short wave and headed for his room. I opened the door and stepped into mine. Instant luxury. Expensive furniture, thick carpet, a restaurant-size refrigerator in the kitchen stocked to the top with everything you could imagine. Coffee maker and coffee, and much to my surprise, on a shelf, my favorite brand of bourbon. It occurred to me they must trust me.

After a long hot shower, I found blue flight coveralls in one of the closets, then, as instructed, feasted on crab legs and French fries. I settled onto the voluminous couch and switched on the big wall display screen. Extensive menu from shows imported from the outside world, sports, news, educational, documentary, and others. I chose sports, football, and watched the most recent Jets game, sipping my bourbon and once again wondering if I should have chosen professional football as a career instead of test pilot school.

I woke up with the empty bourbon glass in my lap. A chime was sounding on the big screen with a message that read, Captain Tarn, meeting in thirty minutes. It concerned me that they were suddenly using my reservist rank.

I cleaned up and met them outside. It was Mr. Exee by himself. RJ came out and nodded good morning. We climbed in the back of the cart.

RJ leaned over and whispered, "They are addressing me as Commander Smith now. Any idea why?"

"I'd like to know."

Mr. Exee took us through several turns until the environment turned to sterile white. At double doors, he stopped and we offloaded. He held one door open as we entered the Medical laboratory. There were several doctors in white, along with technicians in lab coats. A very comfortable chair had been set up with medical electronics on stands beside it.

Exee said, "Would you take the seat, please, Commander Smith."

RJ glanced at me with raised eyebrows and took the seat. I suddenly discovered Eb3 standing next to me. Same gray skin-tight suit as before.

A few sensors were attached to RJ. A small respirator mask was gently placed over his nose and mouth. Respiration began reading out on one display.

Mr. Exee came alongside and said, "It will keep the patient relaxed and will help coalesce his thoughts after the procedure."

"Will he remember anything?"

Exee replied, "He will remember everything, but not in a compartmentalized mindset. It will all be as normal memory."

A stool was brought out and positioned directly in front of RJ. Eb3 sat, his big black almond eyes focused exclusively on RJ's eyes. Everyone in the room stopped and watched. When the mind meld began, the Gray's expression did not change at all. I had seen those big black eyes blink several times, but during the meld they did not. I do not believe RJ ever blinked either. The process was quick, maybe three or four minutes. Eb3 stood, looked at Exee, and left the room. The tech team gathered around RJ, who appeared to be asleep. His chair was lowered into a bed. Side doors slid open, and RJ was pushed to a long cart waiting outside.

I turned to Exee. He spoke, "Commander Smith will sleep for quite a while. They are taking him back to his room. He will be monitored remotely and watched via cameras. You are welcome to visit him to check on him as often as you like. When he wakes, he will be his normal self. Eb3 will transfer the downloaded information into a special system, and it will be printed out in hard copy format. Members of our team will be studying it as it is printing out. I'll take you back to your room now. It would be greatly appreciated if you would dictate your complete report into the communicator I gave you. You will see the report print out on the wall-mounted monitor in your room as you make it. The team will need your report to supplement Commander Smith's information. The Commander will be asked to do the same when he wakes. Do you have any questions?"

"What happens after all this info is analyzed?"

"We cannot say until then."

Exee drove me back. I sat on the couch and began narrating my report, being very careful to leave out the Optos and keep to the fabrication RJ had created. I wondered if Eb3 had seen anything of the Optos while in the meld. At the end of my narration, I ended it by adding, "Report complete." The screen cleared.

A quick check on RJ found him sleeping peacefully, the respirator still attached to his face. Back on the couch, I found a good computer chess game on the big screen, set the level to 2000, and played. I won one, lost one, and the third was a draw. I fell asleep and woke up at 3:14 A.M. Earth Central time, according to the clock on the end table. Checked on RJ again, no change, flopped down on the unused huge bed in the bedroom, and slept for a good stretch.

Woke to the smell of bacon frying. RJ was in the kitchen, cracking eggs into a frying pan. He smirked at me, and I could tell he was his old self. I made the coffee. We sat at the kitchen table and enjoyed the hot food.

"You don't look any worse than usual," I commented.

"My Einstein hair still refuses to be managed," he replied.

"What do you remember?"

"Everything, only it's comfortable now."

"What don't I know?"

"You have the main gist of it. There were some formulas in there, some diagrams, and some photographs of things you wouldn't like."

"Like what?"

"Man-eating snakes with tiny hands and fingers."

"Schedule dates that were much closer than we'd like."

"What else?"

"A list of planets and planetary groups that despise the Ocards and will probably help with the problem. Beyond that, there's too much detail to go through."

I sipped my coffee. "So I guess we are here in the wait mode."

"And who knows what exactly we're waiting for?"

"I wonder how they'd feel about me nosing around this place."

RJ laughed, "I have a feeling if you set one foot out the door, your communicator would go off with someone asking if you needed assistance. Personally, I'm going to head next door and read a book."

So I spent the day milling around, trying to amuse myself. It began to occur to me that perhaps I was done here. They were just getting ready to show up and cut us loose. The mission was complete. No reason for Ocards or Deep State A.I. to come after us now. We had already delivered. Their secret was out.

But no one showed. Tried to sleep, wondering why. Woke up the next day to the fine smell of RJ's bacon, eggs, potatoes, and toast again. He and I sat eating quietly this time, both wondering why we were still here.

Finally, after lunch, our communicators bleeped and the big screen read, Captain Tarn, meeting in thirty minutes.

Chapter 15

Mr. Exee showed up and ushered us into the cart.

"What's going on, Exee?"

"Too much to explain," he replied. "Just wait."

Exee drove us past the Medical section and stopped outside a large meeting room. Inside, screens on every wall were dark, and a large meeting table with many chairs had lights embedded within the surface. There were three men waiting for us wearing military uniforms of high rank, though they were unfamiliar to me. No handshakes were offered. One of the military men gestured to the seats opposite them at the table. Exee waited at the door.

RJ and I sat. The three military men looked stolid. They were all in their fifties, I would guess. They all had partially gray hair, and their faces were weathered.

The man in the center spoke, "Captain Tarn, Commander Smith, first we would like to express our gratitude to you for completing this intelligence mission. We have all read both of your accounts, and we understand how difficult that was. The information you brought back has been thoroughly researched. Combined with our own intelligence efforts, we have a good picture of the assault that is planned on Earth. There have been serious developments in the past two days, much of it described in the intelligence you brought us. We now know that the Ocards virus has already been planted on Earth and has already affected the majority of our population, including those of us in this room."

RJ exclaimed, "What!?"

Before the speaker could continue, a door opposite the room opened, and a staff member stuck his head in. "General Hatch, you are needed in the operations room as soon as you're finished here." The staff member backed out and shut the door.

The General turned back to us and paused for a moment. "Gentlemen, I apologize for not introducing us. I am General Hatch, on my right is General Woods, and on my left here is Colonel Washburn."

I managed to squeeze in a question. "General, I do not recognize your uniforms. What branch are you from?"

The General nodded. "We are Space NSAX."

RJ asked, "NSAX?"

The General smiled. "The general expression is No Such Agency. But in reality, it's a section of the National Security Agency."

Colonel Washburn added, "In other words, we do not exist."

General Hatch continued, "As I was saying, the virus you made us aware of has already been deployed all around the world. We would not have detected it had we not been looking for something. It is not a virus that is easy to isolate and possibly impossible to vaccinate against. Everyone on Earth will have it probably within the next month or so. It seems to have no harmful effects other than to produce certain hormones in people around the age of 40 or older. We cannot rely on eliminating this virus as our means of countering the threat against us. We have several other off-world species that are allies, and they are aiding in studying this virus. But we have to assume it will exist when the next assault is attempted on Earth. Next, I need to update you on the Deep State A.I. you also made us aware of. We have been able to detect traces of this intelligence within our computer networks. The DSAI has not made any significant moves on our systems yet, but we can say with certainty it still is looking for the two of you. Apparently, its mandate is to eliminate anyone who knows about this attack plan if possible."

I sat back in my chair. "Well, that's disappointing."

The General gave me a suspicious look, as though he was about to announce something unexpected. "Yes, Captain Tarn, if you attempt to leave this facility, you could bring destruction down all around you. It is a miracle the two of you escaped the cargo ship and did not happen to be on the mining ship when it was destroyed."

RJ said, "So we remain here in your employ, General."

The General smiled, as though he had made his case. "Yes and no, gentlemen. We have a mission for the two of you, one that fits your talents perfectly. There is a planet in the Dega system which may have something that will help us prevent this attack. In both your reports, you suggested that the aliens that teleported you here were using biological components in their systems, which helped protect you from the DSAI. We have a ship which was a gift from a friendly planet we helped defend during a war, and it is basically constructed of biologic systems. We want you to take this ship to the planet Dega in the Dega system and acquire whatever it is they have that will help us."

I couldn't help myself. I had to ask, "General, are you saying we sent an army to help fight a war on some other planet?"

The General returned a cold stare. "Yes, Captain Tarn."

RJ asked, "Where is the Dega system, General? How long?"

I interrupted, "Why does the Dega system sound so familiar?"

Colonel Washburn answered, "The name was made famous from an old classic movie. Since that time, however, it has been assigned to a system beyond the Pleiades. To answer your question, Commander Smith, it will be a trip of several weeks."

I asked, "What type of ship are we talking about?"

Colonel Washburn looked at the General and said, "General, since you're needed in ops, maybe I should take over here so you can go."

The General nodded. "Good idea." He looked at General Woods. "Do you have anything to add, Mark?"

"Just this, gentlemen: I would be greatly surprised if either of you declined this mission. For if you do, you will be sitting here trapped, waiting for one of the most diabolical attacks against the Earth to take place."

General Hatch looked at us with a half smile. "He has a way with words, doesn't he?"

With that, the two generals rose, nodded to us, and left. Colonel Washburn swung the chair next to him around, leaned back, and put his feet up. He raised his left hand and spoke into his watch, "Screens on."

Two display screens rose out of the table in front of us. All of the big screens on the walls lit up with a circular emblem enclosing an image of the Milky Way galaxy. Colonel Washburn again spoke into his watch, "First."

An image of a luxury starship appeared on all of the screens. As we looked, the Colonel spoke into his watch once more, "Please ask Dr. Eisner to come in."

Colonel Washburn said, "The starship Acura, gentlemen. State-of-the-art biologic computer systems. This ship was designed for transporting emissaries and VIPs. It came with advanced shields and screens, but very little weaponry. We have since modified it to include maximum weaponry."

I gazed at the ride. It was completely contoured. There was not a sharp edge on it. Aside from cooling radiators, the cream-colored skin had no interruptions, no piping, no external packages. If I focused carefully, I believed I could make out the outline of some compartment doors. The huge nose of the ship was an arrowhead with many windows. The aft end was just as large, with two engine nacelles on either side. Between them was a rectangular service section. Usually, the nacelles are mounted away from the spacecraft body so that hangar receiving ports can open for visiting spacecraft. As it was, this design looked as though the engine nacelles were too close to the back end for there to be hangars with external doors there.

The meeting room door opened, and a very attractive woman with black hair entered. She was wearing a dark violet, form-fitting dress that came down above the knee. A V-shaped cut lay between the shoulder straps. Her dress had similar insignia as those of the generals and colonel. She had bright green eyes below eyebrows that slanted upward. Small nose, small mouth, very tanned skin tone. Her high heels clicked on the floor as she came over to our table. She looked at us and noticed our stare but was indifferent to it. She tapped a button on the table to raise her display screen, pulled out a chair, and sat looking at the ship.

"So this is the one, then?" she commented.

Colonel Washburn stifled a laugh at her arrogance. "Gentlemen, let me introduce you to Makayla Eisner, better known to her friends as Mack."

Eisner looked up sternly. "No one here is authorized to use that nickname. I am Dr. Eisner to you."

Washburn had to put a hand over his mouth to stifle his laugh. Eisner shot him a glance.

RJ spoke, hoping to diffuse the situation. "What is the crew complement for this ship, Colonel?"

"It houses sixty-eight, Commander. Dr. Eisner will be joining you on this mission. She holds doctorates in both biology and zoology, with specialization in herpetology and serpentology."

Way in the back of my mind, an alarm sounded. It took me a second to bring it to the surface. I stood and slapped my hand on the table. "Serpentology! Now I remember where I heard about the Dega System. There is a planet there inhabited and run by smart snakes. God, please tell me that's not where you want to go."

There was a long silence. I frowned and slowly sat down. Washburn could no longer hold it in. He blurted out laughing and looked down at the floor, embarrassed by it.

RJ stepped in again. "The captain has a particular aversion to snakes."

Eisner left haughtily. "Oh yeah, big strong men, hand-to-hand combat in ditches, but you try to give them a shot and they faint. Ask them to catch a spider, and they run the other way. Captain Tarn, you have no idea how valuable a species snakes are on our planet, do you?"

"If you must know, a snake saved my life once. I had to eat one on a survival mission. They're not bad cooked on an open fire."

Both RJ and Washburn laughed.

Eisner was not impressed. "And there we have it, a man's second most motivating feature, his stomach."

This time RJ laughed out loud. He caught himself and asked, "So that is the destination for this mission, then?"

Eisner answered, "Where else would you find the best defense resources against a snake invasion, Commander Smith?"

Washburn said, "The planet is referred to as Dega, a name given to it by one of the few expeditions that have actually gone there."

Eisner added, "I've dreamed of going to this place all my life. There are almost no opportunities."

I said, "Gee, I wonder why."

RJ came to the rescue. "Colonel, if the virus has already been released, are you sure we'd have time to make this trip?"

Washburn nodded. "The intelligence group has calculated how long it will take for the virus to spread to the rest of the planet. They are in the process of creating a network to detect ships that might not be who they claim to be. I'm sure you know the great number of vessels that arrive and depart every day. It's a big job, but it's achievable. The intelligence group believes there's no reason not to try this mission. In addition to the target planet, you will need to make a stop along the way to pick up two ambassadors who have dealt with Dega before. They will be critical to the mission."

I asked, "Colonel, where is the Acura right now?"

"She is in Earth space dock. The final preparations are still underway. You have two days to study the ship's design and the information on your flight path."

Eisner jumped in. "By the way, Captain. There is one member of my team who has flown with you before. Lieutenant Paulson has a degree in serpentology. Do you remember him?"

I looked at RJ. He stared in thought. "Yes, yes, I do remember Ensign Paulson. That was aboard the Electra. He had a terrarium on board. His snake escaped. It took days to find it."

I added, "In the women's shower, if I remember correctly."

Eisner laughed, which surprised us all. She collected herself, looked a little bit embarrassed, then continued, "Colonel, do you have anything else? I need to get back to packing."

Washburn sat up. "Gentlemen, be advised we dare not send you up to the Acura by conventional means. We don't believe the camera maskers are enough to make it safe. Two medical transport tubes are being converted so that they will isolate you from any outside influences. You will have to endure the ride up inside them until you get there. Any questions before I go?"

I asked, "Are you coming with us?"

"Not on this mission, Captain. I've been assigned as captain on the Achilles. Perhaps we will run across each other on your way back."

Washburn stood, gave us a last look, nodded to Eisner, and left.

Chapter 16

Eisner shifted in her seat. "About the planet, gentlemen. It is earth-like in quite a few ways. There are oceans, large forests, occasional deserts, and lakes. There are several species of birds but almost no other wildlife. The birds are a very necessary component in the environmental structure. They eliminate bugs, insects, and other rodents. The serpentines we will be dealing with actually live off of the product of an unusual kind of plant which grows bulbs that are very much like flesh. It is the exclusive diet of the inhabitants. It grows naturally and is always in abundance. The species of snake that governs the planet is divided by continents. There have been quite a few wars between them. Because of their physical limitations, they do not have much technology, but they do have some from bartering with outside civilizations. They have solar power and some electronic devices built to suit their size and abilities. They travel along the ground often in the same posture as a cobra that has risen up, getting ready to strike. So you should not interpret that as aggressive. It's just their normal posture. They can, of course, still move flat on the ground. The upper part of their body usually has four small hands with small fingers that can be tucked into their body to move faster or can be extended for using tools. We really don't have much more information than that, but the two passengers we are going to pick up have a great deal of knowledge about this species. That's all I can give you right now. As I said, I need to get back to preparations." Eisner stood and waited for a moment for questions.

RJ answered, "Thank you for your help, Doctor."

Eisner left without looking back.

I looked at RJ. "What just happened?"

"I believe we are going where no man has gone before."

"Did we really decide that?"

"Was there ever a choice, really?"

"Well, when we get there, you talk to the snakes."

RJ scoffed and paused to think about it.

Exee drove us back to our rooms. As we unloaded, he said, "Your reservist ranks have been officially reactivated, and you have been transferred to Space NSAX. You will find new luggage in both your rooms. One of them contains a complete set of Space NSAX uniforms. You'll want to start wearing those immediately in case you have meetings with some of your crew. All the specs, crew complement, and layouts for the Acura have been loaded into your screens. If you need clarification on anything, you can contact Colonel Washburn on your communicator. Good luck, gentlemen. I will be around if you need me."

Exee drove off.

The cramming began. RJ studied in his room. I studied in mine. We took turns calling each other when there was something not perfectly understood. I dedicated my first studies to learning my way around the Acura. To my surprise, when I asked the screen for a 3D recreation of the Acura interior, a lens lit up on the bottom of the screen and created a hologram of the ship. I was able to enlarge portions of it to the size of a real-life vehicle, and I could walk within the display to study the various decks.

I was still imagining myself walking the decks of the hologram when there was a knock on my door. I opened it to find Colonel Washburn wearing new captain's bars on his flight suit. He was carrying two thick manuals bound by blue plastic ring binders with blue cardboard covers. We took seats at the coffee table across from each other. He flipped open his communicator and spoke, "Commander Smith, could you stop by next door?"

Washburn's head was partially within the hologram. He looked it over, then back at me and said, "Learning your way around, I see."

I grabbed the communicator and said, "Hologram off."

RJ came in the door and took a seat next to me. Washburn asked, "What you got to drink around here, Adrian?"

With a questioning stare, I asked, "Bourbon?"

"That would do nicely. We're actually on duty, but it is allowed in moderation; otherwise, all the higher-ups would be court-martialed."

I went to the kitchen and came back with three short glasses.

Washburn sipped and spoke, "These manuals are the Space NSAX regulations. Because we deal with so many unknowns, many of us consider them recommendations instead of regulations."

RJ picked up a manual and flipped through it. "Colonel..."

Washburn interrupted, "It's Stephen, RJ."

RJ smiled. "Stephen, how long has this place been here?"

Washburn took a sip of his drink and leaned back. "Long story, RJ. The secret space program began back in the late 1930s. The Germans were way ahead of everyone back then. It was possible they had already made contact with some non-human species. In any case, they were searching China and India and other areas for ancient documentation about flying craft and power sources. At some point, they recovered a UFO. We also did. They continued searching and studying, and they remained ahead of everyone. The Allies were lucky to have won that war. Germany had jet fighters and some anti-gravity technology. The main reason we won was that we could build bombers faster than they could destroy them. And we just plain had more soldiers. Near the end of the war, some of Hitler's top people abandoned him, gathered up all the advanced technology, and managed to set up an installation in Antarctica. In 1946, Admiral Byrd was sent to Antarctica in Operation Highjump with 4,700 men, 13 ships, and 33 aircraft to attack and destroy the German base. A battle took place, and one US destroyer was sunk with all hands on board. They fought anti-gravity aircraft and basically lost. They either retreated or were recalled. So the secret space program has been in existence since that time. The knowledge of the existence of non-human species was considered to be too detrimental to human society. So the secret space program remained secret, but it advanced quickly because of contact with non-human species and recovered advanced spacecraft and materials."

I asked, "It seems like the veil of secrecy is breaking down, Colonel."

"It is a roller coaster ride, Adrian. All of these secrets have been slowly getting released intentionally and then claimed to be fake so that people who couldn't handle the truth have a way to disbelieve it if they choose to. But with A.I., there have been quite a few more breakthroughs. We are at the point where we can only do our best and see what happens. In fact, someone got into one of our research labs recently and took something very important that is above top secret. We combed this facility for days and have not found them or it yet."

"What did they steal?"

"I am not allowed to know. That's the way it is here."

RJ said, "About the secrecy thing. Everyone knows of other non-human races now. It doesn't seem to be that harmful to society."

Washburn nodded. "They don't know the real extent of it, however. And some people still believe that any species that is not human is automatically comprised of demons."

We sat and thought for a moment.

Washburn said, "There's a few things I need to go over with you two. For one thing, we cannot transport you up to the ship by conventional means. They are modifying medical canisters designed for transporting seriously injured or ill people. These canisters will be set up so they cannot be scanned in any way. We will put you two in them here at the facility and then transport them up to the Acura, where you should be safe from detection. The other thing is communications with the Acura must be kept to an absolute bare minimum. Even though the ship is highly resistant to hacking, we should not take any chances. During your trip, you will stop off to pick up two diplomats. They are non-human. One is a Tantaloid, the species that looks like a praying mantis. They are about six feet tall. The other is a Reptoid. They have a human-like physique with scales, except their heads are similar to the head of a lizard. Both of these species are capable of shape-shifting into human form. They will use their human form for the most part during the trip to make interaction easier. They are both telepathic. Your staff will include members who are efficient in that kind of communication. Both of these individuals will be able to give you much more information about the species you are going to contact. I know this may be a lot to absorb for you two, but I also know you've seen more than most people. Welcome to Space NSAX."

Washburn finished his drink and stood. "I need to get going, and you two need to get back to studying." He paused for a moment, nodded to us, and left.

I looked at RJ and finished my drink. "How can I go on knowing how little I know?"

RJ sipped his drink. "Wasn't it you who complained about people panicking when they saw an alien by saying nothing has changed except they know?"

"So, I don't like where I'm going, and I don't like who I'm going with. What's left?"

"It's a very nice starship."

"Yes, yes, it is a very nice starship."

"Did you notice it has two very large arboretums?"

I nodded dutifully. "I did touch on that."

"It's probably a great crew."

"Yes, I would think so at that level of spacecraft."

RJ sat up straight. "I'm going to get back to studying."

"I'm going to get another drink."

"I'll take one too."

We returned to our studies. When I felt I had the layout down, I went on to crew complement. Sixty-four names to learn. If you do not do that, you can end up making some of the crew feel unimportant and invisible. They all had some small physical effect that helped attach a name to the face. When I began to get a handle on matching names to people, I called in to Exee and asked if there was a VR headset for my video system. Ten minutes later, he brought me two units. I knocked on our adjoining door and handed one to RJ, then sat down to negotiate with the display system.

There was a multilevel menu in the headset. Hand controls allowed me to choose. To my surprise, the system gave me a 3D representation of the Acura interior. I was able to sit back on the couch and walk myself all over the ship's deck levels. The depictions felt very real. The topmost corridor had cream-colored walls, slightly lighted, and ceilings that looked like rough, lighted crystal. The floor was a very thin gold carpet. I checked a ship's guide on the wall and realized the carpet floor color told you what deck you were on. To my further surprise, the system allowed me to add the entire crew complement and place them in their assigned stations.

The entrance to the Bridge was down the corridor to my right. I headed that way. At the entrance, the doors slid open, and I stepped onto the Bridge.

A security person off to my left called out, "Captain on the Bridge."

It startled me, and the Bridge crew all stood. I had to call out, "As you were."

They sat and resumed their normal duties.

My first look at the Bridge layout—it was stunning. The usual forward view screen wrapped around the cabin one hundred and eighty degrees. The program had placed a star field in the view. Gold carpet covered the floors. The walls were the same semi-lighted tan color, and the overhead was the lighted cracked crystal. The control stations were nearly typical: helm control in the center, navigation right of it, engineering left, communications far right, weapons far left. The captain's chair was in the center of the room, with additional seats to the left and right of it. The security console and main computer interface were at the back of the room. These console setups weren't typical. They were all of the same cream-colored material, and they were all contained in a one-piece molded configuration that wrapped around the front of the Bridge. The display screens were all suspended in midair, with no borders around them. The seats were also cream-colored and did not look metallic. On the back walls, smaller screens filled that space, showing various systems information.

I repositioned myself beside the captain's chair. Looking over the Bridge and the people on it brought back memories. It had been quite a while since I had command of a large starship. I'd forgotten the closeness and allegiance members of the Bridge crew had together. Standing there, taking it all in, I suddenly became one with the ship and crew, as all captains should. I had already committed the first-shift Bridge crew names to memory. On a whim, I called out, "Mr. Porter, ship status?"

Cameron Porter, helm officer, turned in his seat and looked at me. "Tractor-mooring in space dock, Captain."

As I smiled to myself, the Bridge doors suddenly slid open. In walked RJ.

"Are you real?" I asked.

"That is correct, sir. I am not a computer representation. I saw an icon on my video screen with your name, clicked on it, and here I am. Pretty amazing simulation, wouldn't you agree?"

"Yeah, I'm trying to learn the crew, and this is almost like cheating."

RJ looked around the Bridge. "I'm assuming they are interactive."

"Yes, I've spoken to the helm."

"You know that's ironic, right? It has to be A.I. for them to interact. So here we are fighting A.I. using A.I."

"I've always enjoyed RJ Smith's philosophy."

"Well, I will take my leave of you. I'm heading down to Engineering. Can't wait to see that." RJ smiled and headed out the door. I used my time practicing the first, second, third, and fourth Bridge crews. I needed to get back to work on the rest of the crew, but before I left, I wanted a quick look at the arboretums. On the wall outside the Bridge, the map showed me that the arboretums occupied space from the top floor and the one below it. I tapped for the seventh deck and instantly found myself there. The arboretums were amazing. Full-grown trees, fruit-bearing bushes, grass trails leading throughout the place, windows covering almost all of it, including the overhead.

I opted out of the headset for the time being and went back to the holograms. Several more hours of memorizing faces and attaching names to them. I would only allow myself the rest of the day to get the crew roster down. There were too many ship technical issues to cover to spend any more time than that.

Chapter 17

Late that evening, I began on the ship's power systems. Antimatter-based, strange non-metallic conduit systems, independent computer control. Eventually, I fell asleep on the couch, memorizing details. Slept there the whole night. Woke up to the smell of RJ's bacon and eggs and toast. We sat in the living room, eating and sipping coffee.

RJ asked, "Have you looked into communications?"

"Only a bit," I replied.

"Did you see that external communications are completely isolated from ship systems?"

"I was going to get back to that."

"They have given the external communication system its own isolated power supply and no connections whatsoever to any shipboard system. In other words, the main computer has no idea of any communications taking place outside of the ship. There is even a warning stating that no outside communication can be played using an external speaker that the ship's main computer could hear."

"They are afraid of a virus coming in through the normal communications network?"

"That is what I make of it. We can only listen to external communications by use of ear pods or by verbal communication with the communications officer. And then there's the scanning and weapons system. Both of those use optical links to protect against incoming viruses. There is a physical space between all the data lines that uses optical pulses to cross the open space. On the receiving side, there is what they call a DCC, deep comparator check. Supposedly, every single pulse that passes through those gaps is instantly checked to match what is supposed to be there, and if something is not supposed to be there, that system is interrupted."

"Well, I hope when we pull the trigger, the gun goes off."

"Supposedly, it can't fail."

"I hate it when someone says that."

RJ nodded. "The other interesting thing is one of the security officers is an Optimus X."

"It's about time. You know I am partial to robotics."

"Yes, we've had our experience with them. Well, it's time for me to get back to work. I'm leaving the dishes for you to insert in the cleaner slot."

"It's been worth it."

RJ wiped his mouth, stood, and headed through our adjoining doors.

Two days of cramming brought reasonable success. I was beginning to burn out. I began to wonder when we would be getting packed like postage and shipped up to the Acura. It happened about 3:00 a.m. A new message on my video screen, along with a persistent beeping, read, "Captain Tarn, are you ready for transfer?" I flipped open my communicator and spoke one word, "Yes." The next message read, "There is luggage in the utility closet; please pack."

Exee came for us about an hour later. We stacked our luggage in the back of the cart, climbed in, and were taken to a new area, a room that looked like a large garage. In it, a gray swept-wing shuttle was parked, waiting to leave, humming as it sat there. Behind it, two torpedo-like transfer containers were positioned on lowered carts. They were red with yellow stripes, had no windows, and no tail fins. When the maintenance workers saw us enter, two of them went to the containers, pushed a button, and the tops popped open to reveal a foam-lined interior. On one side of it, a very skinny oxygen bottle ran down the side with an oxygen mask attached to it. On the opposite side, there was a vent that looked like a heat or cooling source.

Next, upper service people collected our bags and loaded them through a side door on the waiting ship. A ramp on the back opened and lowered, revealing a cargo entrance. Exee came to us and said, "It is time, gentlemen. Is there anything you need, or do you have any questions?"

I looked down at our containers. "I don't think I know enough to ask questions."

Exee understood. "Dr. Eisner and her team have already been taken up. If the two of you would climb in, please."

RJ and I went to the side of our containers, bent over, and rolled in. The foam was very soft and comfortable. Exee came alongside my container and handed me a small piece of folded, sealed paper.

"This contains your command codes, Captain. Please store them in the breast pocket of your flight suit so that we know where they are until you are able to memorize them and destroy that paper."

He gave me a thumbs-up signal and went to RJ's container to give the same speech. Two technicians came up alongside me; one pulled out a belt strap and fastened it across my lower legs, the other fastened one across my chest. He then picked up the oxygen mask, placed it on my face, and looped the elastic behind my head. With the last inspection, he nodded to me, reached up, and closed the container. Lights immediately came on within. There was nothing to see, of course, but it was much better than making the transfer in total darkness.

Next came the feeling of being lifted and slid across the floor, pushed into a cargo bay with clicking and fastening. I could hear the hum of the cargo bay door closing. A loud clunk told me it was sealed. The engines on our transport wound up. The taxi jiggled me around in my coffin. A slight downward force as we began ascent.

My brain began to consider possibilities. What if we hadn't masked this transfer as well as we hoped? What if my transfer vehicle was suddenly blown out of the sky? Would I become an inert missile pointed down, heading for the ground? Or, what if we made orbit and then there was an assault and the ship was destroyed? Would I then be a satellite in a slowly decaying orbit, waiting to burn up?

The rest of the ride was smooth. I switched to wondering about my posture in accepting command of the Acura. It had been some time since my last command. My last two commands had been aboard the Electra. During the first, I had inherited the ship after its captain and first officer were eliminated under the worst of circumstances. My second command was again of the Electra after she'd been through an extensive refit. That trip was supposed to be a peaceful ferry back to Earth but turned out to be anything of the kind and ended up in a war at the planet XiTau. I decided the odds were in my favor this time. This could be an easy trip.

I became weightless. A body floating in a coffin. For some reason, that made me laugh out loud. I was floating in space, inside a canister. My body would lightly brush against one side, then the top, then the other side.

Deceleration changed everything. There were no inertia dampeners in this tin can. Whoever was doing the flying knew that. My head, protected by my raised hands, was pushed against the front of the container to about two Gs. To my relief, I heard metal-on-metal sounds as we clunked onto the deck of a hangar bay.

After a silent pause that seemed to last forever, there were the clicking sounds of latches being undone. The cover of my coffin lifted, and an attractive woman stared down at me. She had black hair cut just below the ears with bangs. Pretty brown eyes and a small red smile. I then noticed the tips of her pointed ears protruding from her hair. She was a non-human and wore a green Ensign insignia. She smiled down at me, and I pulled off my O2 mask and asked, "Permission to come aboard?"

"Captain, I'm Ensign Lee. Yes, you have my permission to come aboard." She laughed and began removing the safety belt across my legs. I undid the one across my chest.

I rolled onto my side, threw a leg over, and climbed out.

"Captain, we do not have a receiving line for you because we were not allowed to know when you would arrive. It is 04:00 shipboard time. Shift three is on station. My instructions are to take you to your quarters because you have been up all night and will need sleep."

I looked for RJ and saw him standing by his container, straightening himself. He looked at me and saluted.

"Lead the way, Lee," I replied.

Lee motioned to the person assisting her and led us across the hardened deck to an elevator on the far side wall. Up we went to the top deck. My brain began to sync up with the computer representation. I knew my way along the upper corridor with gold carpet.

"I think you'll both like your quarters. They are opposite each other near the Bridge. You both have a small conference room that opens into the Bridge, and also opens to your quarters. And both of your quarters have large sliding glass doors that open to an arboretum."

We followed her until the main entrance to the Bridge came into view. The two doors on opposite sides were ours. Lee stopped and smiled. "Your bags have already been delivered and unpacked. There are handheld communicators on your kitchen counter. You can contact an orderly for anything you need either using them or through the ship's main computer. Your doors will only open for you or your voice command. I should give you some privacy. Is there anything you need before I go?"

I smiled at Lee. "You have been very helpful, Lee. Thank you."

"Yes, my thanks as well," added RJ.

Lee gave a short bow and left.

RJ said, "Well, we haven't been blasted out of the sky today."

"As one old movie star once said, day ain't over yet."

"Well, I shall go now and inspect my new living quarters right up to the moment I spot the bed." RJ turned, approached his door, and it slid open.

"Don't forget your command codes."

"There you go, wearing the Captain's hat already." He waved me off, and the door slid shut behind him.

My quarters were the most luxurious I had ever seen. The place had the faint smell of jasmine. The air was cool. Door to the conference room to my right. Living area spacious for any starship. All-around video screens or posters on the off-white walls, most with ship diagrams and general information. Off-white carpet. The squared-off gold-colored couch looked 1950ish. Transparent coffee table. Frail-looking metallic end tables beside the couch. Small kitchen by the far right wall. Bedroom door centered on the left side wall. Wrap-around desk and two chairs next to it, curtains hiding the arboretum to the left. Ceiling dimly lit.

I went to the stunted refrigerator, reminding myself that alcohol could no longer be on my menu. Found a cold bottle of water and headed for the bedroom.

It was nice also. Long closet door left open, showing the variety of uniforms I would be needing. No video screens here, just artwork; ocean waves breaking, forest trails, canyon views. Big bed. I turned in place and fell backwards onto it.

I could tell it was morning aboard the Acura. My doorbell was chiming. In all fairness, the bedside digital clock did say 07:30 A.M. I decided to try the ship's computer. "Computer, please inform the person at my door I will need twenty minutes."

"Yeoman Breize has acknowledged your request."

I forced myself up and hurried through a quick hot shower in the cramped glass shower booth with eight intake fans sucking all the water they could out of my shower. In my closet, I selected the least formal captain's uniform and pulled it on. It was black with gold trim, one zipper down the right side hidden by a flap, high collar, and fairly tight matching slacks that fit down into the black boots provided. The Gestapo look made me uncomfortable. My black hair was a bit too long; all I could do was brush it out and go with it.

In the living area, I called out, "Open door," and found Yeoman Breizc still standing there holding a tray with food that still appeared to be hot on it.

"Good morning, Captain. Forgive me for waking you. I expect you will be having a busy day today." She entered and carried the tray over to the small dinette table and set it down. "The food will stay hot until you're ready to eat it, Captain." She reached into the breast pocket of her flight coveralls and pulled out a black wristwatch. "Here is your wristwatch, Captain. It arrived a little late." She approached me and handed it over. "The button on the right is your menu button. The button on the left is your Comm button." She went back to the dinette and arranged the food on the platter, then came back and asked, "Is there anything else you need, Captain?"

"Not at the moment, Yeoman. That coffee smells very good. Thank you for being so patient."

Breize smiled and left.

Somehow they had mixed my coffee exactly the way I liked it. I took a few sips and tried the easy-over eggs and found them just as hot as she had promised. I sat back and looked at my new wristwatch and decided to give it a try. I pressed the call button and said, "Tarn to Commander Smith."

It took him about two minutes. "I see they got you up as well, Adrian."

"Yes, but the coffee made it worthwhile. We need to put together a couple of meetings this morning for ship status and navigation."

"Pick a time."

"I have a few things to go over first. How about one hour from now?"

"Does 09:00 sound okay?"

"That should do."

Chapter 18

The conference room adjoining the Bridge and my quarters was set up nicely. Long simulated wood table, chairs, and at the end, a computer for me. Hanging on the wall were mainly uplifting simulated oil paintings. I took a seat at the computer and began running through a few things I hadn't touched on yet. When I got to ship's log entries, there was something that bothered me. I clicked the comm button on my watch and called the Chief Engineer. "Captain to Lieutenant Marquis."

The answer was almost immediate. "Marquis here, Captain."

"I'm sure you're busy, Travis, but do you have a minute to answer a question for me?"

"My pleasure, sir."

"I'm going through ship's logs, and for some reason I can't find anything from the ship's last captain. Am I looking in the wrong place?"

"Oh... Captain, there was no last captain. The Acura was towed here from the original shipyard. Apparently, it was much cheaper than filling out a crew just for the delivery. So they towed her here to our space dock."

That took me back for a moment. "Travis, you're saying this will be the Acura's maiden flight?"

"Yes, sir. I'm surprised they did not inform you of that."

"Arrangements have been very hectic, Travis. Has Commander Smith informed you of the meeting this morning?"

"Yes, Captain. I will be there."

"I'll see you here."

With that, I immediately called up the ship's checkout and simulation testing records. They were reassuringly extensive. Occasional glitches had been remedied. Green tests had been repeated several times to be sure. My impression was that the crew had worked very hard to have this ship ready for departure, whenever that might be.

My coffee addiction kicked in. I went to the coffee machine in my kitchenette, tapped enough buttons to order what I wanted, then almost forgot to put a mug under the thing. I found one with an Acura image on it and got it in place just as the first flow of drip had started. It made me laugh out loud.

The department heads RJ had asked for began showing up about ten minutes early. There was a lot of handshaking and pleasantries. The last to arrive was Chief Steward Reno Marada, carrying a tray of more hot coffees. They were passed around as everyone sat. With RJ seated nearest me, I looked over the room and was suddenly reminded who I had become.

There was no need for a start signal, nor was there a need to call for attention. They were all sitting silently, staring at me.

"Thank you all for coming. Commander Smith and I are glad to be here with you. I have reviewed your prelaunch progress, and I found it to be impressive. So, let's get right down to business. Mr. Marquis, ship's status?"

Chief Engineer Marquis leaned forward with a look of confidence. "The Acura is ready for departure at your command. We have an open flag on a coolant storage tank sensor in the environmental storage bay. That's being replaced and will be cleared shortly. We also had a problem with the number three antimatter temperature controller, but I'm expecting that to be cleared shortly."

RJ interrupted, "What exactly was the problem with that computer, Travis?"

Marquis paused in surprise, either because RJ had used his first name or because of the interest in a computer problem. "It appears to have been a stuck keypad button, a stuck keypad bubble button. They are replacing the keypad. That should clear it."

RJ added, "Has there been any other engineering computer-related issues?"

Again, Marquis looked a little puzzled. "None, Commander."

"Travis, please be sure to immediately advise Captain Tarn or myself of any computer-related problems you encounter, no matter how small."

"Yes, sir."

I asked, "Any other flags, Travis?"

"The only other problem was a bad connection in a biofiber junction box. They hadn't polished the end of the biofiber well enough, so it didn't seat into the connection. They just had to redo it, so it's been corrected. That's all the flags we need to account for, Captain."

Next, I went to Visa Rell, our weapons officer lead. She had black hair straight down to her shoulders, parted in the middle. Her makeup was conservative because she was attractive enough even without it. Attractive weapons officers always bother me. You would think they would be too distracted by people wanting to be close to them, but I've been wrong before. "Lieutenant Rell, how are weapon systems?"

"We are good to go, Captain. No flags. The only issue we've had is that we've received too many torpedoes. Somehow, we managed to receive two extra quantum antimatter torpedoes. They are so new I doubted we would get what we asked for, much less two extra. Not a problem, though. There was enough room in the environmental control weapons locker to fit them in. That's right behind the tubes, so they're in the perfect place. I might mention we are not allowed to fire this new type of torpedo aft because they cannot be transferred past the engine cell fields. Do you have any questions, Captain?"

"Thank you, Visa. If I think of any, I'll ask you when I come to visit you in weapon storage. Lieutenant Zelest, status of our comm systems."

"We remain rigged for silent running Captain, but both the internal and external comm systems have no issues."

RJ asked, "Zay, have there been any extraneous signals on any of the systems? And how about noise levels? Have you encountered any unusual noise levels, or are both systems as flat line as they should be?"

"Both networks are perfectly clean, Commander. No extraneous signals of any kind."

RJ said, "As with Engineering, would you please advise Captain Tarn or myself if you encounter any signals at all that should not be there, or any noise of any kind? Advise us right away."

"Yes, Commander."

I was proud of RJ. In this first meeting, he had already made it clear he was not a yes-man. He was an officer in command, and there was no doubting that. Any secret reservations any of the crew had as to whether he could be consulted in my absence were now eliminated. I looked to our Chief Navigator, Keaton Williams. "Mr. Williams, I've studied our flight plan. Any changes?"

"We are good to go, Captain. Flight plan approved. Our stopover at Alpha Draconis takes us quite far out of the way of our main destination, the planet Dega, but there are not many areas of spatial conflict on either leg. So, no changes to our approved flight plan."

I nodded and continued, this time to Security. "Mr. Carter, how do we look?"

Carter brushed his semi-gray crew cut back and ran one of his fingers across an eyebrow. His weathered expression gave no clue. "No issues in Security," he replied. "We are also monitoring the comms, both internal and external."

"Are we set up for our visitors?"

"Of course. Special quarters, specially monitored."

Next was the helm. "Are you ready, Camaron?"

"The boards are all green, Captain."

I turned to Reno Marada. "Reno, thanks for bringing the coffee. How are we on ship's stores?"

"We are fully packed, Captain. I'm very happy with how we did. I should be able to accommodate the special diets of our guests when they arrive. I do not foresee any coming shortages."

"In that case, ladies and gentlemen, if no one has any reservations, I suggest we prepare for a detachment and departure from space dock at noon. Thank you all for coming well prepared."

As they rose to leave, I motioned RJ to stay. We sipped our coffee until everyone had left and the door slid shut.

"What do you think?"

RJ stroked his beard. "I think we're okay."

"I haven't seen a single hint of an attack."

"Not a one."

"Did you know we will be making the maiden voyage of this spacecraft?"

"I deduced it from the receiving documentation. Nothing surprises me anymore."

I swished the coffee around in my cup. "Still, I don't see any reason we shouldn't go."

"We have to go."

"By the way, did you notice in the crew complement they included two diplomatic envoys who specialize in telepathy?"

"I sure wouldn't want to mind meld with a six-foot praying mantis next."

"Let's bring them up here for a meeting once we've settled in underway."

"Let me know. I'll be here."

RJ stood and headed for the door. "I'll see you on the Bridge, Captain."

I nodded.

I returned to my quarters and just sat to clear my head. As noon drew near, I went out to the main corridor just in time to see RJ come out. Together, we went to the Bridge main entrance. The doors slid open, and we stepped in. A voice on my right called out, "Captain on the Bridge."

The crew began to rise. I answered, "As you were."

There were a full complement of console lights on around the room. The wide wraparound forward view screen had dim stars ahead and sections of space dock on each side. I took center seat as RJ sat on my right. There were no warning lights on my chair armrest. I asked Helmsman Porter, "Are we still go, Cameron?"

"All green, Captain."

I looked at RJ. "You want to make the announcement?"

RJ said, "Lieutenant Zelest, please give me ship-wide."

"Ready, Commander."

"Attention all personnel. Stand by for departure from space dock and transition to warp."

RJ smiled. "It's all yours."

I looked to Comm Officer Zelest. "Zay, please signal Space Dock Control we are ready to disengage." From my position, I managed to see four red lights on the helmsman's console turn green.

"Tractors disengaged, Captain. We are free," declared Porter.

"Thrust us out slowly, Mr. Porter. We need to give the refit crews time to celebrate."

"Aye, Captain."

The metal work of the space dock began to slowly pass behind us.

"Mr. Porter, when we are well clear of the orbital exclusion zone, please set course and take us to warp two."

"Aye, sir."

We watched the framework of space dock disappear behind us, our side view then briefly replaced by Earth's ocean on the right and faded stars on the left. As we gained distance, the stars began to brighten and become denser. There was a heavy silence on the Bridge as we all waited for the Acura's first jump to beyond light speed.

It was a smooth transition. Helm called out, "Field forming." A second later, the big black tunnel glowed ahead of us as we dove into it. On the side monitors, it began to look like stars raining past. It took only a few moments to settle in. Space became a dense carpet. Stars moved along our side views. There had been no sensation of acceleration at all. Our inertia dampeners had been that good.

Helm called out, "Steady at warp two, Captain."

"Very good, Mr. Porter. Let's ride here for a while to see how she runs."

"Aye, sir."

RJ commented, "So far, so good."

The Bridge crew relaxed and became more animated as they checked their consoles against their checklists. I sat back and enjoyed the ride into the warp hole. On my right armrest, a 3D screen had lit up, showing our flight plan and where we were with reference to it. We were a little blue dot moving along a thin green line.

I gave it about thirty minutes. "Mr. Marquis, are you happy?"

"Engineering is very happy, Captain."

"Mr. Porter, take us to warp five."

"Warp five, Captain."

We transitioned to the higher speed smoothly. No flags showed up.

I clicked the left button on my watch. "Captain to Steward Marada."

"Go ahead, Captain."

"Mr. Marada, my coffee addiction is kicking in. Could you have someone bring up coffee for the Bridge crew?"

"On our way, Captain. Marada out."

For the next hour, we sipped coffee and quietly rode the warp five.

Finally I decided that was enough. “Mr. Marquee, is there any reason you know of not to take this ship to standard cruise speed?”

Marquee turned in his seat and looked at me. “None whatsoever, Captain.”

“Mr. Porter, take us to warp eight, please.”

“With pleasure, Captain. Warp eight.”

Chapter 19

We cruised at eight with no flags at all for two hours. There was important information that needed to be gathered elsewhere. I leaned over to RJ. "Who has the shift four Bridge command assignment?"

RJ tapped some keys on his armrest. "Lieutenant Commander Mark Jameson."

"Would you type him a request to come relieve us?"

RJ thought for a moment, analyzing what I was up to. He typed in the request.

Jameson showed up about twenty minutes later. RJ and I both rose. I shook Jameson's hand. "You have the Bridge, Mr. Jameson."

"I have the Bridge, Captain."

As RJ and I left for my conference room, I heard Jameson ask, "Ship status, Mr. Porter?" The door slid shut behind us.

RJ and I withdrew to my quarters. I grabbed two bottles of water from the mini fridge and handed him one. We sat across from one another in the living area.

"I think we need to start with a meeting with our two envoys. What do you think?"

RJ nodded. "Our two envoys who specialize in telepathy. Yes, I would love to hear what they have to say."

"Should we set this up ourselves, or would that be shunning my Yeoman?"

"Hell hath no fury like a woman scorned."

I raised an eyebrow and clicked the left button on my watch. "Captain to Yeoman Breize."

Her response was almost immediate. "Yes, Captain?"

"Would you see if our two special envoys are available for a meeting in, say, thirty minutes in my quarters?"

"Yes, Captain. Standby."

I looked up at RJ. "Maybe we should include Dr. Eisner in this."

RJ nodded.

"Captain, both Rell Marks and Tori Kurh say they will be there."

"And, Yeoman, we are thinking we should include Dr. Eisner."

"I'll take care of it, Captain. Breize out."

Dr. Eisner arrived early. Within the first minute, I realized I should have expected that. She'd brought Lieutenant Paulson along with her, a former ensign of mine. Eisner came to me, raised one finger, and opened her mouth but was cut off by Paulson.

"Captain Tarn, it is a privilege to be flying with you again." He turned to RJ. "Commander Smith, with you as well. I'm glad to be here."

I asked, "Lieutenant, do you still have the snake?"

"Why, yes, sir! You remember Goldy, then?"

"The same snake? You have the same snake?"

"Yes, Captain. Golden corn snakes can live in captivity for twenty or thirty years or more. I've brought her with me, of course."

I nodded. "Yes, of course."

Eisner stepped in. "If I can get a word in here. Captain, I am not pleased with how my group and I are being treated on this mission."

RJ tried to protect me. "Was there a problem, Doctor?"

"For one thing, I was given no notice of our departure time at all."

RJ did his best. "There was no set departure time, Doctor. Our orders were to leave as soon as possible. We did not know what our departure time would be until the ship and crew were ready. We then departed immediately. That was what the ship-wide announcement was for."

"Well, is that any way to run a mission, I ask you?"

I tried to help. "Doctor Eisner, this is an emergency mission. It was put together in extreme haste. I'm amazed they got us off as quickly as they did. There are no set departure standards for emergencies."

"Well, I hope you can do better now that we are on our way."

RJ jumped in again. "Were there any other problems, Doctor?"

"Just that I know so little about our mission. How can anyone prepare under these circumstances? Why are we here?"

RJ answered, "That's exactly why we've invited you to this meeting, Doctor. So that you will have as much information as we will."

She had more to say, but a tap at the door mercifully interrupted.

"Come in."

The doors opened to our two envoys, Rell Marks and Tori Kurh. They stepped in and took a moment to look around the captain's quarters. Rell Marks was tall and lanky. He had black hair down to his shoulders. He had shadows below his green eyes, like someone who stares at a computer screen for too long. Tori Kurh was quite different. A gray woman's business suit. Red hair past the shoulders. Light skin, which highlighted her permanent makeup.

Before Eisner could get started again, I said, "Let's all move to the conference room."

We took seats: RJ on my right, no one on my left, Tori and Rell across from each other, Eisner and Paulson across from each other.

After a brief scan around the table, I said, "So, we're here to share some info on the mission. Our first stop is to pick up two non-human diplomats on the planet Alpha Draconis. From there, we go on to Dega to negotiate. Rell or Tori, do either of you know what we are to negotiate for?"

Tori spoke right up. "It's actually not a negotiation, Captain. The agreement has already been reached."

"So what is it we are to pick up?"

Rell spoke. "We do not know, Captain. We are to deliver the transfer cases and accept whatever is offered to us."

"I'm sorry, transfer cases?"

Rell continued. "Yes, Captain. In the secure environmental holding bay inside the screened-off area are two large transfer cases. They are to be handed over to the Serpetoids after the ceremonial greetings have been completed."

"And let me guess, we are not allowed to know what is in the cases?"

Tori sounded apologetic. "Both Rell and I know what those cases contain, but we are not allowed to disclose that until we reach Dega."

I shook my head. "Another typical mission. We are to deliver something, but we don't know what it is, in order to pick up something, but we don't know what it is."

RJ coughed and had to cover his mouth to hold back an outright laugh.

Both Rell and Tori sat silently, looking perplexed.

"Ridiculous!" said Eisner, and I was surprised she stopped there.

RJ tried to defuse the situation. "Rell, is there any danger of an unauthorized person gaining access to those cases?"

"If anyone gets into the caged area and attempts to bypass the locks on those cases, they will be seriously injured by the theft prevention system. There are large warning signs all over those cases."

RJ continued, "Rell, you mentioned ceremonial greeting. Can you tell us what that will involve?"

Rell answered, "We have only guesswork about that, Commander. The diplomats we will be picking up are likely to give us a full picture of what to expect. We were told that the Captain and First Officer should attend the initial greeting ceremony; otherwise, there could be a danger of offending the Serpentoid hierarchy. We were also warned to expect they might ask for a tour of the ship, which we would need to provide for them. Apparently, these Serpitoids limit their contact with outside worlds so we will need to proceed with great care."

I winced and asked, "A tour of this ship? You mean transport them up by shuttle and tour this ship?"

Tori answered, "Yes, Captain, but that's just a guess. It's one of the reasons we requested Lieutenant Paulson come along on this mission. He has extensive experience in handling snakes and being able to detect their moods and needs."

Paulson added, "I am greatly looking forward to it, Captain."

I replied, "I, for one, am glad you are here, Lieutenant."

Dr. Eisner cut in, "Captain, my team and I are hoping to spend some time on the planet. It is an invaluable chance to study advanced evolution of reptiles."

"That will have to be up to them, Doctor."

RJ asked, "The two of you are experts at telepathy. I assume you will be conversing with both the two emissaries we pick up, as well as with the Serpentoids."

Tori answered, "Yes, we have both been trained to some extent for that purpose."

RJ asked, "How much can you tell us about these two emissaries?"

Rell answered, "As I believe you know, one is a Tantaloid of the praying mantis type, the other a Raptoid. Both are capable of shifting into humanoid form, and we expect they will both do that to make interactions with humans easier."

I asked, "Why are they helping us?"

Rell replied, "They are being compensated. They are free agents, not associated with any governing body. Completely independent."

RJ asked, "Will we hear them communicating with you in our heads?"

Tori answered, "No, not unless they direct their ability directly toward you."

RJ asked, "But we would hear them in our minds if they did that?"

Tori replied, "Yes. Telepathy is the universal language. Someone who speaks only French, for example, but is telepathic, might speak to you in French, but you would understand everything that person said, or at least what that person meant. Telepathy is very tiring to a non-practitioner, however. The mind is not used to it."

RJ asked, "So telepathy is a common language for all species that use it?"

Tori answered, "It's actually not that simple, Commander. For example, in the case of our emissaries and the Serpentoids, both those species have emotions, and when communicating with telepathy there is an emotional aspect to the transmission based on the nature of the creature using it. And, since one species may not be very familiar with the other, that emotional effect on the language can lead to misinterpretation or confusion. For instance, a warlike species is likely to frighten a peaceful species without intending to. So even telepathy is not perfect."

I asked, "So when we reach Dega, essentially our emissaries will be talking back and forth with the Serpitoids without us hearing what they are actually saying?"

Rell nodded. "That's true. We will have to rely on their interpretations. The translators in our ears that we use will not work there."

I asked, "What will happen when we reach Alpha Draconis? Will the two of you need to go down to the surface?"

"No, Captain," replied Tori. "The emissaries will be waiting for us in orbit. The ship that they are on will dock with us unless there is a mechanical compatibility issue. Rell and I will greet the emissaries and escort them to the rooms that have been specially prepared for them. All of the food products and other supplies they'll need have already been stored in those quarters. The emissaries will remain in their quarters except for meetings we request."

Eisner could not remain quiet any longer. "Tori, what can you tell us about the Serpentoids we will meet on Dega?"

"There isn't much, Doctor Eisner. Much of what we know is from rumors more than anything. We have been told that in public these particular Serpentoids move along the ground in an upright position, much like a cobra rising up in a strike position. They can move along the ground in a typical snake fashion, but in public they supposedly move with the front half of their bodies erect. They have four very small arms on the underside of their bodies near the head and four tiny hands with four fingers each. They have supposedly constructed large miniature cities, but we don't know anything about those. They are the dominant species on the planet. We do not know what other species inhabit the planet with them. They do not like to interact with other planetary species, probably because they fear they are at some disadvantage physically. That is why we must conduct ourselves very carefully during this meeting."

"I can't wait," commented Eisner.

Lori said, "The emissaries will be able to brief us with a great deal more information."

Rell added, "I also need to mention that our two emissaries do not have names that can be pronounced phonetically, so we will be addressing them by the standard BE title, for Biological Entity. The Tantaloid will be BEP, the P to identify praying mantis type, and the Reptoid will be BER, the R for reptilian type."

Eisner cut in, "Lori, if my team and I would like to stay on Dega for a time to study the species, do you think that might be allowed?"

Lori replied, "Doctor, has your team indicated a willingness to do something like that?"

"I have not asked them, but I'm sure they would love to."

RJ leaned over to me and whispered, "Oh my God..."

Lori continued, "There is no way to know if something like that could be arranged. The emissaries may know."

I said, "So when we reach Alpha Draconis, Lori and Rell will meet and escort the emissaries to their quarters. I will have two security people there to accompany them. Is everyone okay with that?"

Everyone looked around. No one objected.

I asked, "Does anyone have anything else?"

No one did. As we stood to leave, RJ added, "As the mission develops, we'll keep you all informed, and we may need to get together again at some point."

We moved back to my quarters and to the exit. Acknowledgments were exchanged, and our guests departed. The doors slid shut.

RJ said, "Well, that was both successful and uncomfortable."

I held up one finger for pause. "Captain to Jameson."

"Go ahead, Captain."

"Any issues, Mark?"

"No, sir. Still green across the board."

"Keep me posted. Tarn out." I looked at RJ. "Successful and uncomfortable?"

"Yes, snakes who travel standing up taking a tour of this ship."

"Not only that, they are similar to the species that Earth is supposedly going to be attacked by."

"What a mission we have drawn."

I nodded. "I'm thinking a tour of Engineering should be next on our list."

"We'd better not show up unannounced."

"You're right." I clicked my watch. "Computer, who is the lead engineer on duty in Engineering?"

"The lead engineer in Engineering is Lieutenant Luca Tomlin."

"Captain to Lieutenant Tomlin."

"Tomlin here, Captain. What can we do for you?"

"Commander Smith and I would like to stop in and visit main Engineering. Would this be a bad time?"

"Not at all, Captain. We are five by five down here. Glad to give you the tour."

"Thank you, Lucas. We'll see you in a few minutes. Turn out."

Chapter 20

RJ and I followed the golden carpet to the translift, dropped down several decks, then sideways for a minute or two. The doors opened to a familiar corridor, except the carpet was gray. We both knew the way. We took a left outside the translift and headed down a short corridor to the big doors of Main Engineering. The doors were covered in big red NO ADMITTANCE and HAZARDOUS AREA signs, along with posters that told the various ways you could die and who to call if you did.

A scanner checked my eyes as I approached. The door made a big click, and we pulled it open. We emerged into Main Engineering halfway up the four decks it occupied. It was a huge circular chamber with a giant power tube in the center that ran from floor to ceiling. The tube glowed a phasing red, orange, and green. The entire area was hospital white, including the conduits that ran around the walls. We had emerged onto a wide white platform without handrails that stretched forward to the center of the power tube and wrapped around it. There were four optical analysis stations at even points around it. Below us, there was another service ramp at the next deck level, and below that, numerous monitor consoles were scattered around the room at various intervals. Above us, two more service platforms gave access to the higher levels. This was one of the few times I had heard RJ say, "Wow!"

On our left and right were stairwells heading up and down. As we stood gawking, Lieutenant Tomlin came up the stairs to greet us. Short brown hair, slightly overweight, he wore lens less glasses with flip-up magnifier eyepieces. With a big smile, he shook both our hands.

"A privilege to meet you both. Glad you are here. I have studied some of your history."

"You must not hold that against us," remarked RJ.

He laughed. "Shall we go down?"

Tomlin took us from station to station, introducing first-shift personnel as we went. I became convinced we had a very good crew. Station readouts were so good it almost bothered me. RJ and I shook a lot of hands and even had some good laughs. At the end, we stood at the base of the power tube looking up. It is something you never get used to.

I asked, "Lucas, you have an OptimusX on staff, do you not?"

"Twenty-four seven, Captain. Let me call him." Tomlin clicked his watch. "X, please report to Lieutenant Tomlin." Tomlin looked at us. "Wherever he is, he will find me."

True to his word, an Optimus suddenly appeared in the traffic. He spotted Tomlin, came over, and stood silently. Unlike the domestic versions, this Optimus still wore the chrome breastplate, sleeves, and leggings. His polished black face was carefully designed not to cast reflections. Tomlin spoke to him, "X, I want to introduce Captain Tarn and Commander Smith to you."

X turned to us, his voice male, soft, and neutral. "Captain Tarn, Commander Smith." X bowed his head slightly.

I asked, "X, what is your current assignment?"

"Continuous surveillance on all data transmission and background noise in the external communications network, all data transmission and background noise in the internal communications network, all data transmission and background noise in the subcomputer control systems, and report any irregularities to the Captain and First Officer immediately."

Every question and answer was printed out on X's black face. In the noisy atmosphere, there was no chance of misunderstanding.

RJ asked, "X, has there been anything at all that seemed irregular?"

"No, Commander."

I had to smile. "Thank you, X. You can return to your assignment."

X turned and headed back the way he had come.

RJ commented, "Somehow that makes me feel more assured."

Tomlin agreed, "He never misses a beat."

We expressed our thanks and withdrew back to the corridor, headed for the translift.

RJ said, "I'm thinking food."

"Your place or mine?"

"I'm thinking we should make an appearance in the main Mess Hall."

"I see your point. Level four it is."

The main Mess Hall was close to elegant. Hospital white, like Engineering. No serving line, strictly open buffet style. As we entered, a few of the dozen crew that were there began to rise. I held up my hand to signal never mind. I took the scrambled eggs and rye toast. RJ went with spaghetti.

We talked about the crew's obvious efficiency. It had been impressive.

RJ said, "I was also impressed by the Optimus."

"Yes."

"I read that they have already sold more than a million of the domestic models."

"Earth is changing."

"What are your plans next?" asked RJ.

"I thought I should finish up my shift in the center seat. I'd feel guilty otherwise."

"I'm sure Lieutenant Jameson doesn't mind being there."

"You're probably right."

RJ added, "I have some technical reading I'd like to do. I'll catch up with you on the Bridge."

I made my way back to my quarters, gathered myself together, and entered the Bridge through the conference room. The accepted tradition is, you do not stand when the Captain enters the Bridge under normal work shift hours. One or two of the Bridge crew began to stand anyway, forcing me to raise a hand in protest. Jameson stood from the center seat and moved over to the left seat.

As I sat, I looked at him and asked, "No issues at all?"

"Not a thing, Captain. Steady at eight."

I sat back and took in the star stream.

We enjoyed a peacefully smooth ride for the next three days. It was strictly second star to the right and straight on til morning. But, on the fourth day, something suspicious cropped up.

Lieutenant Zelest turned in her seat at the comm station. "Captain, we are getting a mayday call for assistance from the external comm system."

"From who, Lieutenant?"

Zelest listened closely to her headset. "They are identifying as the freighter Morales out of Alpha Draconis. They are reporting an explosion and are dead in space."

"Lieutenant, do not reply to the distress call until I tell you to."

"Yes, Captain."

"Commander Smith to the Bridge."

RJ appeared a minute later and took his seat.

"We're getting a distress call from a freighter reportedly out of Alpha Draconis asking for assistance."

RJ shook his head. "Kind of a coincidence, don't you think?"

"Yes, but it's fifty-fifty, and as you well know, by space maritime law we are obligated to respond."

RJ sat back. "I don't like it."

"We could be looking at a full crew compliment wanting a ride back to Alpha Draconis."

"What could be worse than picking up a small army of strangers?"

I shook my head. "I'm thinking we have to at least stop." I called out to Lieutenant Williams at navigation, "Keaton, do you have their location, and how long to get there?"

"I have them on long range, Captain. Ninety minutes to get there at eight."

"What do you think, Commander Jameson?"

"They could fire on us as we approach, once they know our identity they could be transmitting it everywhere, they could hold a rescue party hostage, they could try to board by force—so many possibilities."

I made the only choice possible. "Mr. Williams, plot us a course to intercept that ship. Helm, make your heading for that ship, drop us out of warp just inside short-range scanning, then all stop and station keeping."

"Aye, Captain."

"Yes, Captain."

I looked at RJ. "If there really was a major explosion, there might be a debris field. We can see that on short range."

"That should be a safe enough distance."

"You want to go take care of security?"

"I'll head down there right now and be back once they're set up."

I winced. "If we have to send a team over there, I want them heavily armed."

RJ nodded. "Goes without saying." He stood and headed out.

I turned to the weapons officer. "Lieutenant Dell, keep a close eye out for any other ships in the area, especially any trying to mask or hide their presence, and bring weapons systems online."

Dell turned to me. "Captain, are we expecting an attack?"

"We are on a classified high-priority mission. We must remain vigilant."

She turned back to her console. "Keeping a close eye, Captain."

RJ returned forty minutes later. He gave me a thumbs up as he sat.

"Were you satisfied?"

He smiled. "More than that. They are tough individuals. I would not want to go up against them in a firefight. They're setting up for recon or rescue—whichever we might need."

"Let's hope no one does go up against us."

We waited through the final stretch to short-range scanning. The ship was still only a star in the view screen at zero magnification. At full power, we could make out her shape, and there did appear to be a small cloud aft.

Lieutenant Dell called out, "There does appear to be external damage and a small debris field, Captain."

RJ leaned over and said, "Remember the very old days when a submarine would eject trash out a torpedo tube to make it look like a sinking?"

"How about a power field?" asked RJ.

"They do have power, Commander, but the engine nacelles are cold."

Before I could comment, Dell called out again. "Captain, there's something else. There is someone in a spacesuit, and he has drifted a long way from the ship. He is drifting without stabilization."

I asked, "Can you tell if he is alive?"

"There is a heat signature, sir."

I looked at RJ. "Bait?"

"It's a perfect setup. We don't know if we're being set up, but we don't dare not go."

"Give the word to your team."

RJ rose from his seat.

I added, "Just the floater. Tell them not to get in any closer. We'll see what he has to say."

RJ understood. He headed for the security office.

The comm officer brought up the best magnification of our target space dancer. We watched the uncontrolled float, waiting for the security shuttle to appear.

They were surprisingly quick. The shuttlecraft appeared in the viewer and headed directly for the floating spaceman. They did not bother sending a teammate out to get him. They simply pulled up alongside and followed along until edging close enough to grab him from the side airlock. They pulled him in and immediately headed back.

I called the Chief Medical Officer, "Captain to Commander Cooper."

"Cooper here, yes, Captain?"

"Please report to the main hangar bay with a team immediately."

"How many, Captain?"

"One."

"On our way."

We watched the ship come around and head back. They disappeared aft to the hangar bay.

I turned to Jameson. "I need to go down and see what we've brought aboard. Keep the weapons are online. If there is any aggression at all from that ship or any other, use them and get us out of here."

"Cooper to Captain Tarn."

"Go ahead, Doctor."

"The patient is humanoid and has vitals, but we cannot see through the visor. This patient needs to be taken directly to Medical immediately."

"I'll meet you there, Doctor. Tarn out."

I turned to Jameson. "You have the Bridge, Mark."

"I have the Bridge, sir."

Chapter 21

I hurried down to deck four, the floor with the light green carpet. I passed though the outer office with just a nod to the receptionist. RJ was already there. They had the patient in a sealed glass exam room with a lot of medical equipment. Our visitor was stretched out on an exam table, still unconscious. Doctor Cooper and three of her assistants were all wearing closed-circuit oxygen masks. They were working to remove the helmet. When it finally unlatched, they worked it off with the gentlest care. I could not see the face or head. They went to work on the suit and, having discovered it pulled off around the shoulders and upper body, they were trying to spread the open sections out as much as possible.

The outside speakers were on. Doctor Cooper said, "Okay, the only way this is going to work is if three of us grip her arms and head while one of us pulls the suit off from her feet."

They maneuvered around and began gently trying to make that happen.

It took about twenty minutes of coaxing, and finally the suit was off, and they stood aside just to look.

She was different than any humanoid I had ever seen. She was dressed in what could be described as a small bikini and nothing else. She had been in that suit wearing only that, bare feet included. Her skin was light golden. Her body was very fit and in perfect proportions. The bikini top was not quite large enough. The bottoms were, barely. She had long golden hair, all tangled up around her and falling off the table. She had pointed ears. Slightly large eyes, now closed. Small nose. Thin pink mouth. Across her upper brow, it looked like flat diamonds had been embedded in her skin. They ran in a line down the sides of her face. The exam light reflected brightly off of them.

Doctor Cooper pulled a sheet up over her legs and upper body. Poking and prodding began. Blood was taken. One assistant left the sealed area with it. Cooper held up a scanning device that looked like a yardstick and slowly ran it over the body from head to foot. Images began to appear on screens behind her. She moved from one side to the other, studying them.

My time was up. I had to get back to the Bridge. I tapped on the glass. She turned and looked at me, then reluctantly came out.

"Any idea how long to wake her up?"

"She appears uninjured, but I would not stimulate her until I've studied the scans further."

"She is healthy, then?"

"As near as I can tell."

My watch bleeped. "Captain Tarn, you are needed on the Bridge."

"This is Tarn. I'm on my way." I nodded to the Doctor and headed out, with RJ close behind.

On the Bridge, Jameson looked anxious. "Captain, Lieutenant Zelest has made contact with another ship. They are asking to speak to you."

RJ and I went to the Com station. I picked up a headset-microphone and handed one to RJ.

"This is Captain Tarn, who are you?"

"Good to hear your voice, Adrian. This is Stephen Washburn commanding the Achilles."

"How can I be talking to Captain Washburn?"

"Because we've been secretly shadowing you since you left Earth. I'm your wingman."

"How far out are you?"

"We are a little over an hour away. My suggestion is you get back underway immediately, and I will take care of the distress call."

"We have one of their passengers onboard, but she appears to be a non-combatant."

"She's along for the ride then, Adrian. You need to get back on course, as you know."

"I guess we will owe you one, Captain."

"A stiff drink in an Earth bar would do it. Washburn out."

RJ looked at me. "Will wonders never cease."

"Communications, give me ship wide."

"You have it, Captain," replied Lieutenant Zelest.

"All hands, this is Captain Tarn. Standby for jump to warp. We are resuming our course to Alpha Draconis. Tarn out. Mr. Williams, set a course to Alpha Draconis. Helm, give us eight and engage when ready."

"Yes, Captain."

"Yes, Captain."

RJ and I took our seats as Jameson moved to the left seat. We all sat back and watched the view screen blur into light speed.

"Steady at eight, Captain."

"Very good, Mr. Porter."

The three of us sat in our command seats and watched space and time pass by. I discovered a boot attached to my seat that had a tablet in it. It took only one fingerprint to open it. Instead of watching the small star field-filled tiny screen on my armrest showing us following the green line of the flight path, I began a more detailed study of the area of space we would be passing through. There were few surprises to be seen.

About an hour later, my watch chimed. "Cooper to Tarn."

"Go ahead, Doctor."

"She's awake."

"On my way."

I turned the Bridge over to RJ and hurried down to level four. Our visitor was still in the glass isolation booth, dressed in someone's light green, veiled nightgown. Dr. Cooper was leaning over a desk, poking at a computer keyboard with one finger. She looked up at me and shook her head in frustration.

"She's a strange one."

"How do you mean?"

"First, we tried to get her to put on some flight coveralls, and she refused. Wouldn't accept it. We had to bring several offerings until she finally agreed to the nightgown, but it had to have the veils."

"Okay..."

"She has vocal cords and can speak, but when she does, it sounds like a narrow band of music, like only a few notes are used, none of them very high and none of them low. None of our voice processors are able to translate it, so we have only been able to communicate with hand signals."

"Hold on a second, Doctor." I clicked my watch. "Tarn to Marks and Kurh."

"Yes, Captain."

"Here, Captain."

"Can you report to Sick Bay right away?"

"Will do, Captain."

"On my way."

I looked back at the Doctor. "They are telepathic specialists."

The Doctor raised her eyebrows. "Oh! Thank goodness, because we can't get anything out of her. She has organs similar to humans, but not arranged in the same way. She has a slightly bigger heart and greater lung capacity. There are a few small organs I can't account for. She utilizes much more of her brain than most humans. She has two small hemispheres different than humans. So this individual is a lot like humans, but very different in some ways."

"Doctor, I am very glad to have at least this much information. Thank you."

Cooper smiled. "I cannot wait for the telepaths."

They arrived quickly. Both came up beside us. Marks took a quick look and turned to me. "She's definitely telepathic."

We all went to the cell entrance and entered. I wondered if we should be wearing masks but looked to find the Doctor was not. Marks took the lead. Kurh looked like he was admiring her figure. At the very first contact, our guest clutched one of Marks' hands, wrinkled her brow, and bowed her head in a sign of relief.

Marks looked at us. "Her name is Astra. She is asking for immediate asylum."

"She is?" I asked in dumb surprise.

Marks resumed the contact and had to hold his hand up to slow her down, but she understood. After less than a minute, he turned to us once more. "She was kidnapped and was being held on that ship as a hostage and slave. She did not expect to survive in that spacesuit and planned on dying."

I asked, "Where did that ship come from?"

Marks asked and replied, "She was sold onto that ship on Alpha Draconis."

I added, "Please convey to her we do not believe in slavery, and no one will be taking her off this ship."

She looked at me wide-eyed and nodded a thank you.

I asked, "Is she hungry and thirsty?"

Marks asked.

Astra nodded, "Yes."

I touched the Doctor's arm. "Can she be taken to quarters?"

"Yes, I or a staff member will need to stay with her at all times until we finish our scans and decide her acclimation is okay."

"Doctor, if it's not too much of an imposition, I'd like to have her on level seven, close by. You are on seven, aren't you?"

The Doctor did not seem put out. "Yes, and I adjoin one of the arboretums. That would probably be good for her. She's welcome to be my house guest. There's a lot more we need to know."

"Someone needs to be with her at all times until we know more, and security will be stationed outside your quarters for the time being."

"I understand."

"We will need to have a meeting with you, Mr. Marks, and Mr. Kurh at end of shift so I and Commander Smith can be brought up to date."

"Of course, Captain. I'll arrange it."

I returned to the Bridge and filled in RJ and Jameson.

Near the end of shift, Dr. Cooper called, "Captain, I'm here with Mr. Marks and Mr. Kurh. Where and when would you like to meet?"

"Give us ten minutes for the next crew to finish tie-in. We'll meet in my quarters. Why don't you go ahead and come on up?"

"On our way, Captain."

We all met at the entrance to my quarters. RJ and I moved some chairs around so we could all sit around the coffee table.

Mr. Kurh began, "She's unlike anyone I've ever met, Captain."

Marks added, "Even she is not sure whether or not she's from this dimension."

RJ asked, "Do you know what planet she's from?"

"Her planet is called Oreonus. There is no listing for it anywhere," replied Marks. "She was abducted by kidnappers because she is part of the ruling family on that planet. Also she has special abilities that we haven't figured out yet."

Dr. Cooper interrupted, "I have seen her move small objects with her mind."

Kurh added, "We haven't been able to verify that. It could have been some type of mental illusion."

"I don't think so," insisted the Doctor.

Marks continued, "In any case, she's been moved around repeatedly since her abduction, partly for value gained and partly because she kept escaping."

"Can you tell how old she is?" asked RJ.

Doctor Cooper replied, "Best guess is late twenties, Earth years, but there's just no way to know."

Marks said, "I was forced to tell her we are headed for Alpha Draconis, and that scared the hell out of her. She says authorities there will demand her return."

I said, "Good to know. Not going to happen."

Marks nodded. "I told her that, but she is still afraid they might try to search the ship. She was partly to blame for the damage to that stranded ship. She was hiding from them when some idiot tried to stun her and hit a coolant line. That caused a chain reaction."

I asked, "Doctor, could you create a convincing disguise for her that will make her look like a human Bridge officer?"

"Without a doubt."

"That will include fooling scanning devices?"

"I'm sure our tech guys can handle that."

"In that case, let's plan on that, Doctor. Let me know if you need anything. One other thing, if Astra has the power of speech, is she capable of learning English?"

Kurh jumped in. "She already is, Captain. From what I've seen, it will be a fast process."

"All of you please do what you can to make that happen. I assume you will continue to debrief her. Please keep me up to date on what you learn. We'll need to document all of your efforts also, of course. For now, I need to have a long talk with Security. Do any of you have anything else?"

They did not.

"Rell and Tori, would you please come with me to the Security office so we can continue this?"

We left and headed for Security Headquarters on level six. "Tarn to Smith."

"Here, Adrian."

"Can you come down to Security? We have an issue coming up."

"Mr. Jameson is still here. I'm on my way."

"Captain Tarn to Carter."

A surprised-sounding voice answered, "Yes, Captain?"

"Are you in your office by any chance?"

"I am, sir."

"Commander Smith and I are on our way to speak with you. Do you have time?"

"Yes, sir. Of course."

"See you shortly."

Chapter 22

Outside the door to Security, we saw RJ approaching. We waited and gave him a quick rundown of our Astra problem.

We went in and greeted the officer in the outer office. She pointed us to Carter's office.

Carter stood from his desk and shook our hands. We sat and tried to relax.

"There hasn't been any problems with our new visitor, has there?" asked Carter.

"No, but there is a situation coming up," I replied.

"I'm not surprised. We were unable to do a normal debriefing on her. First she was unconscious, then she turned out to be telepathic, so I'd planned to set up a meeting with the four of you, but it seems you've beaten me to it."

"She was in that space suit trying to escape slavery. She has asked for asylum, which I am inclined to give her. She's clearly a non-combatant."

"So what's the problem?"

"She was involved in the damage to that ship while trying to escape. That ship is out of Alpha Draconis. So, her captors want her back, and probably the Alpha Draconis authorities have been told she was the cause of the ship's damage, and they want her too."

"I see where this is going."

RJ said, "As I see it, this is a two-tier problem. One, we do not want them taking her back, and two, they are likely to insist on coming aboard to look for her, which violates all our isolation mandates."

Carter sat back. "Hmm, this is looking difficult."

I added, "Doctor Cooper is sure she can disguise Astra to be a Bridge officer, and she believes the tech guys can set her up to fool any scans."

Carter replied, "Of course my guys can help with that."

RJ said, "If all of that is trustworthy, then our real problem is with aliens coming aboard and planting a virus for the Deep State A.I."

Cooper responded, "I'd say it's more than that, Commander. We cannot let the names Smith or Tarn be picked up by anyone online or on board. We will need to set up a surrogate Captain and First Officer, because they'll probably be scanning some people. Deep State A.I. could recognize your DNA. We will also need to wipe your names from the computer records and replace them with substitute names."

We all paused for a moment, realizing that was true.

I said, "I think I'd like to see Mark Jameson sit in as Captain, and I'm thinking you would be the best choice for Second in Command, Jalin. It would keep you in the center of everything that's happening and put you in a good position to react. Somehow I'd like Astra, the Commander, and myself to be at stations on the Bridge so we can see everything that's going on. We'll need good disguises as well."

Cooper answered, "I agree. We'll make you security personnel."

RJ said, "I believe Adrian and I should also be in disguise so that we can be mobile during the event."

Everyone nodded in agreement.

Telepath Rell Marks asked, "Is there any way of preventing them from coming aboard?"

RJ answered, "I should mention that when we encountered the stranded ship, we never identified ourselves. We just picked up Astra and left when we knew the Achillies was going to take care of it."

Telepath Tori Kurh added, "My information is that most of the species inhabiting Alpha Draconis are telepathic. So if there is a search of the ship, it will most likely be by telepaths."

RJ asked, "Would they intrusively read our minds?"

Kurh replied, "They are not supposed to. It is considered bad manners to focus directly on someone and invade their mind. They can ask a question or make a statement, but anything more than that is considered abusive."

Marks said, "I doubt these people will be courteous."

I asked, "How do we stop them from digging into our minds?"

Kurh answered, "There are medications that can make areas of the brain associated with higher reasoning difficult to access."

RJ shook his head. "This is all sounding too complicated."

"There is one other possible solution, Commander. As telepaths, Rell and I could set up a session with every crew member aboard, and using telepathy we could implant the idea that no passenger was ever picked up by the Acura. It's a form of telepathic hypnosis. How many crew do you have?" asked Tori.

RJ paused in thought. "We have sixty-eight."

"So that would be thirty-four crew members for each of us at approximately ten minutes per person. That would be almost six hours of telepathy. We'd have to divide it up—that's too much for one person. We'll be exhausted afterward."

"And that would work? If they were interrogated, they would show no memory of picking anyone up?"

"A ninety-five percent probability. So yes."

I said, "I have one more concern. Rell, or Tori, if our uninvited inspectors end up in the environmental storage area and scan those two unidentified cases, could that cause us more problems?"

I could tell by their expressions they had not thought of that. Rell leaned over, and they spoke in whispers. Rell straightened back up and said, "We'll unseal them and have the technical people install devices that make them look like wine. Then we'll reseal them."

It made us all wonder what the hell was in those cases that we were about to hand over to the serpentoids. We sat in silence for a few moments. Finally, I asked, "If no one has anything else right now, let's put these plans into action. Please keep Commander Smith and myself up to date."

Everyone rose to leave the Security office. I motioned to Security Chief Carter. "Jalin, I need another moment or two."

RJ sat back down.

When the three of us were alone, I sat back and took a deep breath. "So when we approach Alpha Draconis, we will need to ask permission to enter their keep-out sphere. Getting in will probably be easy. Getting out may not be. My last concern is, what happens if our plans fail and they try to take control of our ship?"

RJ added, "The more complex a plan, the more chances for problems."

Carter responded, "If they try to take the ship and we resist, it will be a firefight against a telepathic attack, along with their weapons. To be honest, I have already looked into this. I've found that there is an outer belt around the Alpha Draconis system which is densely made up of ice, similar to Earth's Kuiper Belt. In a worst-case scenario, if we could immobilize their inspection team, we could make a run for that belt, shut down systems, and make the ship as cold as possible to hide within that belt. That's the best worst-case scenario I've been able to come up with."

RJ commented, "That's a two-part tricky."

I asked, "Could we take out their inspection team?"

Carter answered, "If we kept our security members with all inspection team members and kept them armed, we could give them a trigger word that, when heard, instructed them to immediately heavy-stun all members of the inspection team. We might catch them off guard enough to take them out."

RJ said, "I see the danger in that. If they mentally scanned someone and caught wind of that keyword and its meaning, they would know."

Carter replied, "Yes."

I thought about it. “Let’s keep it in our back pocket for now. We’ll talk again.”

RJ and I rose and headed out. In the corridor, RJ asked, “What do you think?”

“I think this was supposed to be a simple pickup. The two emissaries pull up alongside us in a shuttle, get in, and we take off.”

“What’s that old World War Two expression? FUBAR?”

“Fucked up beyond all recognition.”

“That’s the one.”

Back in my quarters, I switched on the coffee maker, filled two cups, and mixed them, then handed one to RJ, and we sat.

We sipped and eyed each other.

RJ said, “So I see two scenarios here. We had to stop for the distress call. We needed to grant the woman asylum. We end up in a big mess at Alpha Draconis. We end up in front of a tribunal on Earth to explain why we did what we did. We explain that space maritime law required us to stop for the ship in distress and to provide asylum for the escaped passenger. Then the tribunal begins with ‘yes, but...’ And they have a thousand buts, so that we are blamed for the situation, thus saving the higher-ups’ asses. Scenario two: We do not stop for the ship in distress; we do not pick up the passenger and give her asylum. Now that disregard for space maritime law creates a gigantic scandal against Earth from our neighboring planetary societies—a great embarrassment to our higher-ups. So we are once again crucified in order to protect those same asses of our higher-ups.”

“I believe you have a good grasp of the situation.”

RJ sipped his coffee. “How many times have we been in a situation like this?”

“I have lost count.”

“There is one reason for hope.”

“I can’t imagine.”

"Of all the times we have been finagled into a situation like this, you have always managed to worm out of it somehow."

We sat in silence and considered it.

RJ said, "I'm going to head for the Commissary and use hot food to put it all out of my mind."

"I think I'll sit here a while and mull."

So we worked on our scam daily. Eventually, we even practiced parts of it. There were problems. Astra understood exactly what we were trying to do and that she was the cause of it. But getting her into a communications officer's uniform was a problem. For some reason, her body could only accept certain types of fabric. We had to locate members of the crew with experience in fashion design. As it turned out, we had quite a few, and an acceptable replica of the uniform was created. Astra also had problems with face covering for a mask. It was either that or covering her face in makeup, which did not work.

RJ and I put in our own good amount of time sitting for the creation of masks. The three of us had specially designed modules that attached to the center of the chest to fool scanners. A great deal of time was spent by Rell Marks and Tori Kurh hypnotizing the crew to forget Astra's presence.

By the time we dropped out of warp to approach Alpha Draconis, we were as ready as we could be. I was Lieutenant Smith; RJ was Lieutenant Jones. Besides our two telepathic envoys, we were the only crew that hadn't been brainwashed to forget Astra. RJ and I took positions on the Bridge on either side of the main entrance. Telepath Kurh was stationed at the side airlock with security to receive our two emissaries. Rell Marks was stationed on the Bridge with us. Captain Jameson was in the center seat; Security Chief Carter was in the right seat. The communications station had been set up for two people. Astra sat left; Zay Zelest was right. Astra had been trained on the comm console. She had been cautioned not to appear nervous, and she understood that completely.

Alpha Draconis was a very large planet. Not much water, jagged mountains, brown desert, and fringes of vegetation. Approaching high orbit, Zay sent a written request for permission to enter an orbital corridor. Written permission to do so was returned. Helm set us up in the orbit we had been advised to use, and we waited, holding our breath.

A few long minutes later, another written request came in asking for permission to dock. On screen, it was a small shuttle, unlikely to be military. We approved, and with our screens set to exterior and the airlock interior, we watched them line up, attach, and enter our airlock. Two individuals in well-worn, humanoid-styled spacesuits—dark gray and dirty. Two dark travel packs were thrown in the airlock after them. As soon as the airlock sealed, the shuttle darted away and dropped down toward the planet.

Chapter 23

Our two nonhuman emissaries wasted no time getting out of their suits. We watched on our screens with great anticipation, wondering what was in them. As the helmets came off and the suits were pulled down, it was quickly apparent they were humanoid but not human. Both had dark green skin and nearly bald heads, with just a slight bristle of white hair. The one on the left had no neck; the one on the right, slightly too much neck. The one on the right had long, skinny arms with tiny hands that had short little bulbs for fingers. He kept his hands pulled up against his chest. His upper body was narrower than a human but longer overall. His green legs were long and wiry, ending in small feet. The individual on the left had a much more stout upper body, with powerful arms that ended in average-sized hands with four long fingers. His legs were muscular, his feet slightly large. It was difficult to tell which parts of them were covered by clothing since it was the same dark green as their skin, but both of their torso areas had emblems and narrow lines of colorful artwork.

When the inner door opened, Kurh and two security members entered. There was a short pause in silence as Kurh faced them. Kurh motioned to security to take their bags, then led the group out of the airlock.

Our plan was to leave orbit the instant the emissaries were out of the airlock. Acting Captain Jameson called out, "Lieutenant Zelest, tell Orbital Control we are ready to break orbit."

"Yes, Captain."

We waited. Nothing happened.

Jameson asked, "Zay, did you tell them?"

"Yes, Captain. There has been no response."

We waited.

Finally, Zelest said, "Captain, receiving a message from Orbital Control. Acura is not authorized for departure at this time?"

"Ask them why, Zay."

We waited.

Zelest said, "The answer is: standby for inspection."

"Ask why, Zay."

We waited.

"Captain, the answer is: standby to be boarded."

It made me wince.

As planned, Jameson said, "Tell them their inspection team is welcome."

"Yes, Captain. No response."

I looked over at RJ. Even with his mask on, I could tell he winced, then shook his head. My face mask was now making the left side of my chin itchy, but I dared not try to scratch it.

We waited in silence for a very long fifteen minutes. Finally, Rell Marks came over to me. He motioned RJ to join us.

"During the telepathic hypnosis, we did go ahead and suggest the doomsday phrase. The phrase is: obey the intruders, do not resist. If that phrase is announced to all personnel, the security people will instantly open fire on the inspection team."

I said, "That's cutting it awful close to a common command phrase."

"Yes, it had to be worded that way so that if the inspection team picked it up on a telepathic scan, it would sound like a harmless, normal command."

At that moment, on our view screen, a fairly large military-style shuttle came into view. Jameson gave the order to open the hangar bay to receive it. We watched the black ship disappear into the hangar. Jameson switched the view screen to the hangar bay in time for us to see the ship settle.

Once the outer doors had closed and the hangar pressurized, a large side door opened, and a dozen of our security people hurried into the hangar and lined up against the side wall. They were barely in place when the ship's tail dropped open to become a ramp. To my great dismay, a large herd of six-foot praying mantis beings burst down the ramp and into the hangar. They were dark in color, with triangle-shaped heads that came to a point, with fearsome-looking teeth along the sides. They kept their arms folded against their chests. They had long, skinny arms with small hands and short fingers with bulbs on the end. Their torso looked like a roach body, with tail pieces like tuxedos. Their legs were long, skinny, and ended in small feet. Tori Kurh approached the charging mass and tried to communicate. He was knocked aside. Our stunned security force tried to join the mass to accompany them but could not. The herd funneled into the open hangar door with the intention of spreading throughout the ship.

Tori Kurh came on the com system. "They are refusing any supervision or escort."

Jameson asked for shipwide and announced, "All hands, this is Captain Jameson. We are being inspected by an Alpha Draconis security force. Do not interfere with them."

I leaned over to RJ. "Suddenly, I'm less bothered by the doomsday trigger phrase."

RJ replied, "Let's hope it doesn't come to that."

Rell Marks looked at us and nodded.

Jameson used his armrest controls to continually put various cameras up on multiple view screens. In most cases, our security was doing an admirable job of trying to keep up with the mantis inspectors, but they were knocked aside whenever in the way. In some cases, the mantis would enter an area, grab one of our people by the arm, turn them roughly around, and use glaring telepathy into their eyes. Some of our people fell to the floor after that encounter.

"They are pushing it," I said.

RJ replied, "They do not seem to be finding anything."

Jameson began making calls to Medical to report to areas where people had collapsed.

They began on the lower decks, and the higher they went, the more annoyed they seemed. Now spread out, security managed to keep up with them reasonably well, although the threat to them was always apparent. Their leader separated from the search and came to the Bridge. He could see we were following them on the view screens, and he seemed to be in contact with all of them telepathically. He gave us all a threatening appraisal but did not attempt any mind or body scans. He positioned himself near Jameson and stood concentrating on his telepathy.

The insect group passed through Sick Bay, ignoring the growing number of crew that had been injured. Doctor Cooper called up to the Bridge, "Our people are in shock, but they will recover quickly," was her summary report.

An interesting event occurred when they entered the two unoccupied arboretums on level seven. They seemed to like the forest and lingered there longer than necessary.

Finally, one of them charged onto the Bridge to join the leader. He stomped around the room, evaluating the consoles and personnel. Satisfied he knew the layout, he began on the far side, scanning and telepathically checking each person and each station. The leader seemed to approve.

All we could do was wait. The intrusive inspection process made it halfway around the room without anyone collapsing. But it was at that point a little alarm went off in the back of my mind. It was a signal I had grown to trust over the years, and it had never been wrong. Somehow I knew when the mantis got to Astra, our concealments would not work. I was now certain of that. It would mean she would be arrested and probably be sent back into slavery, and we would be charged with harboring a fugitive. They would probably confiscate the ship and imprison the crew.

When the mantis was two crew members away from Astra, I dared to walk over to the com station. The two bug men ignored me. I leaned over to Zelest and quietly said, "Zay, do not open a channel yet, but get ready for a ship-wide announcement."

"Yes, sir."

The mantis was now one crewman away from Astra. I opened my mouth to tell Zay to open a ship-wide channel but was interrupted by the Bridge doors sliding open. A new praying mantis creature entered the room. He was a lighter green than the others and wore a sash from the left shoulder to the waist. He had more emblems on his body than the others. I assumed he was the grand bug leader.

He went directly to the mantis that had been running things, and a long, silent conversation took place. There was a lot of flinching and body movements. Abruptly, the inspection team leader turned to the bug doing the scans, and the two of them stopped, then surprisingly headed for the exit, followed by the supreme bug man. They all left without saying a telepathic word to Rell Marks. On our screens, the other bugs began withdrawing.

Rell Marks came to me, his hand on his chest in exasperated relief.

"What the hell just happened?" I asked.

Rell had to catch his breath. "That last tantaloid was one of our emissaries. He was very angry about the delay to leave orbit. He explained to the leader that if they did not leave immediately and give us permission to depart, the leader would be inspecting waste management haulers beginning tomorrow morning. Apparently, he has some pull because you saw what happened."

Jameson had switched the view screen to the hangar deck. The cluster of bugs were crowding back onto their ship.

Zay called out from the com, "We have been cleared to leave orbit, Captain."

Both Jameson and I responded, "Helm..."

Jameson turned in his seat and smiled at me. I nodded approval.

Jameson turned back forward. "Helm, take us out of here as soon as that ship is clear."

"With pleasure, Captain."

As the ship swung around and pushed forward, I tore the irritating mask off my face one piece at a time. I looked over and saw RJ blissfully doing the same. Well away from Alpha Draconis, we paused while helm loaded in the new flight path. Jameson made a ship-wide announcement: "All hands, standby for the jump to warp."

In my mind, I thought I heard a chorus of voices cheering. Astra passed by me, pulling her mask off and unzipping her uncomfortable uniform. She left the Bridge without speaking to Rell. The view screen was switched to wide forward. A moment later, the stars swirled into warp-speed view. We all let out a silent breath of relief.

It took five days to reset all the computers and people. On day six, RJ and I shared a pizza in the Mess Hall.

RJ said, "For the time being, only one thing left to worry about, really."

"Yes, but I haven't seen any indications that we were infected."

RJ dropped his piece of pizza back on the plate because it was too hot. "We had an alien ship in the hangar, and a large group of hostiles scanning everything in sight."

"It wouldn't have been an intentionally deposited Deep A.I. virus. The bugs were completely intent on finding Astra."

RJ blew on his pizza. It made me laugh. "So it would have had to be a virus in their stuff that automatically infiltrated ours."

"Yes, but our Optimus X has been programmed to look specifically for anything left by them, and he says we're clean."

RJ smirked. "And the fact that we haven't blown up yet supports that."

"What an elegant way of pointing that out."

"You're welcome."

I took a bite of pizza and spoke with my mouth full. "So I think it's time we got together with our telepaths and emissaries and learned more about the snake people."

"This *is* great pizza. I agree. We'd better invite Dr. Eisner. Hell has no fury..."

I took a moment to finish chewing, sipped my coffee, and clicked my watch. "Tarn to Rell Marks and Tori Kurh."

"Marks here, Captain."

"This is Tori Kurh, Captain."

"Gentlemen, could you arrange a meeting with our emissaries so that we can better prepare for contacting the snake people?"

"We can do that, Captain. When would you like to do it?" replied Marks.

"Whenever it is convenient for them."

"I'll get back to you, Captain."

RJ and I sat back and sipped our coffee.

RJ said, "We should have Security there as well."

"Of course. Anyone else?"

"How about your favorite snake handler, Lieutenant Paulson?"

"Good idea. We may need him to save us if any get loose."

Thirty minutes later, Marks called back. "They would be receptive to a meeting at any time today, Captain."

"Okay, how about in one hour in the main meeting room on level 4?"

"We'll be there, sir."

"Captain to Doctor Eisner."

"Hello?"

"Doctor, we're having a familiarization meeting with our two emissaries, and I think you should join us."

"Well, it's about time! When?"

"One hour. Main meeting room, level four."

"Very well."

And she was gone.

"Captain to Carter."

"Go ahead, Captain."

"Main meeting room, level four. One hour."

"Yes, sir. I heard about it. I'll be there. Carter out."

RJ tilted his head forward in surprise. "He's heard about it? How is that possible?"

"Never try to understand a ship's rumor mill. It's worse than a time paradox."

"Captain to Lieutenant Paulson."

This time, the reply took a good five minutes. "Lieutenant Paulson here, Captain."

"Main meeting room, level four. One hour."

"Yes, sir."

Chapter 24

RJ and I arrived early. The meeting room was a comfortable place. Softly lit walls and ceiling so that there were no shadows. Long imitation wood-grained table with large projection screens on the walls at each end. Cushion swivel, tilt-back high-back seats all around. A drink dispenser against one wall offered many kinds of beverages. I chose more coffee, sat at the head with RJ, and set up the tablet and electric pen I'd brought. I created a file and named it: 'I hate this.'

Doctor Eisner showed up next. She took a seat but was not talkative. Short answers to the standard greetings. A few minutes later, Lieutenant Paulson came cruising in, and to my surprise, he had Goldie, his golden corn snake, draped over his shoulders. He spotted the beverage dispenser, went to it, and poured himself water, offered some to Goldie, then sat and smiled at us. "I'm hoping to desensitize you guys," he said.

Before anyone could answer, Carter walked in, stopped abruptly at the sight, then tried to act normal and took a seat. A moment later, Rell Marks and Tori Kurh entered, followed by our two emissaries. To my relief, they were both in humanoid form, looking just as they had in the airlock. They took seats, with Marks and Kurh sitting opposite them.

After a silent moment for everyone to settle, I said, "I don't think we need introductions."

RJ jumped in. "Mark and Tori, I think we should begin by expressing our thanks to our emissaries for assisting us during this trip."

There was a second of silence, and Rell said, "Both BER and BEP have acknowledged your gratitude."

I could tell Eisner was on edge, ready to dominate the meeting. Before she could speak, I suggested, "BER and BEP, can you give us an idea of what planet Dega is like?"

After a short span of telepathic silence, Marks spoke using their words. "We must first consider our arrival at Dega. Because the inhabitant serpentoids are physically less able to defend themselves, they use defensive systems obtained from other races. Their planet is rich in gold and other minerals, so although they are less advanced due to their physiology, they are very wealthy by any standard. One method they have acquired for protection of their planet is the use of a planet-wide temporal isolation field. Any ship approaching an orbital corridor is captured by a temporal loop in which the ship will repeatedly loop back in time every twenty minutes by Earth standard time. The ship will remain in that loop until given clearance to enter an orbital corridor, after which the loop will be discontinued."

I glanced at RJ with eyebrows raised.

Marks continued, "Once in a stable orbit, communications with the serpentoids is established using standard text messages. However, the serpentoids do not know the English language, so a substitute language that your translators are able to translate will need to be used. Obviously, that restriction will also be in effect on the planet's surface, although most communications there will be telepathic."

Marks held up one hand for pause and stood to fill a cup of water for himself. He also filled two more and placed each in front of an emissary. The emissaries kept eyeing Paulson's snake, which seemed to be of interest to them.

Kurh continued the description. "Once formal contact is made with the surface, a ceremonial invitation to land a shuttle will be made at specific coordinates given. Your response must also be ceremonial in nature to make the first meeting between humans and these serpentoids an official declaration of cooperation. If they are satisfied, you will be invited down so that the leaders of both parties can meet and observe the ceremony of cooperation."

RJ dared to interrupt. "BEP and BER, exactly what will be expected of us at this ceremony?"

There was a short pause. Marks spoke, "The Captain and First Officer must be the primary attendees. Anyone of lower stature and you would risk offending them. For the most part, you will only be there to observe the formalities. There will be some form of honorary seating for the two of you. Your telepaths will be expected to stand behind you. As previous visitors, the two of us will be allowed to sit on either side of you. A procession of leadership serpentoids will pass in front of us. You may receive gifts, but usually you are not required to reciprocate in kind. Usually, you are not expected to do anything but observe and act impressed."

Marks picked up the communication. "When the ceremony is concluded, usually both sides take a break, returning to their own habitats. When a signal is sent, the exchange of promised items is to take place. Whatever you have brought them is to be offloaded and set down in an area they will have designated. They will inspect all the merchandise and may request a demonstration of it from you. If it is found to be acceptable, it will be taken away. Next, a group of probably four soldiers will approach in formation, bringing the item you have come to receive. It must be presented to the Captain, or if too large, it is placed in front of him for his own group of designated soldiers to pick up and take aboard your shuttle."

There was another significant pause.

Kurh began again, "Usually, after the exchange, a sort of party is held. All of your people will be invited to disembark and watch. They are allowed to bring drink and food with them for the festivities. The serpentoids will put on some form of entertainment. The serpentoids' leadership will likely ask for a tour of your ship, not the shuttle—your ship. It would be unwise to refuse or show any revulsion at the suggestion. They will not cause any disturbances on the tour. They will be courteous and not intrusive. The tour does not need to be conducted by the Captain or First Officer unless that seems necessary. When the tour is finished, they will be brought back to the surface, and as the celebration concludes, you will be free to return to the ship."

Eisner couldn't hold back any longer. "Mr. Marks, ask them what kind of infrastructure is there where they live?"

Our two emissaries paused to evaluate the Doctor. After a few moments of stolid stares, Marks began to speak. It was clear this time he was not relaying their message. This time, they were speaking through him.

Marks said, "The answer to such a question is lengthy and complicated. To begin with, we believe you have been advised that these serpentoids move in an upright posture. They can still move along the ground, but in public that is looked down upon. Also, you already should know that a short distance below the head, on the stomach, they have two very small appendages with small fingers, and below those, a short distance, there is another identical set. The Dega calligraphy is varied and designed to facilitate their style of movement. The cities are large and expansive. The region we are expected to land in will have serpentoid constructs all around and far into the distance. A great deal of forestry is maintained within and around the city. Most wildlife that exists there is protected. A great variety of birds can be seen around the city, and birds are particularly protected. They are important in regulating insect and other intrusive species. The city is comprised largely of private dwellings constructed largely from earthenware, ceramic, and stoneware. The serpentoids' dwellings have windows and doors, but they are open. There is very little glass on Dega. Where glass is used, it has been obtained and installed from off-world suppliers. There are also metallic components and structures, all supplied from off-world.

The average serpentoid dwelling is typically three to five feet high. Many have more than one level. Government buildings are generally metal and ceramic and have some glass. They are typically taller than the surrounding structures. Streets wind through all of the city and are usually grass, sometimes dirt. Dega has several freshwater oceans separating four large continents. Each continent supports its own political society. These societies do not always get along. There have been large-scale serpentoid wars on Dega, but none in a very long time. The serpentoids on Dega do not eat meat. There are trees on Dega that produce a plentiful flesh-like fruit shaped like a cone. This is the primary diet of the serpentoids. Water cisterns are located around the cities, as the serpentoids do not need water frequently. In addition, there are extensive networks of tunnels below the cities. There are many more idiosyncrasies concerning Dega, too many to list. Has this been sufficient in answering your question?"

Eisner was furiously scribbling on a tablet. The rest of us just stared blankly, trying to fathom what we had just heard.

RJ said, "Can I ask how the serpentoids handle ships that invade their space or planet?"

Kurh answered immediately, "If a ship is able to get through the temporal protective shield, a worldwide alarm is sent out. Nations from all continents join forces to repel or destroy the invaders. There is a report of one such intrusion many years ago where transgressors put their ship down on the water, thinking it would protect them. Serpentoids are very good swimmers. As the report states, within a few hours there were so many serpentoid defenders surrounding the ship that it would have been possible to walk on the water. Serpentoids have no problem sacrificing themselves for such a cause. Some used their bodies to block open ports and valves, and eventually the ship was breached. By the time it was over, a side airlock door sprang open to reveal the airlock, like the rest of the ship's interior, was filled with serpentoids from floor to overhead. That ship remains at the bottom of the ocean."

There was another long pause. Even Eisner failed to come up with a response.

Finally, I asked, "BEP and BER, what will the communication arrangement be when we get there?"

Once again, the emissaries chose to speak through Tori Kurh rather than relay the information. We could not tell which emissary was speaking. Kurh said, "As you all know, all animals are telepathic at some level. Mr. Kurh and Mr. Marks have not yet had the privilege of conversing with the serpentoids on Dega. For that reason, the style of telepathy that those individuals use will likely be unfamiliar to them. For that reason, it seems logical for us to begin the communications on Dega to give them the opportunity to familiarize themselves with the serpentoids' telepathics. Logically, we would lead the conversations and pass them on to Mr. Marks and Mr. Kurh, who would in turn translate them for the rest of you. This seems especially important because the Dega serpentoids do not yet understand the English language as we do, although they are at present working to add it to their translators, and some of the leadership are trying to learn it as well. Once Mr. Marks and Mr. Kurh have adapted to Dega telepathy, we can carefully transition to a more direct communication arrangement."

I said, "That certainly makes sense to me."

Either BEA or BEP spoke again, this time through Marks. "One other unusual Dega communication method needs to be mentioned here. Just as the serpentoid race has evolved on Dega, so has some of the wildlife. As we mentioned, the Dega serpentoids are particularly fond of their birds, even though on some planets where wildlife is less evolved, reptiles are often considered a food source by some birds. On Dega, there is a species of raven that has advanced significantly. On most worlds, ravens are able to imitate a spoken language very accurately, but they do not associate spoken terms with ideas or objects. On Dega, the ravens not only speak a learned language accurately, they understand keywords and phrases. Ravens have always been considered highly telepathic. For these reasons, the Dega serpentoids have trained ravens to receive their telepathy and translate it to actual speech. We mention this because on Dega you could encounter a raven speaking to you in some other language, which your in-ear translators are able to translate. In a case like that, look around. A nearby serpentoid is speaking to you through the raven. And, you may be able to answer them telepathically yourself. This is something we needed to mention to avoid confusion if it happens."

"Wow!" said Paulsen. "I could get to speak to a snake directly! Well... I already do, actually."

"Oh my word," added Eisner. "It's the chance of a lifetime."

One of the BEs spoke through Marks. "Your golden serpent is very beautiful, Mr. Paulson. She is dedicated to you."

"And I to her," replied Paulson.

For a moment, there seemed to be a connection between Paulson and BER.

I leaned forward in my seat. "Well, everyone, I think we've covered enough for today. We could all use a break. BEP and BER, I can't thank you enough for this exceptional briefing, allowing us to understand what's ahead. If there is anything at all you need, please let me know. If no one else has anything else, this meeting is adjourned."

Everyone rose. Paulson was the first one out, talking to Goldie as he went.

Chapter 25

RJ and I remained seated and watched our shape-shifting guests leave. Once we were alone, RJ said, "That was a lot to process."

"I'm still trying to process talking to a snake through a raven."

RJ nodded. "Even on Earth, some people say they are as smart as people in some ways. I was told by someone that wild ravens will find a pack of hunting wolves, make themselves known to the wolves, then fly out seeking game. When they spot game, they call to the wolves to come and capture it. Then, when the wolves are done feeding, the ravens get an easy meal on what's left."

"The meeting room has recorded all of it. I'm going to need to listen to it again."

"As will I. You want to hit the Mess Hall?"

"No thanks. I think I'll heat something up in my quarters and begin sorting out everything we just heard."

RJ gave a comical salute and headed out.

In my quarters, I made a quick call to the Bridge.

"On course, no issues, Captain."

I shoved a spaghetti dinner into the mini oven and poured myself water on ice. When the bing went off, I sat at the tiny kitchen table and called up the emissaries' debrief on my tablet as I rolled spaghetti onto my fork.

The emissaries' use of English was quite accomplished. A city of snakes. Fairly large ones. Snake heads peering out open windows. Snakes sliding along grass city streets, their heads three or four feet above the ground. Snakes that were evolved enough that their telepathy had matured, even though ours had not. What were we bringing them? What would they be giving us in return? Who arranged all this? I was a Captain with too few answers and no way to get them.

It suddenly dawned on me that in all the time I had spent in my quarters, I had never pulled back the curtains blocking the arboretum windows. I went to them and pulled them wide apart. Suddenly, before me was a forest canopy. It was beautiful. Tree tops, branches, and every kind of flower and community of plants. Imitation cobblestone paths winding through them.

Astra stood in the center of the garden wearing the same veiled nightgown she had worn before. As I watched the beauty of her, a small bird flew past. It was yet another surprise. I followed it back to a nest in one of the trees, where it disappeared inside. Astra was visiting flower after flower and testing their aroma, though she did not pick any of them. I left the curtains open, went and plopped down on the couch, put my feet up, and fell asleep.

We needed two weeks to get to Dega. Two weeks of impatiently waiting to get somewhere I did not want to be. The Acura ran flawlessly. It was like a simulator with no challenge.

One week in, I'd almost adjusted to the routine.

"Carter to Captain."

"Go ahead, Jalin. I'm not busy."

"Could you come down to Security?"

I looked at RJ sitting next to me. "The Bridge is yours."

RJ nodded. "I have the Bridge."

Entering the outer security office, I could tell something was up. Carter was in his office with a tech officer and someone from Engineering. They were leaning over, looking at Carter's computer screen. They looked up as I entered.

I asked, "Is it good news or bad news?"

Carter tapped a key on his keyboard, and the large screen on the side wall of his office switched on. We were looking at a section of the ship's topside, aft, near an engine nacelle. An area there contained a large section of temperature control radiators. The off-white section of the ship was covered by molded conduits and low barriers between service boxes and cooling equipment. I studied the area being shown and, to my relief, saw no damage anywhere.

"It's hard to see, Captain," said Carter. "You know, of course, we conduct video inspections of the ship's exterior at regular intervals using the external cameras. This hasn't been seen before, so either it's new or has moved somehow."

"Jalin, I see no damage whatsoever."

Carter picked up a laser pointer from his desk and began circling an area on the screen.

There was something. A disproportionate, shoe-shaped device jammed in between the cooling panels and a containment wall.

"What is it?" I asked.

Carter zoomed in on the spot. It began to look more like a heavy boot.

"That can't be what I'm thinking."

"We're not sure, Captain, but I believe every one of us is thinking spacesuit boot."

"It's certainly not standard space equipment."

"We're thinking it may be a space dock work suit. They are black and gray and heavier than standard."

There was a moment of silence in which we were all hoping that wasn't a correct guess.

"Has IT searched for telemetry from an unassigned spacesuit?"

One of the people standing next to Carter answered, "We have searched. There are no active spacesuits transmitting. The suit batteries could be dead."

Carter added, "Or maybe it's just part of a suit that got left behind somehow."

I shook my head in disbelief. "Well, we all know what has to happen."

"Yes, that would be me, Captain."

"I'll be joining you, Jalin."

"Captain, this does not warrant endangering the ship's captain."

"I want firsthand information on this, Jalin."

"I understand, sir. I planned to bring Optimus X with me. He can see things we might miss."

"Does the Optimus have a maneuvering unit?"

"Oh yes, of course. He's certified to do external repairs. The truth is, he could get there without one anyway—we just wouldn't risk that."

"We will want to keep this quiet."

"Yes."

I rubbed my mouth in thought. "Give me thirty minutes to check in on the Bridge, and I'll meet you in the starboard airlock."

On the Bridge, I took the center seat and motioned RJ to lean in. I quietly gave him a rundown of what was going on. With a puzzled look, he said, "How come you get to have all the fun?"

"Careful what you wish for."

"Oh... yeah..."

By the time I reached the airlock ready room, they were already there, suiting up. The Acura's ready room and airlock were the nicest I had ever seen. Hospital white, with all conduits and sensors molded into the walls so that there were no sharp edges anywhere. Lighted walls and ceiling, so no shadows and no way to miss anything. The air felt cool and smelled particularly clean. The sounds of equipment being maneuvered around were echoing slightly off the walls. The techs had my suit ready. I only had to strip and pull on the thermal undergarment and plug in the hose. Optimus X already had his maneuvering unit on. It was surprisingly small compared to ours. As the techs pulled the torso down over my head, I asked, "X, have you been fully briefed on what we're doing?"

"Yes, Captain."

"Have you evaluated the object?"

"My analysis indicates we are recovering a space dock work suit. There is a ninety-five percent chance that the boot is attached to a full suit."

"X, how did you reach that conclusion?"

"The angle at which the boot is at rest can only be maintained if it is supported by attachment to a suit."

As the techs helped me get the gloves on, I watched Jalin's helmet being brought down over his head. He was laughing inside at Optimus X having better insight than we did. I had to agree with him.

I bent my head forward to fit into my helmet. They clicked it into place, and immediately the suit began to fill. The bar graphs near my chin showed the pressure gradually come up to twelve pounds. Next, the five bar graphs showing oxygen and other mixtures in the air came up to assigned levels. When everything was stable, the suit automatically began lowering suit pressure as the nitrogen removal system did its job. The suit EVA team withdrew and shut the inner hatch while we waited for the suits to get down to five, the pressure level needed so we wouldn't be trapped inside balloons too rigid to move in. As the pressure approached five, our tiny world had become habitable. Cooling system bar graphs were right on. We were ready.

Carter called on the intercom. "You got me, Captain?"

"Five by five, Jalin."

"Are you with us, X?"

"Communications have been established."

We rocked back into our maneuvering units attached to the walls, latched them on, and stepped forward. The control arms came down from the stowed position without a problem. Tiny taps at the joysticks on either arm showed that the cold gas control jets were responding.

Carter asked, "So whether it's a suit or a body, we're going to bring it back with us, correct, Captain?"

"Correct. We should isolate the suit by keeping it here in the airlock. If it is a person, we will let Medical isolate the body and move it back to Sick Bay."

Carter went to the outer door, unlatched it, and pulled it aside. After a quick look, he stepped out and jetted a short distance away. I stepped forward, took a quick look at the big empty space out there, backdropped by stars in every direction, and leaned into the emptiness. A few taps at the joysticks brought me alongside Carter. We watched X come out after us. Carter joked, "Up, up and away."

The three of us rose vertically. The ship looked darker in outer space. Irregular shadowy surface features running along the side walls passed by us. From above, we looked out over the flatlands of the ship's topside. The cooling radiators we needed were off to our right. Carter took off, leading the way, as all good security officers insisted on. But we allowed X to make the final approach to the mysterious space suit boot. Somehow, X held himself to the ship's surface and maneuvered to pull and push on the item in question.

"This is a space dock work suit with a humanoid form within," declared X. "The suit is well used. The visor is set to dark. I cannot make out details within the helmet. Suit pressure is one point four pounds. There are no life signs within the suit."

"Can you bring him out, X?" asked Carter.

"Yes, Lieutenant, but gender has not been established."

I asked, "What is holding it in place, X?"

"One arm is wedged between two cooling coils, but it can be released for removal."

"Please do so," said Carter.

It took X a minute or two. Finally, he pulled the body out by the torso and moved into a position for transfer. The worn, gray spacesuit floated with the arms spread out and the legs parted. The face shield was frosted white. Carter clipped a tether onto the suit, and we headed back.

We cruised low across the superstructure of the Acura, watching the irregular dark surface pass by below us. Our new crewman followed along behind Carter, its arms out as though flying. At the edge, we dove down and rendezvoused at the airlock entrance. X and I waited for Carter to enter and drag his strange friend in as artificial gravity dropped the body to the floor. When the dragging was done and the new passenger fixed against one wall, X and I took turns entering. To my surprise, X closed the outer door without having been told to.

We waited for recompression and for our suits to very slowly bring suit pressure up to match it without making nitrogen bubbles in our bloodstream. I can never decide which I want to remove first, my gloves or my helmet. Both bring a wonderful feeling of relief.

With helmet off, I asked, "X, would you contact Medical and let them know we're ready for them?"

"Yes, Captain."

I watched as X silently stood and sent the message.

Chapter 26

Medical arrived ready to go, led by Doctor Cooper. Inside the airlock, we shut the inner door, and the med techs worked at removing the suit. We set the airlock air feed as internal and with as much filtering as possible, but with the first click of the helmet, the air became stale and foul.

It was a human male. Shrunken face and hands. Doctor Cooper suggested it would be best to cut the suit undergarment off in the med lab. We were happy to agree. They zipped our John Doe up in an airtight bag, lifted him onto a gurney, and with no atmosphere warnings, we opened up and went out, but resealed the airlock with filtration still running.

As the three of us gathered outside the airlock, I asked, "X, did you get anything else off the suit or body?"

"All suit batteries depleted. External power would need to be applied to interrogate suit computers. External damage to the suit wearer: frost burns and radiation injury. No other analysis possible."

Carter added, "I'll take X down to Medical with me. We'll keep you updated. The tech guys will store the suit."

Back in my quarters, I brewed up some hot chocolate, tried to relax, and went to stare down into the arboretum. Astra was there again, this time wearing a blue nightgown and veils, obviously borrowed from someone else. On a whim, I grabbed another hot chocolate and headed to the arboretum.

As I approached, Astra was separating some flowers to give them more space. I startled her slightly. She smiled.

"Hello, Captain."

Her voice stunned me. It was like three voices combined in harmony. The highest-pitch voice had a slight sawtooth wave to it that tickled my ears. "Astra, you can speak."

"My English is coming along nicely, I am told."

"You can understand everything I say?"

"I cheat. What I do not understand, I fill in with telepathy."

I smiled. "Would you try this? It's called hot chocolate. Be careful, it's still very hot." I held out the cup.

She sipped carefully. Her eyebrows raised. "It is wonderful. Thank you. I have been wanting to thank you for rescuing me."

"We do not believe in slavery, Astra."

She nodded and sipped.

"I'm going to go and leave you to the arboretum. It's been a long day."

She smiled.

In my quarters, I made it to the bed and collapsed onto it.

Morning seemed to come seconds later. Why was I not awakened with the autopsy report? I made it through the morning routine of trying to look like Captain Infallible. On my way to the Mess Hall, I called Medical. "Captain to Doctor Cooper."

"You want the results on John Doe, Captain, I know. We're not done yet, but death by asphyxiation and heart failure, just what you would expect from a spacesuit out of air. We're still waiting on the DNA."

"Thank you, Doctor. Keep me posted."

Struck gold in the Mess Hall. Eggs over easy, bacon substitute, fries, rye toast, and blessed coffee. There were a half dozen other crew there. I took a spot at a wide, empty section of table and plunked my tray down. The food was hot and smelled great. I dove in like a starving man.

Zay Zelest passed by on her way to friends. "Good morning, Captain."

"Morning, Zay."

She paused. "Captain, I must tell you. I know we're above top secret. But this is the scariest mission I've ever been on."

"Oh, the Dega inspection."

"Yes, the rumors are that they were about to begin strip searches until it ended suddenly."

"Probably just rumors, Zay."

"Enjoy your breakfast, Captain."

Nothing could distract me from the eggs. They were seasoned perfectly.

Dr. Eisner plunked her tray down across from me without being invited. "Captain, something wonderful is happening."

"Yes, we survived the Alpha Draconis inspection."

She looked confused for a moment. "Oh, yes... no."

"I'm sorry if you were frightened by all that."

"No, really, we weren't. We were in my quarters, my staff and Mr. Poulson. The mantis people came in, but it was clear they did not like Mr. Poulson's snake, and they left very quickly."

"Believe I'll make a mental note of that."

"No, what I'm talking about—I've been able to speak more with the emissaries through Mr. Marks and Mr. Kurh. I am collecting information on the Dega Serpentoids that will rock the world of the next herpetology convention. Certainly, I will have to publish a paper on this."

"What have you learned, Doctor?"

"There is a clear and defined social difference between the males and females. And the females, using those tiny hands and fingers, are able to knit and sew to a certain extent. They create colorful collars that are worn between the two sets of arms and above them. The females wear light colors, the males brighter, darker colors. They are also used to designate rank among their military and governing bodies."

I tried to interrupt, but it was no use.

"They generally do not have electronics in their homes, but in the metal and glass official buildings, they do have small receivers and video screens. Their power comes from solar energy provided in dealings with other worlds. They have some pictures of you and Commander Smith, by the way."

"I'm sorry, what?"

"They are very particular about dealing with only those individuals actually in charge of a collaboration. They requested images of those who would be in charge of this mission, so your photos were sent to them via subspace. That way, they will be assured when we arrive that they are dealing with the supreme commanders. That is their term for their top leaders."

"I guess..."

"But the most exciting thing right now is that the emissaries have said the serpentoids' leadership may let me remain on Dega while they are brought up to tour the ship. I will get to be alone with them. It's never been done before. It's a world-class first."

I had to stand to get a word in edgewise. "Well, good luck with your research, Doctor." Tray in hand, I slipped away.

On the Bridge, RJ was already there, sitting right seat.

"How are we doing?"

"Steady as she goes. If it wasn't for the mysterious stowaway, the praying mantis inspections with near strip searches, and the dead people flying on the hull, this would almost be a routine mission."

As I sat, I shook my head. "No, it wouldn't really."

"Well, yeah."

"Anything new?"

"I was going over the Dega defensive temporal barrier thing in my head, and questions began popping up, so I had Marks inquire to the emissaries. The thing is, if we fly into a temporal loop and we keep looping back in time every twenty minutes, that means we are stuck in a certain spot in space while the planet Dega is continuing on its path without us. That's one thing. The other is, how do they send us clearance to assume orbit when we're back in time?"

I shook my head in agreement. "These are critical questions I hadn't got to yet."

"Well, the emissaries have been very forthcoming. According to them, the temporal protection field was a gift from a people known as the Guardians. The Dega serpentoids were being treated very harshly over the early years by other planets. The Guardians set up this barrier to protect them and make the planet their own. That allowed the serpentoids to evolve much more quickly. This temporal barrier is almost completely automated, as you would expect. Part of the control system includes a temporal transmitter. It locks on to any ship that enters, and when the time comes, it transmits an acceptance message or a declined message back in time to the location of the looping ship. If declined, they are allowed to leave through a neutralized corridor. If accepted, they are allowed to enter orbital space through a neutralized corridor. If too much time passes and Dega moves too far away, the looping ship remains trapped in a bubble but can still be released by the system. The last, but no less important, bit of information was that the system can also destroy any ship caught within it, if the serpentoids so wish."

"Well, that's both enlightening and disturbing."

RJ tapped one finger against his lips in thought. "I wonder if there's anything we can do to be prepared for the time loop."

"If you come up with something, by all means let me know. In the meantime, it's time to get an update on our mysterious body. Captain to Dr. Cooper."

"Go ahead, Captain."

"Anything new on our deceased stowaway?"

"You have it all, Captain. Nothing else out of the ordinary, but you may need to check in with security. They are trying to identify him."

"Thanks, Doctor. Tarn out. Captain to Carter."

"Yes, Captain?"

"Any ID on our stowaway?"

"We've run prints, reconstructive imaging, and DNA through all our databases. Nothing. But we cannot send it to headquarters because we're still silent running."

"I guess the mystery will remain for now."

"Yes, Captain, but there is one other mystery to be included. In going through his spacesuit, one of our guys found a key sewn into the interior layer of fabric. We have no idea what this key belongs to. We've been trying to match it up in the storage bays, but nothing yet."

"Okay, Jalin. Keep us posted. Tarn out."

RJ looked at me with eyebrows raised in question. "What do you think?"

"Right now, our biggest concern has to be our approach to Dega. We are not allowed to know the parameter of the temporal field. We only know their keep-out zone."

"And obviously we will be in that temporal field before we reach the keep-out zone. But since we must visit Dega, we must enter that temporal field."

"I see no way around it. Keep trying to come up with something that might help us while we are in that damned loop."

Two Earth days later, we could see the speck that was Dega on our long-range scanners. When we were close enough, we dropped out of warp and continued ahead on thrusters. We called the two emissaries and Rell Marks and Tori Kurh to the Bridge, and six of us gathered around Zay Zelest and the com console.

I said to Marks, "Ask them if we're close enough to call in."

After a quick glance at Marks, one of the emissaries leaned over and used an electronic pen to write something on the com input screen. It was a language I'd never seen before.

A minute or two later, a reply appeared on the coms incoming screen. The emissary looked at Marks.

Marks looked at me. “It says, ‘Hold your position and await further instructions.’”

I called out to Porter, “Helm, all stop and station keeping.”

“Yes, Captain.”

Chapter 27

The two emissaries looked at Marks and me. Marks said, "They say we are in the temporal field. There is no way to know how long it will take before we're given clearance inside the keep out zone. They are returning to their quarters to wait."

I nodded a thank you to the emissaries. The two of them left. I thanked Marks and Kurh, and they headed for their quarters also. RJ and I returned to our command seats.

I looked at RJ. "Well, here we are."

"Or have we been here before? You don't know."

Dega was now a ball of green and blue centered in the view screen. The surrounding stars were dimmed by its reflected light. I noticed the Bridge crew seemed on edge. That was confirmed when Yeoman Breize entered the Bridge with a tray of coffees. On her way to me, she fumbled the tray, and one coffee tipped over the edge and splashed on the floor. She let out a moan of despair as the service port near the floor popped open and a robot vacuum sped out to clean up the mess.

"Sorry, Captain." She handed me and RJ coffee.

"That's okay, Yeoman. Thanks for thinking to bring this. Perfect timing."

She went about handing the other coffees out.

As the Bridge doors slid open for her to leave, I noticed Doctor Eisner standing just outside. She did not enter as the doors closed.

It was too much mystery to me. I got up, went to the doors so they would open, but Eisner was gone.

Sitting back down, I asked RJ, "Did you see that?"

"What?"

"A nervous Eisner standing at the door, then not entering."

"I missed that. Eisner missing a chance to speak? Something must be wrong."

My watch switched on. "Carter to Captain."

"Go ahead, Jalin."

"Update on the unidentified key. We still have not found a lock that it fits, but we are still looking. We did a metallurgical analysis on it and found it contains an unidentified alloy not found on Earth. I know that doesn't help much, but we'll keep looking. Carter out."

RJ said, "The thing may unlock something on another planet for all we know."

"Damn strange that it was stored inside an Earth spacesuit."

"Pandora's box, maybe."

"That we do not need. I hate sitting here in empty space."

RJ called out to navigation, "Mr. Williams, are you running long-range scans?"

"Yes, Commander. As planned."

"And there are no other ships out there?"

"No, sir."

RJ smiled at me. "Well, at least there's..."

I called out to Porter, "Helm, all stop and station keeping."

"Yes, Captain."

The two emissaries looked at Marks and me. Marks said, "They say we are in the temporal field. There is no way to know how long it will take before we're given clearance inside the keep out zone. They are returning to their quarters to wait."

I nodded a thank you to the emissaries. The two of them left. I thanked Marks and Kurh, and they headed for their quarters also. RJ and I returned to our command seats.

I looked at RJ. "Well, here we are."

"Or have we been here before? You don't know."

Dega was now a ball of green and blue centered in the view screen. The surrounding stars were dimmed by its reflected light. I noticed the Bridge crew seemed on edge. The Bridge doors opened, and Yeoman Breize entered with a tray of coffees. I suddenly had an urge to stand and meet her, probably because the coffee smelled so good. I took two coffees from her tray, handed one to RJ, and sat back down while she passed out the rest.

"Do you need anything else?" Breize asked.

"No, Yeoman, but you're a blessing for bringing the coffee. Perfect timing."

She smiled and headed for the doors.

When the doors slid open, I noticed Doctor Eisner standing outside, reluctant to enter. She seemed nervous and about to let the doors close, but at the last minute entered and came to us.

"Captain, I am concerned about something."

"Yes?"

"In my further discussions with the emissaries, I have learned that these serpentoids still possess their venom glands, their alveoli. They also have retracted fangs which remain retracted unless they mentally extend them. The venom has become extremely potent over the centuries, and according to the emissaries, a single bite means certain death within seconds. There is no antidote. So during our visit, we will be surrounded by dozens of these creatures, any of which could strike in an instant, effecting instant death. Should we perhaps reconsider our visit there, perhaps find another method of meeting?"

I looked at RJ. He shrugged and replied, "Doctor, perhaps you are looking at this from the wrong perspective. If we were meeting dignitaries with bodyguards who were carrying weapons, any of them could, without warning, draw and fire, killing us in seconds. There would essentially be no difference."

The idea seemed to register with Eisner. She thought for a moment before speaking, a pleasant change for her. Rubbing her hands together, she replied, "Yes, yes, I see that. You are correct, Commander. Why am I thinking these serpentoids are more dangerous than anyone else? Of all people, I'm a graduate serpentologist. I should never have been so shallow-minded. Thank you, Commander. Good day, Captain." She turned and left, seemingly in deep thought.

My watch bleeped. "Carter to Captain."

"Go ahead, Jalin."

"Update on the unidentified key. We still have not found a lock that it fits, but we are still looking. We did a metallurgical analysis on it and found it contains an unidentified alloy not found on Earth. I know that doesn't help much, but we'll keep looking. Carter out."

RJ said, "The thing may unlock something on another planet for all we know."

"Don't you find it strange that it was stored inside an Earth spacesuit?"

"Pandora's box, maybe."

"That we do not need."

RJ called out to navigation, "Mr. Williams, are you running long-range scans?"

"Yes, Commander."

"And there are no other ships out there?"

"No, sir."

RJ smiled at me. "Well, at least there's..."

I called out to Porter, "Helm, all stop and station keeping."

RJ called out to navigation, "Mr. Williams, are you running long-range scans?"

"Yes, Commander."

"And there are no other ships out there?"

"No, sir."

RJ smiled at me. "Well, at least there's..."

I called out to Porter, "Helm, all stop and station keeping."

"Yes, Captain."

The two emissaries looked at Marks and me. Marks said, "They say we are in the temporal field. There is no way to know how long it will take before we're given clearance inside the keep-out zone. They are returning to their quarters to wait."

I nodded a thank you to the emissary. The two of them left. I thanked Marks and Kurh, and they headed for their quarters also. RJ and I returned to our command seats.

I looked at RJ. "Well, here we are."

"Or have we been here before? You don't know."

Dega was now a ball of green and blue centered in the viewscreen. The surrounding stars were dimmed by its reflected light. I noticed the Bridge crew seemed on edge. The Bridge doors opened, and Yeoman Breize entered with a tray of coffees. I suddenly had an urge to stand and meet her; the coffee smelled so good. I took two coffees from her tray, handed one to RJ, and sat back down while she passed out the rest.

"Will that be all, Captain?" Breize asked.

"Yes, Yeoman, and thank you for bringing the coffee."

She smiled and headed for the doors.

When the doors slid open, I noticed Doctor Eisner standing outside, reluctant to enter. She seemed nervous and about to let the doors close but, at the last minute, entered and came to us.

"Captain, I was concerned about something."

"Yes?"

"In my further discussions with the emissaries, I have learned that these serpentoids still possess their venom glands, their alveoli. They also have retracted fangs, which remain retracted unless they mentally extend them. The venom has become extremely potent over the centuries, and according to the emissaries, a single bite means certain death within seconds. There is no antidote. I began to think the danger was too great, but then I realized that in all official meetings, many guards and others also have weapons. But I thought I should let you know about this."

"I appreciate that, Doctor. Please do keep us informed."

She headed for the door. My watch bleeped. "Carter to Captain."

"Go ahead, Jalin."

"Did I recently update you on the key we found?"

"No, Jalin. Go ahead."

"We still have not found a lock that it fits, but we are still looking. We did a metallurgical analysis on it and found it contains an unidentified alloy not found on Earth. I know that's not much, but we'll keep looking. Carter out."

RJ said, "The thing may unlock something in another dimension for all we know."

"Strange that it was stored inside an Earth spacesuit."

"Pandora's box, maybe."

"That we do not need."

RJ called out to navigation, "Mr. Williams, are you running long-range scans?"

"Yes, Commander."

"And there are no other ships out there?"

"No, sir."

RJ smiled at me. "Well, at least there's..."

I called out to Porter, "Helm, all stop and station keeping."

"Yes, Captain."

The two emissaries looked at Marks and me. Marks said, "They say we are in the temporal field. There is no way to know how long it will take before we're given clearance inside the keep-out zone. They are returning to their quarters to wait."

I nodded a thank you to the emissary. The two of them left. I thanked Marks and Kurh, and they headed for their quarters also. RJ and I returned to our command seats.

I looked at RJ. "Well, here we are."

"Or have we been here before? You don't know."

Dega was now a ball of green and blue centered in the viewscreen. The surrounding stars were dimmed by its reflected light.

I noticed the Bridge crew seemed edgy. The Bridge doors opened, and Yeoman Breize entered with a tray of coffees. I stood to meet her. The coffee smelled so good. I took two coffees from her tray, handed one to RJ, and stood sipping while she passed out the rest.

"Will that be all, Captain?" Breize asked.

"Yes, Yeoman, you are a saint for bringing the coffee."

She smiled and headed for the doors.

When the doors slid open for her, for some reason I expected to see Doctor Eisner enter, but there was no one.

My watch bleeped. "Carter to Captain."

"Go ahead, Jalin."

"Have you been updated on the key we found?"

"No, Jalin. Go ahead."

"We still have not found a lock that it fits, but we are still looking. We did a metallurgical analysis on it and found it contains an unidentified alloy not found on Earth. We're still looking. Carter out."

RJ said, "The thing may unlock something in another dimension for all we know."

"Why inside an Earth spacesuit?"

"It goes to Pandora's box, maybe."

"That we do not need."

RJ called out to navigation, "Mr. Williams, are you running long-range scans?"

"Yes, Commander."

"And there are no other ships out there?"

"No, sir."

Zelest called out, "Captain, we are receiving a written message from Dega."

"Contact Kurh and Marks immediately."

"Yes, sir."

RJ and I gathered around the com station, waiting for Marks and Kurh, knowing they would bring the emissaries with them. When they arrived, the seven of us stood staring at the screens. Finally, Kurh looked up and said, "We are cleared for orbital insertion. They are sending coordinates for a geosynchronous orbit, landing coordinates, and a time clock for us to reset our chronometers."

We looked up at the main viewscreen just in time to see the green-blue ball of Dega instantly disappear, leaving a star-filled sky.

"Zay, please transfer the coordinates to helm."

"Yes, Captain."

"Captain to Marquis."

"Yes, Captain?"

"Com is sending you a time clock. Please use it to reset our chronometers."

"I understand, Captain."

RJ asked, "Mr. Marks, how much time did we lose?"

"It appears one hour and twenty minutes, Earth time, Commander."

Kurh called out, "Also, they are asking for a landing two Earth hours from now, Captain."

"Understood. Thank you. Captain to security."

Carter answered, "Standing by, Captain."

"Jalin, I believe we are ready to move those transfer containers onto a shuttle. Departure in two hours."

"In process, Captain."

I looked at RJ. "You realize we have to put on those tight, uncomfortable dress uniforms, right?"

"I know there's a joke in there somewhere, but I am unable to find my sense of humor."

"Helm, take us forward, then find the right place to park."

"Yes, Captain."

Chapter 28

As we moved forward, Dega came into view off to our right, where it had moved during our temporal absence.

RJ commented, "The Guardians left the serpentoids one hell of a defense system. They imprison you and you never know it."

"Yes, and if the victims are really being looped back in time, they would never age no matter how long they were trapped."

We watched Dega move to the center of the main viewer. Green and blue now steadied below us as our geosynchronous orbit held us in place. There were rivers, and deserts, and massive forests. It was very much like Earth except it didn't feel like Earth.

We called Jameson to the Bridge. RJ and I headed to our quarters to put on our party clothes. We met in the corridor and began the long walk to the shuttle bay. The carpet was gold, but it felt like we were walking the green mile.

I said, "I sure would like to be wearing a weapon for this."

"Thought about that. Emissaries said we could, but they did not recommend it. Besides, there will probably be so many snakes there we could never stun them all, even with wide beam."

"Well, that's both informative and disturbing."

The shuttle bay was busy with numerous service personnel. We used the aft ramp to gain access. The two large transfer containers were already loaded so that we had to maneuver around them. I was surprised at how crowded the shuttle was. Along either side, Kurh and Marks, our two emissaries in blessed humanoid form, Security Chief Carter and three of his crew, all armed, Doctor Eisner and one assistant, and Lieutenant Paulson with Goldie around his neck. They had left us the two most forward seats near the flight deck. The two pilots glanced back at us as we sat.

We watched the ramp come up and close us in, then waited for the hangar to decompress. The bay doors opened, though we could not see until the shuttle lifted and rotated. The air in shuttles always smells a little oily once the cabin is pressurized. Through the pilots' viewers, we watched the shuttle slide forward and out of the bay. They nosed us right down and banked to the right. The down view of Dega began speeding past until we pulled up into our parking orbit and became fixed over one specific spot on Dega. Then it was down and down and down, where the world slowly became bigger than the sky.

We all glanced at each other in silence, all with expressions of concerned wonder. When we finally felt the shuttle bump down onto the ground, it made some people jump slightly—not that they were concerned about the shuttle crashing, more that they wondered what was outside.

After a long series of procedures by the pilots, the back hatch ramp came moaning to life as it gushed open to planetary air, slowly lowering itself down to expose us. When the ramp finally thumped down onto the ground, the pilots did not bother to welcome us to Dega. They said nothing at all, just kept with their checklists.

The two emissaries stood and headed for the ramp. Kurh and Marks followed them. As Captain and Commander, RJ and I were not allowed to show fear of disembarkment. We stood and headed for the ramp, followed by Paulson and Goldie, both seemingly unaffected by the whole affair.

Security Chief Carter called out to me, "Captain, we will remain aboard to guard the shipment. We'll monitor you from here."

I nodded approval.

A few steps down the ramp, I looked up. Instantly, it reminded me of Dorothy opening the black-and-white door of her crashed house to peer out at colorful Oz. It was almost like stepping into a cartoon.

We were parked in the middle of a grass-covered clearing. In every direction there was a colorful miniature city, with full-size trees and vegetation scattered within. Most buildings were no higher than six feet, with many shorter than that. They were all multicolored in red, green, and blue. Here and there, a few metal buildings with glass interrupted the flow of the topography. Far in the distance, forests marked the city line. Many birds populated the area.

There were snakes everywhere. I was shocked. I had expected dark-skinned, plain snakes. None of them were. They were the most beautiful snakes I had ever seen. Intricate colors and designs—rainbow swirls, stars, triangles, fractals, and every other geometric form imaginable. The colors were vibrant and intricate. Their flared necks made them even more beautiful.

Colorful snake heads were peering out of open windows. A constant flow of snake traffic filled the avenues between buildings. Groups had formed in many places to stare at the shuttle. Not far from us, a main pathway in the grass was filled with passing snake gawkers. Occasionally, a black bird would land near a group as if to say hello.

I looked around and noticed that the only one of us not mesmerized was Paulson. He was pointing out things and laughing out loud. He was completely enjoying himself. Doctor Eisner seemed reluctant but engrossed. Finally, our two emissaries headed off to the right, where odd-looking short stools had been set up for us. We all followed.

The center seats were left open for RJ and me. Marks was on my left, RJ on my right, and Kurh on his right. The emissaries were just beyond. We sat and continued to watch the spectacle of a land we could not have imagined.

A delegation of snakes arrived in front of us. Their leader was distinguished by a triple gold collar. His associates had similarly unique-looking collars. The leader approached the first of our two emissaries and moved in close. The emissary held out his right hand with his index finger extended. The snake closed the fingers of one of his tiny hands around it, bowed slightly, then went on to the next emissary to repeat the greeting. Next was Kurh, who did the same, then came RJ. RJ did not hesitate; he did the symbolic handshake as well. The snake approached me, and I had no choice. The tiny snake fingers felt very strange, almost sticky. The greeting ceremony continued until everyone had made physical contact with our host. There did not seem to be any ill effects.

A short time later, the two emissaries arose and went to meet the delegation. A few minutes of what seemed to be telepathic discussion took place. Abruptly, Marks and Kurh rose. Marks looked at me. "Captain, it's time to deliver the goods."

I nodded and clicked my watch. "Captain to Carter."

"Go ahead, Captain."

"It's time to unload the cargo."

"Understood. In process."

They brought the two large shipping containers down and set them in an area designated by the emissaries. Marks and Kurh broke the seals and unlocked them. Three new snakes with special neck bands that made me think of military insignia went to the cases as the emissaries opened them and left them open.

The lead snake leaned over an open container and drew something out in his tiny hand. It looked like a miniature pistol. He maneuvered away from the case and turned to face an open area beyond the shuttle. He spent a few minutes fiddling with the device, turning his head sideways for a better look with one eye. Finally, he raised the weapon, pointed it at an empty patch of grass, and fired. A blue beam flashed out, hit the ground, and made a small explosion. There was excited movement by the rest of the snakes.

Marks sat down next to me.

I asked, "We're supplying them with weapons?"

"We should talk about this later, Captain. Keep your thoughts positive. Sometimes negative thoughts can be picked up by telepaths."

I shut up. The cases were closed. The two emissaries carried them off somewhere, one at a time under the direction of the military snakes.

As we watched, a new delegation appeared and approached me. The lead snake was carrying a small plastic case about the size of a cigar box. It was gray, ribbed, and sealed. The leader came close, bowed slightly, and pushed forward so that I could take the box. With a final slight bow, they were gone.

"It's fragile, Captain. Keep it close. It must not be opened until we are back on Earth. It needs to be stored in the captain's wall safe until then."

"I understand."

"When the emissaries return, three of our hosts will be expecting a tour of the ship. They have asked that Mr. Poulson and Goldie conduct the tour."

"I will thank Mr. Poulson later."

"After the tour, you and Commander Smith will be expected to return for the closing ceremonies. It's important because it means that Dega has now formally established relations with Earth. The ceremony won't last long, and then we'll be free to depart."

When the time came, Doctor Eisner and one staff member were allowed to remain on Dega until we returned. We loaded up into the now spacious shuttle. Last to board were the three visitors. As we got situated and the shuttle powered up, the three brightly colored snakes lowered down and each maneuvered into a circular pattern flat on the floor. Marks leaned over to me. "They've done this before."

It was a quiet ride up, except for Poulson talking to Goldie.

Marks leaned over again and said, "Captain, Mr. Kurh and I are adapting to the serpentoids' telepathy. We are able to exchange short sentences now. This expansion of our telepathic ability will be a great asset to Earth."

I shook my head in agreement and clicked my watch. "Captain to Jameson."

"Go ahead, Captain."

"Ship status?"

"Nothing to report. All systems nominal."

"We will dock shortly. Has the crew been prepared for the tour?"

"Yes, Captain. Medical has been thorough. There is apprehension, but we should not have any problems."

"Very good. See you on the Bridge, Mark. Tarn out."

The tour went smoothly enough. A number of crew hid out. Poulson seemed to enjoy it more than our guests. After depositing the precious, unexplained case in my wall safe, RJ and I waited in our stiff dress uniforms on the Bridge. When our visitors were adequately ingratiated with Acura scenery, we were called back to the hangar bay for the trip back down. Aboard the shuttle, our visitors appeared tired. I believe one or two of them slept in their curled-up position on the deck.

When the shuttle hatch lowered, it looked like a party was going on all around us. The snakes were clearly happy. We took our positions in the same seating area and watched the snake celebration continue. Marks said, "There is telepathic music being played. I can hear it now."

We were greeted by quite a few dignitaries who just wanted to be able to brag that they had met us. I almost got used to the tiny squeeze of those little hands on my index finger, but having the head of a large snake that close was never easy. I hoped I would not dream about it.

As the ceremony began to dwindle, one of the emissaries came up to us, said something to Marks, then left. Marks leaned over again. "Some surprises, Captain, that you may not care for. The snakes are bringing you a thank-you gift. We don't know what it is, but you must accept it with pleasure no matter what it is, or they may be greatly offended."

"No problem, Rell. What else?"

"This news is a bit concerning. Our emissaries will not be returning with us as planned. They have been contracted for another job and will be picked up by another ship."

That one caught me off guard. I looked at RJ. "Suddenly, the emissaries will not be returning with us."

RJ rubbed his eyes and pinched the bridge of his nose in thought. "Why does that immediately greatly worry me?"

"Well, we're in agreement then."

As I pondered our unescorted trip back to Earth, a new procession of snakes approached us, pushing a fragile cart with something hidden by a loose gold silk covering. It took two of them to push it, and they had to keep changing off with others as they tired. My impression was that these were females.

"It's your gift, Captain," said Marks.

They stopped a few feet in front of me and performed some silent custom of telepathic words and movements. Finally, the silk covering was pulled away to reveal a golden wired cage with a large black bird in it.

Mark looked at me and said nervously, "It's a raven, Captain."

I thought to myself, "At least it's in a cage."

One of the snake attendants maneuvered into place and opened the cage door.

The raven took one look at me, took off, and landed on my left shoulder. It repeated the name, "Adrian, Adrian, Adrian," and seemed content to rest there.

I looked at Marks in desperation and could tell he was communicating with our hosts.

Finally, he looked at me sympathetically. "This raven has been trained by them to answer to you and only you. They had your photo and name, so the raven was trained using those. They say this raven will quickly learn many English words and phrases and will understand them. Not many visitors have been privileged to be gifted a Dega raven, the most intelligent raven anywhere. They hope you enjoy your gift."

I nodded profusely and tried to smile. I held out my index finger and did the snake shake. The gifters backed away.

RJ looked over, stifling a laugh. "You are truly a pirate now. Bernard Porre will never let you live this down."

Marks said, "It's time to go, Captain."

"Yes, Rell, yes, it surely is."

I had no idea what to do with my new bird. I stood. The raven remained unconcerned. I walked toward the shuttle. The raven matched my body movements, completely content to be going somewhere. We all took our seats. The shuttle lifted off.

Dr. Eisner was sitting opposite me. "My God, Captain. That is the most beautiful raven I have ever seen. Do you see how reflective the black feathers are? And the small feathers at the front of the neck are usually ruffled, but on yours they are perfectly smooth."

"That's all fine and well, Doctor, but what do I do with it?"

"Well, first you need to determine the gender so you can stop calling your raven 'it.' Then you need to find an appropriate spot to create an aviary. That will be his home base."

"I take it you can help with that?"

"I would be glad to."

"Thank you, Doctor."

Chapter 29

When we settled into the hanger bay and the chamber had repressurized, it was time to get off. I looked at Eisner and asked, "What do I do about this?"

Eisner giggled, a very unusual reaction for her. "You are his keeper. You can't just drop him off in a strange place and leave. Where do you need to be next?"

"Captain's conference room meeting."

"You must allow him to accompany you. As soon as you're done there, I'll meet you in your quarters, and we'll figure out an aviary. You'll be able to leave him there as needed."

"So I have no choice but to walk around with a raven on my shoulder in front of the crew?"

RJ cut off a laugh that had escaped.

"That is the best way," replied Eisner.

I scowled. "Jalin, meeting in Captain's conference room, immediately."

"I'll be there."

I looked at RJ. He'd managed to put away his smirk.

"I'll be there."

"Rell and Tori, would you please join us there?"

"Yes, Captain."

"Yes, Captain."

I clicked my watch. "Mr. Williams, Mr. Porter, and Mr. Marquis, please report to the Captain's conference room immediately."

They all acknowledged.

We waited to be last to disembark. I'd hoped the hanger crew had dispersed. They had not. I came down the ramp with a big black bird on my shoulder, and every single person doing something stopped. Dead silence as I walked across the hanger. Finally, some joker yelled out, "Oh Captain, you have a bird on your shoulder."

Several others let out muffled laughter. To my surprise, the raven looked over in their direction and gave out a loud chaw that somehow sounded angry. I turned my head toward him and whispered, "Thank you." Again, to my surprise, the raven answered, "Adrian."

In the conference room, the jokes were mercifully withheld. As we waited for everyone to show up, Eisner came in and reached out to hand me something. I opened my hand, and she dumped a bunch of food pellets in it.

"Fruit dog food pellets, Captain. One of a raven's favorites. Try one."

I looked down at the pellets, decided there was no choice, and held one out for the raven. He gobbled it up without a moment's hesitation.

Eisner waved me on. "Well? Go ahead. More."

I handed the bird several more with everyone watching. Eisner began to leave.

"Doctor, why don't you stay and sit in on this meeting? It's of interest to everyone."

The doctor looked surprised but took the nearest empty seat.

When everyone was present, I looked over at RJ. "You want to start this off? I'm exhausted, and I need to feed my bird."

RJ choked back a laugh. "Okay, everyone. We're having this meeting because we are not comfortable with the emissaries suddenly deciding not to return to Alpha Draconis with us. It may simply be a benefit in that we do not need to stop at Alpha Draconis at all. We can head straight for Earth. Mr. Marks or Mr. Kurh, what is our status with Dega regarding our departure?"

Marks answered, "We are cleared to depart at our convenience. We can take any departure heading we wish; a corridor in the temporal field will open for us automatically."

"Mr. Carter, any thoughts on our departure?"

"Like you, I do not like the sudden cancellation. I do not like surprises. When you think about our threats from DSAI and from people who want Astra back, you have to wonder if the emissary cancellation is somehow related to those. I suggest we do not depart Dega and take our precalculated flight plan back. I believe we should depart Dega and head away from Earth. We travel out a light year, then come around and plot a new flight plan that allows us to travel parallel to our originally planned course. We fly a distance that will allow us to continually monitor our original course using long-range scans to see if anyone unexpected is out there lying in wait for us."

RJ looked at me.

I nodded. "I like it. That would also allow us to keep an eye out for the Achilles. Captain Washburn may be out there waiting to escort us." My raven pecked lovingly on my neck.

RJ asked, "Can anyone think of a problem with that plan?"

Williams said, "It will delay our arrival on Earth a little bit, but we're already ahead of schedule if we don't have to stop at Alpha Draconis."

RJ responded, "Anyone else?"

Porter added, "I suggest we get the heck away from Dega before they change their mind."

I said, "Okay, that's our plan then. If anyone has any other ideas, please contact me or Commander Smith directly. Meeting adjourned to the Bridge."

We took our places on the Bridge. Only a few uniformed crew stared at the creature on my shoulder. Thankfully, no one made any remarks. It took navigation a few minutes to create a new flight plan. When he was ready, we used thrusters to move through the area of temporal shields. As best we could tell, we had to assume we were not locked in a time loop. The Dega snakes had been very serious about establishing relations with Earth. I doubted they would send one of their prized ravens to an assault of some kind on our ship.

Mr. Porter called out, "Ready to jump, Captain."

"Please proceed, Mr. Porter."

Our view screen warped a bit with the jump. We slid into a star field alive around us. I had to wonder what it would be like jumping to warp over and over in a time trap. The idea overloaded my brain.

"Mr. Williams, any hits on long-range scanners?"

"Nothing, Captain."

We cruised without incident to our turnaround point, stopped, came about, and locked into our new flight plan. A second jump brought us on course toward Earth. Two hours later, no sign of enemies along our path.

"Doctor Eisner to the Captain."

"Yes, Doctor?"

"Yeoman Breize and I are outside your quarters. Would you have a few minutes to join us?"

"I'll be right there, Doctor." I gave RJ a curious look. "You have the Bridge."

"I have the Bridge. I do not envy you."

In the corridor, I spotted Breize and Eisner waiting outside my door. The raven seemed excited for some reason. Breize was holding a three-foot-wide half-moon contraption. I joined them and commanded the door to open. We went in.

Eisner said, "Captain, did you know one of your windows overlooking the arboretum opens?"

"I never looked that closely, Doctor."

"We've made this platform for your raven. See the perches all around it, the small walled-off compartments for food, and the larger two tub shapes for water?"

"It looks amazing, Doctor."

Breize said, "Watch this, Captain."

The three of us went to the arboretum window, where Breize opened the rightmost window wide and maneuvered the platform into the arboretum area, where she attached it to the window ledge. Eisner began filling the compartments with raven food, while Breize added water to the tubs.

Before they could finish, the raven jumped from my shoulder out the window and onto the platform. Immediately, water was the main interest.

"Damn, I didn't have a chance to put out water."

"Problem solved, Captain. I'll be sure the waterers are filled when I check your quarters every day," said Breize.

"By the way," added Eisner, "congratulations, it's a boy. I used the ship's imaging to make physical comparisons. No doubt, he's a he."

The raven hopped around on the platform and began eating selected items.

"I feel like getting down on one knee to thank you two."

Eisner said, "Just wait, Captain. I suspect the best is yet to come."

We watched as the raven tired of eating. He hopped around on his platform and began studying the arboretum. To my surprise, he leapt from the platform and dove down into the trees, eventually landing on a branch out of sight.

Breize and Eisner clapped and laughed.

Eisner asked, "What have you named him, Captain?"

"I was thinking just Raven. Does that sound alright?"

She nodded. "Yes, that is commonly done. It allows strangers to address him by his correct name."

"Once again, I am deeply in debt to you two. Thank you from both of us."

"Just leave this window open all the time so he knows he's not locked out from your space, and you should be able to come and go with or without Raven."

"Doctor..."

"I think it's about time you started calling me Makayla, Captain."

"Well, thank you, I will."

Eisner and Breize headed for the door, celebrating their success. They waved and left. I searched the arboretum but could not spot Raven. Feeling strangely alone, I returned to the Bridge.

"You've lost your bird," said RJ.

"Arboretum."

"That's cool."

"God, it is."

I sat back and enjoyed the view of open space in a warp bubble. The crew began to relax. The ship's very faint hum was reassuring. We finished our shift with no technical problems and no enemies lying in wait. One by one, the crew exchanged places with second shift.

RJ asked, "Mess Hall?"

"I wasn't kidding about being exhausted. I'm heading for the horizontal."

"May your sleep be undisturbed."

We ran for several more days with no issues and no sign of any other ships. I had just come in, coffee in hand, to relieve my shift-three counterpart when a security call came in.

"Carter to the Captain."

"Go ahead, Jalin."

"Could you come to the port arboretum? The raven has found something."

"Raven found something in the arboretum?"

"Yes, Captain. He was digging in the dirt and found something buried."

RJ looked at me. "Now I have heard everything."

"You have the Bridge."

"I have the Bridge."

When I entered the arboretum, Raven was sitting on top of Carter's hat. Carter had a big smile and was struggling not to laugh. Unable to speak, he pointed down at a flower bed. I looked. A fancy metal box the size of a shoebox had been partially uncovered in the dirt.

Raven flew onto my shoulder and said, "Adrian."

"Let me guess, Jalin, we have no idea what this is?"

"That would be correct, Captain. It has both NSAX and alien markings on it."

"I bet it needs a key to open it."

"Right again, Captain. And we just happen to have an unexplained key."

"Well, we don't dare move the thing."

"I agree. We'll need to bring in a portable scanner to see what's inside, and even that is dangerous."

Raven began rubbing his head against my cheek.

Carter smirked.

"Obviously, we can't just leave it here. Call for the scanner, Jalin."

"Already have, Captain."

They set up the scanner system, and we all gathered outside the arboretum for the scanning. The tech ran several types of scans using his remote control and finally looked up at us, puzzled.

"Come on, what do you have, Mr. Edwards?"

"I've got nothing, Chief. Nothing mechanical, nothing electrical, and the atmosphere appears normal. There is nothing in this box."

So we gathered the thing up and took it to Security for opening. The mystery key was brought out. Carter inserted it in the box lock and slowly turned it. The lock clicked open, and the lid popped up slightly. Cautiously, Carter raised it.

The only thing visible inside was a piece of fabric. Exasperated, I could stand waiting no longer. I reached in, grabbed the fabric, and pulled it out. As it came out, it unfolded into a strange bodysuit. The suit was off-white with small black squares all over it. It had a full hood with a face covering but no eye, nose, or mouth holes. There was a split in the front of it from the neck down to the waist. I spread it open to reveal a totally black interior, so black that you could not focus on it. It looked like total darkness inside the suit.

Carter took it from me and inserted one arm into one of the suit's sleeves. It fit well but did nothing other than cover his arm. "As near as I can tell, this is just a piece of apparel. It must be some official alien uniform for something." He moved it around and inspected it further but found nothing. "We'll run some additional tests on it, Captain, and let you know."

I thanked him and headed back to the Bridge.

"It has to be some extremely valuable alien uniform that somebody was hoping to cash in on," said RJ after I updated him.

"Best answer I can think of."

Chapter 30

We finished our shift debating more about what had been found, then headed for the Commissary for dinner. We stopped by my place to pick up Raven just for the fun of it. I wondered how he would do in the turbolift this time. He was very attentive as I asked the turbolift for, "Deck four, please."

In the Mess Hall, Raven turned the place into an instant party. People were laughing and holding up bits of food. When Raven spotted something interesting, he would fly over and take it from them, resulting in cheers from onlookers.

About the time we were finishing up our meals, my watch bleeped.

"Carter to Captain."

"Go ahead, Jalin."

"Could you stop by Security this evening sometime? I'd like to test a theory."

"Anything new on the suit?"

"There is some form of circuitry in it, but nothing we're familiar with. I'll explain more when you get here."

"Be there shortly."

As we rose to leave, Raven was across the room flirting with an attractive Lieutenant. He spotted us and caught up to my shoulder. Everyone laughed in delight.

RJ said, "I think I see why old sailing ships often had mascots."

Carter was in the laboratory section of Security. He had the suit spread out on a metal exam table. He looked up as we entered.

"So, news, Jalin?"

"We tried to analyze the material. We ran the suit under an infrared light, and we could see fibers finer than human hairs running all through the thing. And the material itself seems to be submolecular pieces bonded together. So, we do not think it's just a suit."

"But it does nothing."

"Maybe not. Watch this." Carter switched on the infrared lamp beneath the suit, summoned us over closer, and said, "Watch closely." He pressed one finger against the suit, and a barely visible dim light circled his finger. He looked up at us. "Every inch of this suit responds like that. In other words, every inch of this suit does something; we just don't know what."

"So, dead end?"

"I tried putting the suit completely on and closing it up. Nada. But then an idea struck me. Every inch of this suit appears intelligent in some way. Now, when we first opened the box, who was the first person to touch the suit?"

"I confess, that was me."

"Right. So humor me, put one arm into this sleeve." He held up the one sleeve of the suit for me to try on. I shrugged, took position, and slid my arm into it.

My arm, and the suit sleeve, vanished.

The three of us stood there in silence for a moment. Finally, Carter slapped the counter and said, "I knew it. I knew it. It had to be! Adrian, you were the first to touch the suit. That was the same as logging on, in a manner of speaking. Now you are the user, the only user. That's why it doesn't work for the rest of us. Come on, you've got to try this thing on so we can see what it does."

"Are we sure it's safe?"

"We know what it's supposed to do, and it appears to be doing it."

I looked at RJ. "You agree?"

"Well, quite a few people would love to see you disappear."

I ignored his joke and, for dignity's sake, looked around. It was only the three of us. I unzipped my flight suit and pulled it off. As

I slid one leg into the strange apparel, my leg and the suit vanished. Carter let out a, "Wow!"

With both legs gone, I pulled the torso up and closed the split. I was now a floating head only. With a last exchange of looks, I pulled the hood up and over and down on my face.

Carter declared, "Captain, you and the suit have vanished completely. Can you hear my voice?"

"I hear you just fine, Jalin. It's a very comfortable fit. I can see everything around me, but not my own hand and arm."

There was a tablet on the table near me. I went to it and picked it up. It became a tablet floating in the air. I discarded the tablet and pulled the face cover back. "Did you hear what I said?"

"We did not hear a thing from you," said RJ. "Try it again."

I pulled the face cover down and spoke in a loud voice, "Okay, can you hear this?"

The two of them stared blankly. Carter said, "We are not hearing a thing, Captain."

I pulled the face cover back again. "Okay, I guess nothing gets out of this suit. No visual, no audio."

RJ said, "Geez, if you were ever seriously injured in that thing, you would not be able to call for help, and no one would know you were there."

I gently pulled the suit off and put my coveralls back on.

Carter said, "It may mean that even telepaths can't read you when you're wearing it. I'll do some more nondestructive testing and keep it in its box stored in the Security vault."

"Gentlemen, I believe we should keep this information to ourselves. Consider it classified. And, Jalin, be careful. That thing is definitely alien technology."

The following morning, we met in the Captain's conference room with the team heads for the weekly tie-in. The meeting could not have been less eventful. Helm had nothing new to offer.

Communications had to realign one channel. Navigation was seeing clear sky to the edge of the scanning range. Weapons Officer Dell said all was well. Chief Medical Officer Jean Cooper had two cases of stomach irritation from a hot sauce contest. But when we got to Chief of Security Carter, he had a sour look on his face. He had that expression that tells you he didn't want to report.

I had to insist, "Okay, out with it, Jalin."

"It was a difference of opinion that ended up as a fistfight, an all-out brawl between two of the crew in Waste Management."

"About what?"

"Somebody was in somebody else's locker."

"I know you don't want to say, but who?"

"Waste Processing techs Hans Jaka and Timothy Pool."

"Did Medical need to get involved?"

Doctor Cooper answered, "One cut over the eye, some bruising, a split lip."

"What have you done with them, Jalin?"

"Oh, they're in lockup, for sure."

"So you're going to write this up for me, right?"

"Of course. Not my favorite thing."

"Anyone else have anything? No? Okay. See most of you on the Bridge."

On the Bridge, I got the fight report a few hours later. I read through it, and on the surface it sounded like a standard hothead dispute. But for some reason, I had a bad feeling about it—something I couldn't put my finger on. I handed the tablet over to RJ. "Check this out."

After a few minutes, RJ handed the tablet back. "It's annoying."

"Because?"

"Annoying that this Pool person attacked someone for going through his locker, except if he hadn't, it probably would not have been brought to our attention."

"So you agree there's something wrong with the whole thing."

"Absolutely. The report says that the Jaka guy said he was in the locker to borrow Pool's deck of cards. Pool says he doesn't own a deck of cards. The disconnect is annoying. Security searched the locker. The only thing he might have wanted to steal was one adult magazine."

"It's just a simple case of two hotheads, but we both have ridiculously suspicious minds. Maybe we're making something out of nothing."

"Or maybe Mr. Pool had something in his locker that he wanted to keep hidden. And maybe Jaka found out about it. There are a number of possibilities."

"Still, could be making a mountain out of a molehill."

"Or Pool and Jaka already had some issue with each other, and Jaka was trying to find something to hold over him."

"This is what happens when we sit too long on a smooth-running Bridge."

"What are you going to do about this?"

I drummed my fingers together. "I was thinking you are by far the best judge of character, whereas I have a solid history of bad such judgments. You feel like talking to these two?"

"I will take it under advisement."

RJ was late showing up for his shift the next day. Yeoman Breize left his coffee in his cup holder. He showed up and sat sipping and staring off into the distance. He looked at me and said, "This is great coffee," and took a few more sips.

I asked, "So what did you take away from your waste disposal visit?"

He sipped some more. "They are both hiding something in their past."

"Any idea what?"

"With Pool it probably has to do with ill-gotten money. With Jaka it's more than that, but I don't know what."

"Would you quietly discuss this with Security and have them keep an eye on things?"

"Already have."

The next several days were smooth sailing. We were almost at the point we could begin thinking about Earth. That sentiment was suddenly interrupted when Navigation called out, "Captain, something on long range."

I went to Mr. Williams' station, sipped my coffee, and stared down at the screen. It was still a tiny unidentifiable blip, but it was indeed something. I called out to Zelest, "Zay, anything on the com?"

"Nothing but some noise, Captain."

RJ came up beside me. "No ID yet?"

"Nope."

"It does happen to be along our previous flight path."

"Yep."

Zelest called out, "Captain, someone is trying to send something, but we're still too far out."

"Stay on it, Zay."

Williams looked up at me from the navigation console. "Captain, I'm getting a transponder code. It's for the Achilles."

"The target is dead in space, Keaton?"

"Yes, sir, and it is drifting slightly."

"Hem, stand by to drop out of warp."

"Standing by, Captain."

"Zay, give me shipwide."

"You have it, sir."

"All hands stand by to drop out of warp. Mr. Porter, take us out of warp and initiate station keeping."

"Out of warp to SK, Captain."

Zelest called out, "Captain, we are getting something now. It's not audio. It's a packet file, highly encrypted."

"Transfer it to my quarters, Zay."

"Yes, Captain."

Before I could call Jameson to the Bridge, he walked in.

"You have the Bridge, Mark."

"I have the Bridge, sir."

I waved RJ to join me. We headed for my quarters.

In my conference room, we called up the file on the table computer. It was titled ATO. I clicked for it to open. It asked for my security level and ID. The decryption took a good five minutes. For a moment, we thought it had locked up the computer. Finally, a document emerged.

To any Earth vessel: The Achilles has been taken over by a group of Quantaloids. They prevented us from generating a warp field, then docked with us using advanced technology. We were not able to prevent them from accessing the starboard airlock. They are highly telepathic and are able to control our movements mentally. They came from a ship that was already highly damaged. It was able to leave to get repairs. We managed to sabotage our warp drive systems and our navigation computers. We are now told that a tow ship will be coming to take us away. We have also been told we will be placed in stasis for the trip. When they first came onboard, they executed six of my crew to show they were serious. When they discovered we had sabotaged our warp drives, they killed six more as punishment. I do not believe they are capable of detecting any approaching ships, but be warned: stay away from the Achilles. These Quantaloids believe a prisoner of theirs has been stolen, a princess by birth who would have become queen of some unidentified planet that is important to them. They planned to use this prisoner as leverage. Any ship that encounters us should stay well clear. They will consider any ship in this area to possibly have their stolen prisoner. Please contact Earth Space Control in the Terran system if possible. –Captain Stephen Washburn epsilon 8 5 9 4 omega 4 7 zero zero zero delta 2 2 2 5 w z Juliet/

Chapter 31

I sat back and rubbed my eyes. "Oh man..."

RJ winced and shook his head.

I looked at him. "We can't leave them."

RJ grimaced.

"Captain to Carter."

"Security here, Captain."

"Would you come to my conference room immediately, please?"

"On my way."

RJ said, "I don't think I see a plan for this."

"The plan is, we don't leave them."

"Did he really post his command codes at the end of this message?"

"Looks like it to me. He must have hoped we would be the ones to pick it up."

"If the quantaloids really are scanner blind, that would be a big advantage."

"They murdered twelve of the crew; chances are they will eventually kill the rest."

"If they really are blind, we could get a shuttle up to a docking port without being seen."

My door tone sounded. "Unlock door."

A moment later, Carter walked in with a curious look on his face.

"Take a seat, Jalin. Read this."

I turned the computer to face him. As he read, his expression became angry, then determined.

"We're not going to leave them, right?" he asked.

One look at us, and he did not need an answer.

"We need Mr. Marks and Mr. Kurh in on this."

I nodded. "I should have thought of that already." I clicked my watch. "Mr. Marks and Mr. Kurh, please report to the Captain's conference room immediately."

Carter asked, "Are those really his command codes at the end of the message?"

RJ replied, "Kind of makes sense, don't you think?"

Carter said, "We'll have a lot of power for a short time if those are still good. We can cancel the airlock indicators on the Bridge and Engineering and then command the airlock doors to open without being detected."

Carter looked at me for approval. I reluctantly agreed. "Yes, that's good, that's good."

Carter continued, "We can do the same for the inner door. We can gain access to the ship without them knowing."

RJ took a deep breath. "There are a lot of ifs in there, Jalin."

I heard the doors to my quarters swish open. Kurh and Marks entered. I motioned them to sit, then pushed the computer over to them.

"Please read, gentlemen."

When they had, they looked up at me with strained expressions.

"We are not going to leave them, are we?" asked Marks.

"We have quite a few close friends on that ship," added Kurh.

"Gentlemen, if we were able to send an assault team over there, would they be taken over by these telepaths?"

There was a long pause before either answered. Finally, Marks said, "As long as they don't know you're there, you would be reasonably safe. They wouldn't be looking for anyone. Once they became aware of the team, they would be mentally searching for them. It would only be a question of time before they began to locate team members. If they were able to incapacitate the entire Achillies crew, then it is likely they would do the same with the assault team, one member at a time."

RJ asked, "How long might we have before they discovered the assault team's presence?"

Kurh answered, "Impossible to say. Even if a team member was hiding, if a telepath passed by too closely, he might sense a foreign species nearby."

Carter added, "So it just means the assault team would have to take them out before being discovered."

RJ suggested, "But if they failed, it would mean the quantaloids would know if an assault team showed up there must be a ship somewhere nearby. They would be on to us."

Carter said, "But we have the Achillies command codes. We could interfere with anything they tried to do."

RJ replied, "Getting really complicated now, Jalin."

There was a long, heavy silence.

Carter sat back in his chair and exhaled in exasperation. He looked at RJ and me. "There is another option I dislike intensely."

"There's no way we can abandon everyone on that ship," insisted Marks.

Another long period of silence.

I sat up. "Tell them, Jalin. They are now officially cleared."

"One man could take all the quantaloids out."

"Instead of a team? Are you kidding?" said Kurh.

RJ looked at me, shaking his head, although I could tell he was not in disagreement. Nor was I.

"Jalin, go get the suit."

Carter sprang from his seat and hurried out.

Marks and Kurh sat, looking confused.

We sat in silence, awaiting Carter's return. When he finally showed, he gently put the fancy box down on the table in front of me. Marks immediately began to get a strange look on his face.

I opened the box, pulled out a tuft of suit, and said, "What we need to know is..."

Marks slapped his hand on the table and stood. "That's it! That's the item somebody took from the reverse engineering lab at the NSAX facility. We searched that entire place trying to locate it or the guy who took it. How could you possibly have gotten your hands on it?" Marks sounded indignant.

We all sat in silence once more, like school kids getting busted.

Carter quipped, "A little bird told us where it was."

Marks was angry. "What!?"

RJ offered consolation. "Rell, for now it's enough to say we have the item and the body of the man who took it. It's complicated. I'll explain later."

After another moment of silence, I asked, "What we need to know is, can a telepath detect me in this suit?"

Kurh answered, "Not a chance. Nothing comes out of that suit, not gamma, beta, alpha, or anything else. You can yell at the top of your lungs in that suit, and no one will hear a thing."

Marks, having calmed down, said, "It will also keep your body temperature at exactly the same level it was when you put it on."

Kurh asked, "Captain, why you? Shouldn't Chief Carter be the one to carry out this mission?"

Another long silence.

Kurh responded, "Oh... I see. Captain, you were the first to touch the material. You established a link with the suit. Well, that's that. There's no resetting it until we're back at NSAX headquarters."

Marks asked, "Captain, even if the suit works, how will you overcome five quantaloids by yourself?"

I sat back. "I will kill them all."

Solemn silence.

Marks was taken aback. "How will you do that?"

"One at a time."

Carter, being the hardened soldier he was, had to cut off a laugh before it began.

I added, "If I'm visualizing this correctly, I see Jalin flying the shuttle through a precision blind approach, dropping me off, and departing the same way."

Carter said, "Captain, there is one other crew member who is immune to telepathy and who could back you up on this mission."

RJ shook his head in agreement. "The Optimus X."

Carter nodded. "Yes, if we fit you with a receiver and earpiece, Optimus X could communicate its observations to you."

I asked, "Can the Optimus be programmed to destroy quantaloids on sight?"

Carter replied, "Yes, it can, though I'm not sure that would be the wisest way to use it."

"What would you suggest?"

"Let the Optimus X appear to be a standard working android. He'd have access to just about everywhere on the ship and could advise where the quantaloids are located and their numbers. You would then probably be able to dispatch them with less chance of them realizing something was wrong."

RJ said, "That's another thing. Because we have the ship's command codes, at a predetermined time we could create a distraction, like a coolant leak or something that would help distract them from realizing any of their associates were missing."

I said, "Gentlemen, I believe we have a good plan of action. The last thing to keep in mind is that, according to the transmission, there is a tow ship coming to take the Achillies away. We need to do this before they get here. And, Commander Smith, you will need to keep all weapons online and combat maneuvers ready."

"Of course."

"Jalin, can you get the Optimus X programming underway and ask the tech guys to bring me a receiver and ear pods? Also, I want two chest holsters, one on the left and one on the right, to fit inside the suit, with two weapons set to kill. Let's try to launch this thing in thirty minutes, if possible."

Carter stood and rushed out.

Kurh and Marks followed.

RJ and I sat in silence for a moment.

I suggested, "If this all goes bad, at some point you may have to decide to cut and run."

"I know."

"We're also going to need some delicate timing on this. There can't be any transmissions between the shuttle and the Acura."

RJ replied, "Right. It's just fortunate that we were already on silent running."

"Yeah, so it will be up to you guys to use the command codes to check the Achillies airlock ready room to be sure it's empty before you open the outer door for me. You'll need to hack into the Achillies airlock cameras to see when we're about to dock so that you know when to open up that airlock outer door. I won't be wearing a spacesuit, so once we've docked, the airlock pressure has to be matched to the shuttle's interior pressure before those doors can be opened."

"I don't see a problem with our tech guys using the command codes to hack into that stuff and balance pressures."

I nodded. "I agree. I trust those guys. Once I'm in the airlock, I'll close the outer door myself. Then the shuttle is free to leave the way it came. From that point on, I can check the airlock observation windows to be sure no one is around before Optimus X and I leave the airlock."

"If you get that far, we should be in good shape, at least for that moment."

"Well, I've got to make a stop in my quarters and switch into an undergarment and some stretch shoes I have. We'll coordinate from the hangar bay before we head out."

"There's not much left to say, is there?"

"We can wish each other luck. That's about it."

"Good luck."

"You too."

I tucked the suit box under my arm. In my quarters, I changed into black tights and a thin black turtleneck, then pulled on the stretch shoes. I stopped to drink as much water as I dared, and headed for the hangar. There were quite a few people in the hangar when I arrived. Tech people were standing with Optimus X, typing keys on a tablet. As soon as Carter saw me, he came over with two of his people and held up holsters with straps. He wrapped them around me so that one holster was on my left and the other on the right, just as I had asked. They were just below breast height. Perfect. He checked the two weapons he had with him, tucked them into the holsters, and snapped them in place—available for a quick draw.

The shuttle was already humming with power.

"They've set up a remote console on the Bridge to tie in to the Achillies systems. That way Commander Smith will be on top of everything that happens," said Carter. "Unless you have something else, we're ready."

We went to the shuttle and climbed up the aft ramp, followed by Optimus X. The bay was well lit in a golden-tinted light. Carter went to the pilot's seat. Optimus X and I stayed in back and took seats on either side, facing each other. Optimus X placed his toolkit on the floor next to him.

As Carter began his checklist, I asked X, "Have you been thoroughly briefed on this mission, X?"

"Yes, Captain."

"Do you understand why we are undertaking this mission?"

"Yes, Captain."

"What reason were you given for this mission?"

"Adversaries have taken control of the spacecraft Achillies and have done great harm there."

"Do you understand I will be wearing a special suit that will make me invisible to you and everyone else?"

"Yes, Captain."

"Do you understand you will be able to communicate with me, but I will not be able to reply to you or communicate with you in any way?"

"Yes, Captain."

"Do you understand your role during this mission is to disguise yourself as a working maintenance robot?"

"Yes, Captain."

"Do you understand that, if it becomes necessary, you will need to destroy any quantaloids you meet onboard the Achillies?"

"Yes, Captain."

"I'm glad to have you with me, X. Thank you."

"You are welcome, Captain."

I added, "I hope we can save the crew of the Achillies."

Chapter 32

Drive sounds picked up inside the cabin. We lifted off slightly and turned in place. The bay doors cracked open and spread apart. Stars appeared out the forward viewers. On the instrument panel, I could see the green-lined map Carter was so carefully following.

It was time to disappear. From the box beside me, I drew out the suit, opened the front seam, and pulled into the legs. The suit came up over my torso easily enough, and I pulled in my arms and the rest over my head, but left my face exposed. After a quick adjustment of my guns, I closed up the seam. I was now a face hanging in midair.

"Coming up underneath the Achillies," said Carter. "If that outer door doesn't open for us, we're done here."

Carter's dock with the Achillies had to be masterful. There could be no bumps or scraping. He had to press the outer seals against the Achillies with no impact at all. After a long few minutes, I felt the shuttle settle against the Achillies. We waited for the tech on Acura to verify the Achillies airlock was at the same pressure as the shuttle.

Finally, there was the faint sound of the Achillies door opening. I held my breath and opened our external door. There beyond was the empty Achillies airlock. No time to waste. Get in it. Optimus X and I hurried off ship, and once in the airlock, tapped the close button. I know Carter left immediately, but he did it with such skill I did not hear or feel a thing.

We were now secretly aboard the Achillies. Out the observation windows, there was no one. That meant they weren't expecting us. I opened the inner door, and as Optimus X and I exited, Optimus X said, "Captain, initiating phase one search program. A false coolant leak alarm is scheduled in twenty-seven minutes from now. I will periodically advise you of the countdown."

Without looking back, Optimus X headed down the corridor and turned right a short distance away where a four-way intersection was located.

I went to the intersection. It was certain there would be quantaloids on the Bridge and in Engineering. If the ones in Engineering could be taken out, there would be a good chance that at least one on the Bridge would leave to find out what was going on. Separating them seemed like a good idea. With that in mind, I headed for Engineering, deck two.

I turned the corner hoping to find the most inconspicuous way to deck two and stopped in shock. Ahead and behind me in the corridor were crew frozen in time. Two were leaning against the wall in midstride, two were on the floor still in a walking posture, one was face against the wall drooping down.

This was the quantaloid version of stasis.

The Achillies was a much older vehicle. Gray metal walls with conduit running along them. No carpet. Occasionally grated decking. Tubular lights overhead. The number on the wall told me I was on deck three. I needed to get to deck two. It occurred to me using a translift was ill advised. Optimus X would be using them, but even if I caught up to him somewhere, the space in the lift would be dangerous. If a quantaloid entered, it would be too small. I needed a Jeffries service tube. They were most commonly located near four-way intersections like this one. It made routing conduit in various directions easier. I had to force myself to look away from the injured crew. There was a service closet not far away. I went there, opened it, and found the lower round hatch that was used for Jeffries tube entry. Closed myself in the closet and, in the dim light, felt around and opened the hatch. Service lights switched on. I looked down into the darkness of the vertical hole and climbed in. One deck lower. Had to use one hand to open the next access hatch. But now I was on deck two. Inside the service closet, I listened for the sound of anyone, then cracked open the narrow door slightly.

More bodies on the floor or crumpled against walls. Had to suppress the anger. There was not a sound here except for the faint hum of ship equipment. Stepping among the unconscious crew, I came to an open door titled Engineering Resources. To my horror, it was stacked with the dead, at least a dozen or more. Many were wearing blue engineering flight coveralls. Most engineering guys never would take no for an answer.

The next intersection gave me what was needed. To my right, in the distance, I could see the entrance to Engineering. There was light and sound there. I had to keep reminding myself I was invisible. I moved along one wall to the entrance and leaned around to peer in. The central power stack was alive and glowing. Frozen crewmen sat at some consoles. A few others were on the floor. One green quantaloid was standing at an engine monitoring console, apparently trying to get something working. A second quantaloid was at the vertical master communication console, fiddling with it.

On the right side of the power column was something I did not recognize. It looked like a golden, crystal chandelier hanging up from the floor. It was a good six feet tall, made of golden rods and colored crystals with a golden base maybe a foot up from the floor. At the top of the thing, a chrome antenna slowly turned three hundred and sixty degrees. It took a moment, but I remembered seeing similar designs of quantum computers where ninety percent of the device was for cooling the main unit at the base. It suddenly dawned on me that this was the quantaloids' version of a stasis generator. If I could shut it down, everyone would wake up. But that would not be a good thing to do right now. Chaos would ensue. Quantaloids would resume their killing.

I could not waste time. A ship was coming. The two of them were too far apart to shoot one and then try for a long shot across the room to get the other.

Optimus X's voice switched in. "Captain, seventeen minutes until false coolant alarm sounds."

Across the chamber, I spotted a room that could be used: the fire control systems room. If I could get in there and set off a fire alarm, the two of them would have to come in to investigate. In a small space like that one, my chances of taking them both out would be fair.

I held my breath and stepped out onto the second-floor catwalk. Very quietly, I made my way down the metal steps to the deck-one floor. I was now out in the open. I moved through consoles toward the fire room, had to step over a crewman's body, passed between the two quantaloids, and reached the other side of Engineering without even a glance from them.

The fire control door was closed. It was a single push-to-open with a window. Both quantaloids were absorbed in their consoles. I leaned carefully back against the door and opened it an inch or two. Then a little more. After several nerve-racking pushes, there was enough space for me to slip through. I almost forgot and let the thing close, but at the last moment caught it and closed it as slowly as I had opened it. With great relief, I took a moment just to breathe.

It was a small room. No consoles, just control panels on the walls. Big red warning label on the door below the window. In front of the master panel, the alarm test button was plain to see. I pulled apart my suit front and drew out the left-side weapon.

Optimus X came on the com. "Captain, five minutes until false coolant leak alarm."

I did not want the coolant alarm just now. I wanted these two quantaloids to enter this fire control room. Without waiting, I pressed the test alarm button. The fire horn began blaring. I hurried to stand next to the door. I could see red light flashing outside above the door. I stood with my weapon raised at quantaloid head level, waiting for the first to come through.

It took only seconds. The door burst inward, and the mantis charged in, taking three insect steps before stopping to look around. My gun went "*zipbang*" and made a one-inch hole in the side of his head. He crumpled down into a pile of twisted insect arms and legs.

Hurry and reset. Get by the door. Raise the weapon. That was all the time I had. The second mantis took one step inside, saw his partner, and "*zipbang*," a one-inch hole in the side of his head. Down he went. Quickly, I dragged him the rest of the way in, moved them both so they couldn't be seen through the window in the door, tucked my weapon back in, and closed my suit front. I stepped outside the fire room and closed the door. I leaned against the wall next to the door to consider what the hell just happened.

Was there any bug brain on me? I checked arms, body, and legs. Looked clean.

Optimus X came on. "Captain, there is a fire alarm sounding. False coolant leak alarm in four minutes."

It snapped me awake. I hurried back into the fire room and canceled the test alarm, then back outside and against the wall again.

Suddenly a new, "whoop, whoop, whoop," alarm sounded. The Acura people were right on time.

Optimus X came on. "Captain, the coolant alarm has sounded. One of the quantaloids on the Bridge is leaving, probably to check on Engineering."

It straightened me up. I hurried across the chamber, climbed the metal stairs, and took a position on the left side of the door, my back against it, my weapon held against the wall to partially conceal it. There was nowhere else the mantis would be headed but here, to Engineering. I checked my gun. Still plenty of charge. I kept the gun high against the wall at mantis head level and waited. It was difficult to estimate where we stood in this battle. They were aware something was wrong. It was possible one of them was already searching cameras to see if they could spot something. My two deceased mantises were well out of sight. They would find nothing amiss, except perhaps their colleagues not visible in Engineering.

I thought I heard the lift stopping. I braced.

The mantis came through the door very quickly and stopped at the railing to survey Engineering. I stepped in behind him and, *zipbang*, to the back of the head. He fell to the left in just the right position that I could push him down the stairs with one foot.

I hurried back to my position beside the open door.

The game was getting more interesting. Now what? Three of five down. One on the Bridge, one missing. Nervously, I checked my weapon again. Still good charge. I waited several minutes. Waiting in these situations is never easy. I looked down and suddenly realized the last mantis had been armed and had dropped his weapon. I stepped out to hurriedly gather it in, turned, and there in front of me, ten yards away in the corridor, was mantis number four holding a weapon pointed at the floor. He saw the weapon I was holding.

We both drew. I won. My first shot hit him square in the chest. Green splatter went everywhere. I walked toward him, firing continuously as I went until he fell backward to the floor, dead.

I leaned against the wall in relief but jerked back up for fear there were more. There was nothing. Stone silence.

Optimus X cut in. "Captain, the quantaloid on the Bridge has become alarmed. He has shifted into humanoid form. He is removing the garment from a dead crew member. He is putting it on. He's taking a weapon from one of the security people. He's leaving the Bridge."

If I could have ordered Optimus X to kill the last mantis, I would have, but as it was, his programming would now prevent him from taking action without knowing the status of the other quantaloids.

So now we were almost equal. I was invisible except for my gun. The last mantis could imitate a crewman in stasis anywhere. He would be almost as invisible as me. I could no longer set him up. I would need to become the hunter. Predator against predator. One of us would have to screw up. He had time on his side.

I stowed my gun and pulled out the fresh one. Could I think like a quantaloid? He knew something was wrong with his friends. No human could do that. Any human would immediately be taken over mentally. It had to be some other telepathic species trying to take the ship for their own. But all that was necessary was to wait. Or maybe catch the new intruder off guard. Where would the best place be? Any intruder would want the Bridge. Play-act stasis near the entrance to the Bridge, then kill them when they showed up.

Was that what the quantaloid was thinking? It was my best guess. I restowed my gun for complete invisibility and headed for the turbolift. Climbing all those decks in a Jeffries tube did not make sense. I had to chance the turbolift. I stepped in, commanded "two," and kept alongside the doors in case wild, blind shooting broke out when they opened.

The doors opened on two. Nothing but silence. I dared to look out the open doors. Five people in the corridor. All crew. Two on the floor against the wall, two others leaning, and a fifth a few feet from the Bridge entrance, free-standing in stasis.

There was one way an invisible man could tell which of them was faking. Even the stasis people were still slightly breathing. If one of these was a fake, he'd be needing more air than the people in stasis. I'd be able to see his lungs move.

I moved out into the corridor. The first crewman was leaning against the wall, still in a walking posture. I moved my head down close to his chest and could just make out shallow breathing taking place about once every minute.

The next crewman was dead on the floor against the wall. He was half against it, face into the corner of the floor, with one arm raised and held up by the wall. There was a small dash of blood near his neck. I stepped ever so carefully, trying to make it to the next victim without betraying my invisibility.

Fate intervened. Though I never touched him, for some reason the dead crewman's hand and arm chose that moment to slide down the wall and punch the floor.

Chapter 33

Shots rang out. Near the end of the corridor, one stasis crewman was no longer in stasis. He shot wildly at the dead crewman. One stray shot caught my lower leg, tore a patch out of my suit, and caused a spray of blood. I dove to the other side of the corridor, leaving a line of red as I went. On my back, I tore at my suit, trying to get a weapon. The wild humanoid followed the blood trail and brought his weapon to bear on me. With one hand on my gun, I had one chance: draw and fire and hope he missed his next shot. As I flinched to do that, there was another '*zipbang*,' and the false crewman's head tipped to one side, rolled over his shoulder, and fell to the floor. His body slumped straight down and began to transition back to quantaloid. Standing behind, in the open entrance to the Bridge, Optimus X stood with his weapon still held out.

I pulled up my face covering. "X, thank you!"

"You are welcome, Captain. Have we completed the recovery mission?"

"Yes, X. Thanks to you."

"Should I treat your wound, Captain?"

I pushed myself up to a sitting position and clamped my hand over my leg. "No, X, go to the hanger bay. Move all of the crew out of there to safety, then depressurize the bay and open the hanger doors for the rescue teams that are coming."

"Yes, Captain." X bent over, replaced his weapon into his service bag, gathered it up, and walked on by me on his way to the hanger.

There was an emergency medical kit just inside the Bridge entrance. I hopped along to it, pulled off the invisibility suit, then sat on the floor and used the kit's pressure bandage device to stop the bleeding.

Next to the communications console, I selected the Acura com frequency and made the call. "Acura, this is Tarn."

"Go ahead, Captain," said Carter.

"We have retaken the Achillies."

The com system suddenly clicked off, probably from loud cheering overloading it. It came back on a moment later to the sound of Carter's voice saying, "Be quiet, be quiet."

"I'm still with you, Jalin. We need a large medical team here ASAP, and a tech group to try to restore these engines."

"They are already assembled and will be there in minutes."

"Optimus X is opening the hanger bay doors for you."

"Are you injured, Captain?"

"No, but a lot of crew are. Have the Medical people meet me in Engineering before they go anywhere or treat anyone. These people are still in stasis."

"Understood. I'm going to hand you over so I can get aboard one of those shuttles."

"That's okay. Switch me over to Commander Smith."

"Smith here."

"RJ, have you been listening?"

"So you're not hurt? Not at all?"

"Once the shuttles are clear, we need to move the Acura over to the Achillies in case we need to provide defense."

"Already in the works."

"Great. I'll get back to you shortly. Tarn out."

I took a moment to scan the Bridge. At the command seat, Captain Washburn was still in his seat, one arm in a sling, a big red patch forming near the elbow. It was a bad break. He stared at me with dead stasis eyes. I put my hand on his shoulder. "You have your ship back, Captain. We'll have you up in a few minutes."

Next stop: Engineering. I headed that way and realized I was limping pretty badly. No time to bother with that. Near the turbolift, there was a janitorial locker. I opened it and found a pair of coveralls. I pulled them on over the pressure bandage device and took the lift.

On deck two, I made my way back to Engineering. As I entered, I felt a shuttle make a hard landing in the hanger bay. It resonated through the ship. That can happen from nerves.

A few minutes later, as I stood by the stasis machine, a flood of medical and technical people came rushing in. I summoned the medical group. The techs came too.

"Okay, everybody. Here's the deal. We've got a lot of injured people under stasis all over the ship. When I disable this stasis unit, there's going to be a lot of screaming, crying, and yelling. Be prepared for that. All of you medical people need to spread out around the ship to find the worst injured. I'll give you ten minutes to do that. I'll make an announcement ship wide when the stasis is going to be switched off. It's going to be chaos. Do your best. Okay, everyone, get going, and good luck."

I grabbed one medic before she could leave. "Lieutenant, Captain Washburn is on the Bridge with a very bad compound fracture of the arm. Would you head there right away, please?"

"Yes, Captain. Certainly."

They rushed out. It gave me a surge of pride in them.

A tech came up to me. "I've looked at this thing, Captain. I believe we could shut it down using a scanner."

"Thank you, but we can't take a chance. It could be booby-trapped to fry everyone's brain. I'm going to blast the antenna off of it, then shoot it until it's dead."

The tech nodded and headed back toward the engine control console.

I gave them their ten minutes, then went to the com station. Found the listing on the screen that said "Ship Wide." Clicked it. "All personnel. The stasis unit is about to be shut down." I drew out one of my weapons, took careful aim, and said, "Three, two, one!" My first shot did indeed blow the antenna off the thing. I kept firing from top to bottom until it was a useless piece of golden garbage. The tech group stood staring, then went back to work.

Crewmen around Engineering began moving and moaning. Someone began swearing at the top of their lungs. The medical people that had remained raced around to treat them. A few appeared uninjured, just dazed.

I returned to the com console. "All personnel. This is Captain Tarn. You have all been under the control of a stasis unit for many hours. We have retaken the Achillies. You are safe now. medical personnel are spread out over the ship and will be coming to treat you shortly. Those of you able to walk but needing treatment can report to Medical or find a medic in your area. Please be assured, you are safe now. We are in control of the ship."

I pushed back, but then decided it was time to lean against something. Someone tapped me on the shoulder. To my surprise, it was Doctor Cooper.

"Captain Tarn, you need to come with me. Can you make it, or should I call for a gurney?"

"What?"

"You are bleeding profusely on the floor. You have left a trail of blood showing everywhere you've been. So which is it, walk or gurney?"

"Doctor, there are many others that need you much more than I do."

"Captain, that trail of blood leads up the stairs and down the corridor. That's how I found you. I've been following it."

"It's okay, Doctor. I put a pressure bandage device on it."

"Well, either you botched the application or it's not enough. Walk or gurney? Remember, I outrank you on this, and if we waste any more time talking, you're going to pass out from loss of blood."

"Well, if you're going to be that way about it..."

And that was the last thing I remember saying.

I woke up in a comfortable bed with white sheets. I felt way too good. It had to be morphine or something else really special. I was ready to gather up some friends and go drink beers and party. I caught a glimpse of my reflection in the polished metal on a cart by the bed. I looked like a drunken barfly. I tried to look around the room, but my head moved like a bobble head character. Finally, I looked at the bed on my left. There was Captain Washburn with his arm in a sling. He was staring back at me with an exaggerated look of confusion. He was as doped up as I was.

"What the hell, Adrian?"

"Huh?"

"You got green shit all over my ship."

I couldn't come up with a response.

"And look! My left damned arm is broken. I can't swing a golf club like this!"

"You do look kinda like shit, Mark."

"Look who's talkin'. At least I can walk." He let out a spitting laugh.

"I don't think either of us can walk, Washburn."

"Hey, let's blow this place and go find some wild women."

"Okay, but I have to ask my wife first."

Washburn choked off another laugh. "What are you, henpecked?"

I tried to stop my bobbing head. "You don't know the half of it." I spit out a laugh.

"Wait a minute, your wife is a famous interplenty diplomater!"

"Oh... yeah... I really hit the jackpot with her."

RJ appeared between our beds.

Washburn cried out, "Smitty! There we go! We got a threesome, Adrian. Let's get out of here."

RJ shook his head. "I think the Doctor may have overdone the medication."

Washburn objected. "No way! I still need a good shot of tequila. Right, Adrian?"

"Bourbon."

"Okay, bourbon. RJ, call the nurse."

Washburn suddenly began to snore.

RJ looked down at me. I could not think of anything to say. I wondered if I had been bad.

"Adrian, the tech guys say that the Acura parts inventories are not compatible with the Achillies equipment. But they've found enough spare parts in storage here to get the engines up and running. Maybe two hours. Maybe one. There have been no detections of any ships approaching yet. We still have a chance to get out of here before anyone else arrives."

"Well, that's good then, right?"

"We're going to need to leave some of our crew with the Achillies. They've lost too many key personnel. But we'll be able to escort each other back to Earth for safety."

"Uh-huh."

"Adrian, there's one other thing. The Achillies acting security chief came to me. He said he had important information to pass along. The Acura hasn't been able to get any updates from Earth because we've been on silent running, but the Achillies has been receiving periodic subspace messages from Earth. Apparently, the Deep State A.I. threat is gone. Earth's own A.I. is very broad and deep. Somehow, they got our A.I. to link up with the DSA.I., and after several discussions, our A.I. convinced the DSA.I. of the error of its ways. The DSA.I. is no longer associated with the Ocards or their ambitions. We have been cleared to come out of silent running."

"Well... that's... good... to... know."

That was the last thing I remember saying.

I woke up because Doctor Cooper was pulling my eyelids up to stare down into my eyes. "Oh, there you are,"

"Hello."

"Yes, hello, Adrian. Are you cognitive enough to listen?"

"Try me."

"Okay, your leg wound was way too bad for a pressure bandage adapter. You lost a fairly large section of muscle mass in that leg. I don't know how you were able to walk with it, never mind the blood loss. What has to be done now is we will make a surgical mold of the missing section and then grow new muscle tissue to fit that area. It will be glued in place until it takes and heals."

"I'm not sure I like the sound of that."

"Once the mold is created, you will not be able to walk until the new tissue is ready to be surgically attached. Walking could alter the injury, which would make the mold an incorrect fit. Do you understand?"

"How long before I can walk?"

"My guess would be at least a week. Fortunately, we can do this procedure here. Do you have any other questions?"

"Let me think about it."

She laughed, gathered up her tablet, and left.

Washburn was allowed out of bed two days later. He pointed and laughed at me for being stuck in bed, although he had a raised arm brace on that made him look like he was planning on punching someone everywhere he went. I countered his taunt by saying, "Please don't hit me."

The same day, Doctor Cooper showed up to escort me on a gurney ride back to the Acura, where the final surgery was to be done. RJ had already recovered the torn invisibility suit and its box. Both ships were scheduled to go to warp after the move was complete.

Three days later, they brought me in to do the hole replacement in my leg. I was required to undergo anesthesia so I wouldn't tense up. When I awoke, they showed me the rather large ellipse-like area of new flesh. It was identical to the rest of my leg except for a fine red outline. The following day, I was allowed to walk if I promised to spend most of my time in the Captain's chair. Back in my quarters, Raven seemed angry that I'd been gone so long.

The Acura and Achillies cruised together without incidence. The tow ship had never shown, but the Achillies was a dark ship for a while. Seventeen crewmen had been killed. Two dozen more had moderate injuries. Counseling was non-stop. There were too many for burial in space. They were stored in a specially designed cold chamber for the return trip.

Chapter 34

I was sitting back in my command seat on the Bridge one afternoon when Raven suddenly landed on my shoulder and said, "Adrian, hello." I asked RJ, "Did you see who let him in?"

"No."

"Did anyone see who let Raven onto the Bridge?"

Everyone shook their heads no.

I clicked my watch. "Tarn to Carter."

"Yes, Captain."

"Would you have a moment to come up to the Bridge?"

"On my way."

I met him at the door with Raven. "Jalin, someone let Raven out of my quarters and onto the Bridge. I'm sure it was just a joke, but that's a bit too far. I need to know who let him out."

We went to my quarters. Carter scanned the door. "When did this happen?"

"About fifteen minutes ago."

"This scan says you voice-commanded your door to open thirteen minutes ago." Carter went to the Bridge entrance and scanned again. "This scan says you voice-commanded the Bridge door to open thirteen minutes ago."

"I did neither."

We looked at each other. Then we looked at Raven. I said, "You don't think..."

"It's the only explanation. The ship's computer still has the waveform of the voice used. It's identified as your voice."

"So, just to be clear, you're saying Raven imitated my voice so perfectly, the ship's computer believed it was me."

"I have no doubt. What are you going to do about this? Are you going to try to break him of the habit?"

I thought about it. "No, I wouldn't want him getting locked in somewhere by accident. I'll just deal with it."

Carter looked at Raven. "You're a very smart bird, Raven."

Raven answered, "Hello."

Back in my control seat, I looked over at RJ. "My bird can command doors to open using my voice."

Two days later, it happened again.

"Yeoman Breize to the Captain."

"Go ahead."

"Captain, Raven is here in the Mess Hall."

"Did you take him there, Yeoman?"

"No, Captain. He just flew in."

"Who brought him down there?"

"We don't know, but Lieutenant Trulane said she saw him fly out of the elevator."

"Is he causing a disturbance?"

"No, Captain. Everyone loves him. He's taking turns visiting people for treats. Do you want me to try to bring him up to you?"

"Thank you, no. I'll come and get him."

I turned to RJ. "Could that bird have commanded the turbolift down to level four so he could visit the Mess Hall?"

RJ smirked. "How many times have you taken him down the turbolift?"

"Four, I think."

"That's one smart bird."

I thought for a moment. "You know, Marks and Kurh said the Dega Ravens are also telepathic. I wonder if they could help me teach him."

"Sounds like a good idea to me. When we get back to Enuro, how do you think Fantasia is going to take to him?"

"Oh, no problem. I can envision her riding her horse down the trails with Raven following overhead. She loves animals, birds, you name it."

"Elachia too. You know she brought back a hedgehog from one of her diplomatic sessions. The thing lives in the castle with us and is like a puppy dog."

"We have amazing wives, RJ."

"You can say that again. What the hell are we doing here?"

"Well, anyway, I've got a week left to try my plan."

"He may take over as Captain before then."

We both held back a laugh.

I said, "So I'm due in Doctor Cooper's exam and scolding room. You have the Bridge."

"I have the Bridge."

"I'll see you at the four o'clock status update with the Achilles."

"I will be there."

I leaned back on the exam table, no pants, with the attractive Doctor Cooper squeezing and playing with my leg. I had to concentrate to prevent myself from coming to attention. It almost felt like she was secretly encouraging that.

"Are you taking the extra water?" she asked.

"Yes, Doctor."

"No need to be so formal, Adrian. You can call me Jean."

"Okay."

"Just make sure you don't miss taking the antibiotics, and you should be fine in a few more days. I do not expect any scarring."

"Thank you, Jean."

"Okay. You can get dressed, and I'll see you in a few days."

"You are coming to the four o'clock update, aren't you?"

"Oh. Yes. Of course. Those poor people on the Achilles."

At four o'clock, we gathered in the main conference room. The wall screens were all linked to the Achilles conference room. We needed all the department leads there, so the room was almost full.

I turned to RJ. "You want to take this? You're much better at it than I am."

"Can I get that in writing?" RJ smirked and stood. "Okay, everyone. Let's get started." When quiet had been achieved, he sat back down. "Let's begin with Achilles Engineering. Captain Washburn, overview?"

"I'll turn that over to Acting Chief Brandon," said Washburn.

Brandon did not stand. "I would start by saying the duct tape and glue are still holding."

A few short laughs answered his joke.

"But seriously, we have an inefficiency in our coolant system that has caused an increase in nacelle temperatures, but they are staying just within limits. We'll continue to troubleshoot, but we expect to be able to hold this warp while we do. We also have a few electrical system problems that were caused by the stasis unit taking over several power distribution circuits. We are presently managing those problems. Our life support was affected by that also, but has now been stabilized. So overall, we see no problem in maintaining warp for the next five days."

RJ asked, "Okay, does anyone else have any system-related issues to bring up?"

No one spoke.

"In that case, let's go on to Medical. Doctor Cooper?"

Cooper replied, "I'll turn this over to Doctor Franklin, who agreed to transfer over to the Achillies to handle things there. Are you with us, Jack?"

"I am here, Jean. Starting with our two most serious cases. We had two head injuries resulting in severe concussions. Both had to be put into medical comas. One patient responded quickly to treatment. We believe he will eventually recover completely. The second, more serious, had bleeding on the brain. We had to relieve pressure. It was touch and go for quite a while, but we have him stabilized now, and we are hopeful for a full recovery also. Beyond that: broken bones, lacerations, deep bruises. All of those patients are either here under observation or have been assigned to their quarters for bed rest. That's the extent of Medical right now."

RJ asked, "Anyone else with any medical concerns?"

No one.

"Last but not least, Security. What have you got for us, Jalin?"

Carter sat up in his seat. "There has been an update just in the last few minutes. First, as many of you already know, the Deep State Artificial Intelligence threat has apparently been eliminated. Discussions between Earth's A.I. and the DSA.I. resulted in an alliance between Earth and the DSA.I. The DSA.I. has discontinued its association with the Ocards race and is now opposed to them. That being said, the new update we just received was not good. Earth managed to intercept four different Ocard-hired spacecraft that would have deposited the serpentoid embryos in Earth's atmosphere. Apparently one ship did somehow get through and managed to seed a cloud base over the southern Chinese area. There have already been reports of these immature serpentoids showing up on the ground. That makes the cargo we obtained from Dega extremely important now. It is fortunate we are only four days from Earth."

RJ said, "I should mention here that everything Security just said is classified and should not leave this room. Does anyone have anything else or any other issues to report?"

Silence.

"In that case, meeting adjourned. Thank you, everyone."

They left with thoughtful expressions on their faces. The prospect of returning to an Earth overrun by man-eating snakes was disturbing.

When we were alone, RJ said, "Overall, it was a good update."

"Yes, and the big finish was a real-life horror story."

"Let's hope the Dega trip was worth it."

"I'm betting 50-50 on that, but I can't imagine what it will be like if whatever we got doesn't work."

RJ took a deep breath. "Do you have any lingering doubts that we should not have rescued Astra? You know, should we have blown right past that stranded ship and not looked back?"

"Do you?"

"No."

"We've been over this. Ignore the ship in distress and get brought up by the Space Council for violating interplanetary law. Stop to provide assistance, and here we are."

RJ rubbed his hands together. "Now if the duct tape and glue just holds together for another five days."

Three days of smooth cruise held up for us. On the fourth day, everyone considered us a shoe-in. The crew was communicating with Earth friends and family on a daily basis. Reports about the alien snake problem were being suppressed.

At the end of day four, I headed back to my quarters, tired from too many excited conversations. I walked into my quarters, and a funny smell made me look up. A jolt hit me. There on my floor was the body of Yoeman Breize. I could not tell if she was alive or dead.

A gruff voice behind me called out, "Well, well, Captain. I didn't think you'd make it this far. All the way back to Earth after all. Let me thank you. It's just what I needed."

I turned and faced a short, scruffy-haired man in dirty off-white coveralls holding a plasma pistol.

I said, "I need to look at her."

"No, ya don't. She's just a little stunned, I think."

"There's a cut on her forehead."

"Yeah, she didn't want to let me into your quarters."

I shook my head. "What the hell are you doing?"

"You don't recognize me, do you?"

"Yes, I do. You're the guy who got in trouble searching somebody's locker. It's Jaka, isn't it? Hans Jaka."

"Well, I am impressed, Tarn. I didn't think you'd remember any of us down in Waste Disposal. That locker thing—I thought I was searching Yoeman Breize's locker for her ID card to get into your quarters. Turns out it was the next locker over."

"So why have you assaulted her, and are holding a gun on me, Jaka?"

I tried to evaluate my chances of taking his gun. It was unfortunate he was keeping too smart a distance. He had his back to the entrance door. One good body slam would put him into it hard, but he would need to miss his first shot.

"No, no, Tarn. Don't go getting that look. You take one step in any direction, and I'll drop you at the hip. Then we'll wait for you to wake up in pain and start again."

"I'll ask again. What the hell do you want?"

"I'm a sleeper."

"A sleeper agent?"

"For the Ocards. They need what you have in your wall safe."

"There's no way you'll ever get off this ship."

"Oh, contraire, Mr. Tarn. There is a cloaked Ocard ship paralleling us right now. I only need to give 'em the signal."

"You'll never get near a com station after this."

"Don't need to. I just press this little button I have in my pocket and voilà."

"And if I refuse to open that safe?"

"Then I will kill her and ask you again." To accent the moment, Jaka fired his pistol into the couch, then quickly returned it to me.

I decided a charge at the right moment was my best chance. "Okay, I'll open it."

My plan was to take two steps toward the safe, then do a sideways lunge at just the gun. I secretly took a deep breath but was suddenly interrupted.

A black ball came flying out of the arboretum window at what seemed like ninety miles an hour and went smack into Jaka's face. There was terrible screeching, clawing, and pecking at his face and eyes. Jaka screamed from the assault on the eyes. I stepped forward and snatched the gun, then wrapped one arm around his chest and took him to the floor. The three of us crashed down, but Raven kept going and Jaka kept screaming. With Jaka captured under my legs, I yelled at Raven to stop. It took a moment, but the bird finally glanced up at me and hopped on the floor. A second later, he looked at Jaka and started up again on his face—more screaming from Jaka.

"Raven, stop, stop, please." I brushed my hand under him, and he flew up to my shoulder. He stared down at Jaka's torn-up face and began cawing threatening sounds. Jaka held his hands to his face, moaning.

I managed to click my watch. "Captain to Security. Emergency in the Captain's quarters. Armed assailant is now secured."

A voice answered so hurriedly I couldn't understand it.

"Captain to Medical. Medical emergency in the Captain's quarters."

"We'll be right there, Captain. Can you tell us the nature of the emergency?"

"Yoeman Breize is unconscious. I don't know anything else."

I heard them click off. I felt around and removed the Ocard trigger from Jaka's breast pocket.

It took less than five minutes for the door to slide open, with Carter and three subordinates charging through with weapons drawn. Jaka gave up struggling and just waited under my leg with his hands over his face, moaning. The security guys pulled me up and away and wrapped a chain around Jaka's waist, then cuffed him to it in the front.

Medical charged in a few minutes later. Two went immediately to Yoeman Breize, while the other tried to get a look at Jaka's face. After a quick glance, he clicked his watch. "Medical, we're going to need another gurney."

Raven and I stood by while both patient and assailant were taken away. Carter stayed behind and took a seat opposite my couch. He motioned me to sit.

"Can you explain all of that to me?" he asked.

I did my best.

"We have a cloaked Ocard ship trailing us, waiting for his signal?"

"That's what he said." I handed over the Ocard trigger.

"I'm going to head down to my office and send out a signal to Earth on a secret noise telemetry channel, and we'll have half a dozen ships here to meet us in a matter of hours. We'll let the Ocards keep waiting and hope they're still here when our guys arrive."

"So, normal operations until then?"

"Yes." Carter stood and hurried out.

I looked at Raven. "You deserve a treat."

Raven replied, "Treat!"

Chapter 35

As soon as things had settled down, I called RJ over. We sat on the couch, and I did my best to fill him in.

He looked me over carefully. "So not a scratch, then?"

"Jaka got all the scratches. Bad ones."

"Did they give you an update on Yoeman Breize?"

"Yes. She was stunned at point-blank range near the back of the head. They treated the cut on the side of her face, and they have her on strong feel-good meds so that she won't have the headache when they let her wake up, and she won't be panicking about what happened."

"I have to say they are pretty damned good down in our Sick Bay."

"Agreed."

RJ leaned back and sipped his iced tea. "But we are in danger."

"Yes. The Ocards are technically advanced and are telepathically powerful, and they're out there cruising along with us."

"But Carter thinks this is the way to go."

"He has a lot more experience with them than most people."

"But they could decide to invade us at any time."

"Except they are signatories on agreements that do not allow them to do that. Everything they try to do has to be by proxy."

RJ sipped. "I hope Carter's plan works."

"We'll know in less than twenty-four hours."

Ten hours later, five Earth battleships dropped out of warp so close to us it rocked the Acura and Achillies badly. There was a short exchange of weapons fire before the Ocard ship captain felt obliged to come out of cloak. The Ocards' telepathic abilities were of little use to them since the Earth ships had a significant contingent of allied Grays. The Ocards were escorted back to Earth for negotiations.

We dropped into Earth orbit an hour or two later. The Achillies went directly to a space dock for easier access to the wounded and to speed repairs. We were commanded to open our shuttle bay doors for imminent arrival of a security shuttle. We were to meet it when it arrived.

When the hangar pressurized and the shuttle ramp lowered, two heavily armed special forces soldiers exited, followed by a Gray. Somehow I recognized him as Eb3, the Gray that had debriefed RJ. We did not speak but used hand gestures only. Together, the five of us went to my quarters, where I opened the safe, removed the Dega case, and handed it to Eb3. The three of them left promptly after indicating we should stay behind.

RJ and I went back to the end-of-mission checklists for crew and ship. Several hours later, another security shuttle arrived. We were scheduled for debriefing on the surface. When would we get back? They couldn't say. I grabbed a few things, went to the arboretum window, and called my bird. RJ met me in the hangar bay. We boarded with a few strange looks from the pilot, although they did not complain about the bird on my shoulder.

It was a large conference room, part of the same underground facility we had prepared for the mission in. RJ and I sat side by side at the big, fake wood-grained table in yet another room where the walls were covered in electronic monitors. Three official-looking gentlemen in military-styled uniforms came in and sat across from us. They were not young, all grayed and weathered. They seemed bemused by the bird on my shoulder.

The central-most character spoke. "I'm General Caine. On my left is General Pail, and on my right, Lieutenant Colonel Walker. We're a little surprised by the bird, Captain."

"It's a gift from the Degans that I was ordered to accept no matter what it was. Surprisingly, it found your missing invisibility suit and saved my life from a sleeper Ocard that you hired into our crew."

The three stiffened a bit but did not contest.

RJ said, "I assume you all have read our reports."

Caine answered, "Yes. I was not certain how to take the Captain's referrals to your raven. I thought it might be code of some kind. I now see it was not."

Raven chose that moment for his greeting. "Hello."

They ignored the greeting.

General Pail spoke. "So, in regards to your mission, you were ordered to maintain silent running and stop for nothing, but you chose to stop for a ship in distress and to take aboard an escaped prisoner."

I replied, "You only have that half correct, General. We stopped for a ship in distress and then rescued an escaped hostage."

"Why did you stop at all?" asked Caine.

RJ answered, "Had we not, we'd now be sitting here explaining why we broke interplanetary maritime law by ignoring a ship in distress."

No argument was given.

Pail spoke again. "You then violated your orders again by stopping to aid the Achillies."

I answered, "All three of you are military. Please, whichever of you would have left the Achillies behind and not aided Captain Washburn, please raise your hand."

Two of them shifted nervously in their seats. No one raised their hand.

Caine asked, "Captain Tarn, using that invisibility suit, you killed those four quantaloids in cold blood. Does that bother you?"

"The crew of the Achillies meant more to me than a clear conscience, so I don't think about it."

RJ asked, "Gentlemen, what about the snake invasion? Is Earth still in danger?"

Pail replied, "The samples you brought back contained the DNA of a number of serpentoids, one of which matched a sample from one of the creatures we captured. Also, a sample of a generalist virus was in that container, which can be mutated to attack any DNA we choose. Using those together, our lab has already created a virus that will kill the invading snakes with their first breath of air, and it will not affect humans or any other Earth species at all. So we expect that threat to be gone shortly."

Lieutenant Colonel Walker gave a deep exhale and said, "All three of us are very aware of Captain Tarn's reputation for creating chaos and somehow coming out of it smelling like a rose. Commander Smith, almost always you accompany him on these notorious occasions. The service records of you both are a confusing collection of mangled rules and regulations that somehow end up achieving the desired end result. And now, having been directly involved with the two of you, the three of us find ourselves faced with exactly the same circumstances that again resulted in multiple unexpected successes. You rescued a hostage planetary princess who is slated to become the ruling queen of the very influential planet Oreonus, a planet we previously had no affiliation with, whom we are now returning to her home planet, which has unexpectedly become an Earth ally, by the way. You retrieved virus samples from the planet Dega and, at the same time, impressed them with your regard for serpentoids. Then, on your way back, you rescued the Achillies and saved her crew, captured a sleeper agent for the Ocards, and made it possible for us to take into custody an Ocard ship with several high-ranking Ocard officials on board. I'm sure you can see how all of this is no less than injurious to our disciplined, military way of thinking."

I folded my arms. "So are we being charged?"

Walker answered, "Not just yet. You'll either be charged, given a medal, or both. We've had a communication from a doctor by the name of Elaia Allay who claims you saved her life but were killed on a mining colony not long after. She wanted to impress on us what wonderful, selfless people you are—were—and that she will always be grateful. She invited us to her planet for a diplomatic exchange."

I kept my arms folded. "So we're free to leave?"

Walker continued, "Well, not exactly. Yesterday, two of the most beautiful women I have ever seen arrived in orbit in a very large starship claiming to be your wives. Of course, we did not believe them, but apparently they are diplomats well known to many Earth officials who confirmed their claim. You are to be turned over to their custody until we can settle this matter."

I said, "Please, not the briar patch."

RJ could not help himself. He laughed out loud. Everyone looked at him. "So my wife Elachia is here?"

Caine answered, "They are a persuasive pair."

RJ answered, "Don't we know."

Caine said, "Gentlemen, if you would stand, please."

We obliged him and stood.

He came around the table and took two small black clip-on devices from his pocket and clipped one on each of our collars. He stood back.

I suddenly began to feel very light. I worried about Raven and placed one hand over his back. There was a gentle glow of blinding light, which collapsed down around us.

We were suddenly standing on two transport pads in a ship filled with gold, chrome, and bright white decorations. Elachia and Fantasia stood in front of us, looking annoyed.

RJ said, "Well, that was different."

Elachia cried, "Fantasia, yours has a bird on his shoulder!"

Fantasia replied, "It's a raven. I love ravens!"

Raven immediately jumped from my shoulder, flew to Fantasia, and sat on her shoulder, rubbing against her cheek.

Elachia scolded, "Well, I hope the two of you have had enough cavorting around the galaxy."

RJ said, "Yes, dear." I nodded vigorously.

Fantasia said, "Well, come this way. We're starved. Elachia, keep an eye on them. Make sure they don't disappear."

We followed as ordered.

RJ said, "I'm never accepting another assignment, ever. That's it. Nada. Never again."

I replied, "Agreed."

RJ thought for a moment. "Haven't we had this conversation before?"

"I do believe we have."

Other Adrian Tarn novels by E.R. Mason:

Fatal Boarding
Deep Crossing
Shock Diamonds
Dark Vengeance
Mu Arae
Six Seconds
Cold Logic
Tirumalai

www.ingramcontent.com/pod-product-compliance
Lightning Source LLC
LaVergne TN
LVHW090558110826
845146LV00001B/171

* 9 7 9 8 2 3 4 0 5 9 4 3 7 *